Praise for the Demon Underground Series

"Wow, I didn't sleep at all last night. I stayed up reading *Fang Me.*"
—*Archimedes, SuccuWiki, Five Stars*

"This series gets a BIG 5 Paws from me."
—*Happy Tails and Tales Blog*

"I recommend this series to anyone and everyone!"
—*Books, Books, and More Books, Five Skulls*

Catch Me

Demon Underground Series, Book Six

by

Parker Blue

Bell Bridge Books

Bell Bridge Books
PO BOX 300921
Memphis, TN 38130
Print ISBN: 978-1-61194-623-9

Bell Bridge Books is an Imprint of BelleBooks, Inc.

Published in the United States of America.

We at BelleBooks enjoy hearing from readers.
Visit our websites
BelleBooks.com
BellBridgeBooks.com
ImaJinnBooks.com

10 9 8 7 6 5 4 3 2 1

Cover design: Debra Dixon
Interior design: Hank Smith
Photo/Art credits:
Girl (manipulated) © Ys1982 | Dreamstime.com
Portal (manipulated) © Agsandrew | Dreamstime.com
Background (manipulated) © Realrocking | Dreamstime.com

:Lmcx:01:

Dedication

For my wonderful fans. You guys rock!

Chapter One

Val

THOUGH THE MOONLESS night was already black as ink, I retreated farther into the deep shadows of a live oak outside my townhouse. My mouth went dry, my heart pounded, and my stomach churned as if a dozen vampires were cavorting about inside me. Yes, it was my most frightening outing yet—a date with Austin.

Beside me, Fang, my trusty hellhound, snorted. YOU'VE TAKEN ON DOZENS OF VAMPIRES, MAGE DEMONS, AND BLOOD DEMONS . . . AND YOU'RE AFRAID OF A DATE WITH THE GUY WHO WANTS TO BE YOUR BOYFRIEND?

I'm not afraid of *him,* I sent Fang telepathically.

THEN WHAT ARE YOU AFRAID OF?

Oh, maybe looking like a child to the vampire who was way over a hundred years old and sexy as hell. What did he see in me, an average-looking eighteen-year-old with virtually no experience in this kind of thing? I'd never really "dated" before, though I had two short-lived relationships—one with Dan Sullivan, a full human, and the other with Shade, the broody shadow demon. Neither had prepared me for a date with a sexy vamp.

After the fabulous Valentine's Day flash mob he'd arranged for me with "zombies" dancing to Michael Jackson's *Thriller* a couple of weeks ago, I'd promised to go out on a real date with him, and this was the first time we'd both been able to arrange it.

Unfortunately, Fang could read all my doubts and insecurities and would call me on every single one of them. I cringed, waiting for it.

YOU'RE NOT HALF BAD-LOOKING, Fang said.

Gee, thanks.

DON'T BE AN IDIOT. WHAT COULD HE POSSIBLY SEE IN YOU? WELL, MAYBE IT'S THE FACT THAT YOU'RE AN AWESOME SLAYER, OR MAYBE BECAUSE YOU'VE SAVED HIS BUTT AND COUNTLESS OTHER VAMP AND DEMON BUTTS IN SAN ANTONIO MANY TIMES IN THE PAST

FEW MONTHS—NOT TO MENTION THAT OF UNSUSPECTING HUMANS. OR MAYBE, JUST MAYBE, HE'S HOT FOR YOUR INNER SUCCUBUS WHO MAKES *HIS* BUTT FEEL SO GOOOOOOD.

"That's a lot of butts," I murmured. But I had to admit my inner succubus—I called her Lola—liked Austin, too. A lot.

YOU DO GET THAT LOLA ISN'T A SEPARATE ENTITY? YOU ARE THE SUCCUBUS—THAT ONE-EIGHTH DEMON PART OF YOU ISN'T SOMETHING OR SOMEONE YOU CAN SEPARATE FROM YOUR HUMAN SELF, NO MATTER HOW MUCH YOU MIGHT WANT TO.

"How can I forget when you keep reminding me?" I muttered. Besides, I'd only wanted to get rid of Lola *before* I'd been kicked out of my home. Everyone else in my family—my mom, stepfather, and half-sister—was fully human, so I'd felt like a freak. But now that I'd discovered the Demon Underground, I didn't feel so much freakish as I did . . . inexperienced.

WELL, Fang drawled. THERE'S ONE WAY TO GET THAT EXPERIENCE, YOU KNOW.

Yeah, I know. I'm doing it, aren't I?

IF YOU STOP HIDING—FROM YOURSELF AND HIM.

Austin drove up then, in one of the black luxury cars the San Antonio vein of vampires kept in their motor pool. He stepped out of the car, wearing jeans that snugged in all the right places, a black leather jacket, snakeskin boots, and his ever-present cowboy hat. My heart beat faster. What a hottie—and so out of my league it was ridiculous.

Fang nudged me with his nose. DON'T BE RIDICULOUS. YOU'RE VAL SHAPIRO, THE SLAYER, THE DEMON UNDERGROUND'S PALADIN ENFORCER. HE'S OUT OF *YOUR* LEAGUE.

Yeah, right. As if I could hide from Austin's keen vampire vision anyway. His gaze found me in the depths of the shadows, and a slow, sexy smile widened his mouth. "Hello, darlin'."

Would any girl not melt into a puddle right then and there? True to form, Lola surged front and center, her interest sharpening. As for me, I swallowed, trying to get some moisture in my mouth. "Hi," I managed. Oh yeah, I am witty beyond belief.

He leaned against the car, waiting for me to come to him. "Shall we go?"

I took a deep breath and sauntered toward him, or tried to. Instead, I tripped over a root of the massive tree. Graceful, I was not.

I felt my face flame hot and wished I could rush back inside without looking like a fool.

TOO LATE, Fang jeered.

Sooooo helpful.

I put a fake smile on my face and managed to leave the darkness of the tree without stumbling again. I headed toward the car under the streetlight, and Austin moved around to the other side to open the door for me.

I hesitated before getting in.

"What's the matter?" he asked, his face hidden in his hat's shadow.

I glanced up at him anyway. "Where are we going? Am I dressed okay?"

I really didn't have much in the way of clothing to choose from. Jeans, a shirt, and one of my many vests was pretty much my go-to uniform, and tonight was no different. I needed the vest to cover the stakes in my back waistband. Not to use on Austin, of course—he was one of the good bloodsuckers in the New Blood Movement—but after being a slayer for several years, I kind of felt naked without them. The rest of my vampire-hunting kit was in the backpack I carried like most girls carried a purse.

"Perfect," Austin said, opening the car door wider.

Good, because I didn't have anything suitable to wear to someplace fancy and didn't know if anything like that was open this late at night anyway.

I slipped inside to let the luxurious leather seat cradle my butt, but it seemed weird to see Fang sitting on the sidewalk instead of jumping in beside me. "Where are we going?" I asked again.

Austin leaned his forearms on the roof and door to dip his head where he could see me. He gave me a slow grin. "Well, darlin', there are these rogue vampires attacking tourists in Brackenridge Park—"

"Near the zoo?" That didn't bode well.

"Yeah, and I thought maybe we could have ourselves a little fun chasing them down."

Relief coursed through me, and I relaxed. Grinning back at him, I said, "Sounds great."

Austin glanced over at Fang, who looked as though he was an eager, tightly-coiled spring about to *boing* loose. "You wanna come?"

DAMN BETCHA, Fang said, though Austin couldn't hear him. He leaped into the car, jumped over my lap, then bounded into the back seat. LET'S GO!

"That's a yes," I told Austin with a laugh.

As Austin went around to get into the driver's side, Fang exclaimed,

WOW. FIRST DATE, AND HE'S TAKING YOU OUT TO HUNT EVIL VAMPIRES WITH YOUR HELLHOUND. DOES HE GET YOU OR WHAT?

He gets me, I confirmed, smiling.

As Austin drove toward the park, I fumbled for something clever to say. "So, how was your day?"

THAT WASN'T IT, Fang said drily.

Yeah, I sounded too perky, even to my own ears.

Austin shrugged. "Same old, same old. Train new vamps how not to get killed, check on the blood banks, sleep like the dead. You?"

I tried to match his tone. "Oh, you know. Read spells in the *Encyclopedia Magicka*, play with the hellpuppies, babysit Shade."

Fang snorted in the back seat. HELLPUPPIES? I LIKE THAT.

Austin cast me a sidelong glance. "Babysit Shade?"

His question didn't sound like a jealousy-over-an-old-boyfriend thing, more like a what-the-hell-is-he-doing-now kind of thing.

"Yeah, ever since his sister was sucked into that other dimension, Shade has been trying to figure out how to get her body back, trying to convince other demons to help him." Luckily, he'd stopped blaming me for her death, but he wasn't talking to anyone much. "Either he's holed up researching the encyclopedia or the Internet, or he's hanging out at the blood mansion."

"Blood mansion?" Austin repeated, sounding bemused.

"You know, the place where we lost his sister and took down the blood demon. I'm not sure what else to call it." When he nodded in comprehension, I added, "Micah is afraid Shade's going to do something stupid there."

"Like what?"

I grimaced. "We don't know for sure, but he wants *me* to make sure Shade doesn't do it." I cast Austin a glance. "I hear Alejandro bought the blood house?"

Austin nodded. "We trashed it when we took down the blood demon and his followers, so Alejandro feels responsible for cleaning it up. Besides, the Movement is growing. We could use another place."

"Maybe your boss could warn Shade off, threaten to have him arrested for trespassing or something?"

"You really think that'd work?"

"Probably not." I sighed. Shade was another guy I didn't know how to deal with. Give me a rogue vamp to slay or an evil demon to fight, and I was good. Personal relationships . . . not so much.

"How'd you get out of babysitting duty tonight?"

"Tessa had the night off from Club Purgatory and volunteered to watch him so I could go out with you. He's probably sleeping, anyway." After all, it was long past the time when most law-abiding citizens were in bed.

Austin cast me a heated sidelong glance. "Remind me to thank Tessa later."

That look made Lola reach greedy fingers toward him, but I reined her in. Now was not the time.

Maybe later.

Luckily, we'd arrived at the park, so I didn't have to respond. Instead, I got out of the car and asked, "What's the situation?"

"We've heard rumors of rogues hunting here, looking for clandestine lovers, oblivious teenagers, and the homeless to snack on."

I nodded. "Let's—"

I broke off as a patrol car pulled up, and an officer leaned out the window. "Hello, folks. What are you doing here at two o'clock in the morning? It's not safe."

"It's okay," I told him. "I'm Val Shapiro . . . used to work for the SCU?" If he was warning people away from the park, he probably knew what kind of "special" crimes the Special Crimes Unit handled and who I was. I leaned down so he could see my face. I vaguely remembered seeing him before.

He recoiled. Yep, he knew me all right. The scuzzies were okay fighting vamps and demons, but they didn't really like having a demon in their midst, especially one who could whup their ass and make them enjoy it at the same time.

His gaze slanted toward Austin.

"My hunting partner tonight," I added. "He can hold his own. Are we free to go, Officer?"

Apparently, he took my word for it, because he nodded. "Good hunting," he said and drove away.

WELL, RESPECT IS BETTER THAN ACCEPTANCE ANY DAY, Fang said.

Yeah, I kept telling myself that.

I turned to Austin. "Any idea where to start looking?"

JUST FOLLOW MY NOSE, Fang said and put snout to ground.

"I take it Fang knows?" Austin said.

"Looks like it."

I headed down a trail after Fang, and Austin held out his hand. "We should pretend we're lovers taking a stroll," Austin said. "Lure them out."

"Oh, okay," I said, ducking my head to hide the flush warming my cheeks. I didn't know whether to feel elated that he'd found an excuse to hold my hand or deflated that he found it necessary to explain. Either way, I'd take his words at face value and act out his little play.

He caught my hand, linking his fingers with mine. Oh, my. It was as if someone had dumped a bucket of hormones inside me, and they all responded at once, surging through my chakras with gut-churning intensity.

Lola liked.

Fighting back the sensations, I tried to focus on why we were here. "Do you have the amulet with you?" I asked casually. For some reason, everyone seemed to think I was addicted to the thing since it constantly pulled at me, begging me to use it. I wasn't, but the crystal was a handy tool now that I'd lost some of my slayer mojo. If it was nearby, I could use it for small things like seeing through a shadow demon's swirliness, but for big things like controlling men, I had to touch it.

"Yes," Austin said equally casual, "but you're not going to get it unless we're way outnumbered."

The crystal called to me then, and I was able to pinpoint its location—deep in Austin's front pocket. Well, crap. I couldn't go after it there without embarrassing the heck out of myself. He knew it, too. I shrugged, pretending it was no big deal.

He caught my glance at his front pocket and grinned.

My face flamed, and Fang chuckled.

Don't even start with me. I'd embarrassed myself enough already.

We walked for about a quarter mile down the path when Fang said, UNDEAD BLOODSUCKERS AT THREE O'CLOCK.

I squeezed Austin's hand in warning.

He leaned down to murmur in my ear, "Yes, I hear them."

And that's when three guys came strolling out from behind the trees, as if they were trying to look chill but not quite succeeding. College guys, probably, and they came in three sizes—small, medium, and large. But they didn't seem like the typical schoolyard bullies—more like the ones who got picked on.

"Hey, girlie, wanna play?" the heavy one asked.

He'd have to catch me first, and that wasn't going to happen. "Oh, great," I said, rolling my eyes. "Geeks on parade." I exchanged glances with Austin. "Are these the vicious predators you were worried about?"

"Naw, can't be," Austin drawled.

"You think you can take me, cowboy?" the medium-sized one asked belligerently.

Sheesh, was that a pocket protector I saw under his squeaky new leather jacket?

Austin nodded slowly. "I do."

"All three of us?"

"Piece of cake."

They rushed him, ignoring Fang and me. Big mistake.

Fang took on the wimpy little guy, jumping up to bite him in the butt, then catching him off balance so he fell down. Fang bared his teeth at the kid's throat as I muttered the spell for super strength, then grabbed medium guy and slammed him down on the hard ground. Austin joined us, easily tripping up the heavy dude so they were all three lying on the ground, side by side, staring up at us.

"Too easy," Austin said.

"Hey," medium guy protested. "Do you know who we are?"

"The Three Stooges?" I guessed.

Anger blazed in medium guy's eyes. "I'll show you who's a stooge." And, of course, he made the mistake of reaching out to control my mind. Fumbled, more like it.

That meant I could now read *his*.

"Sorry, Chris. That doesn't work on me." I glanced at the other two. "Go ahead, Carlos and Charlie, try to control me."

They seemed shocked that I knew their names but narrowed their gazes at me.

"Don't tell me," Austin said with a small smile and shake of his head. "They actually tried it."

"Yep," I confirmed. Now I could read all three tiny little minds. I sighed. "These are not the droids we're looking for."

Austin cast me a puzzled glance.

I shrugged. "Sorry, their geekiness is kinda overwhelming."

"Who *are* you people?" the small guy, Carlos, asked.

"Ever heard of the Slayer?" Austin replied with a raised eyebrow.

"Her?" he said, his voice ending in a squeak.

"Me," I confirmed. "And Austin here is what you strive for but can never be."

"What does that mean?" chunky Charlie demanded.

"He's a vampire, too, only he's been doing it a whole lot longer than you have. *And* he doesn't try to pick on innocent people to get his rocks off."

Speaking of that, medium guy—Chris—was inside my energy field, so it was obvious he was starting to get mighty interested in me. Well, Lola, anyway.

"We haven't hurt anyone," Chris said, leering.

He was trying too hard to be sexy, and it grossed me out. Sometimes it sucked being part lust demon. "That's true, you haven't—not yet, anyway. But you were planning on it, weren't you?"

These pathetic excuses for vampires wanted to be at the top of the pecking order for once, instead of being pecked on. But to do that, they needed larger . . . peckers.

Fang snorted.

Austin sighed heavily. "They really haven't hurt anyone?"

"Not yet," I confirmed. "This was their first foray as baby vamps." They were hungry as hell but couldn't quite bring themselves to drink blood . . . yet.

"Think there's hope for them?"

"Maybe."

Carlos looked back and forth between the two of us, seeming a little less frightened now that Fang had backed off so he was only sitting on the kid's chest. "What are you talking about?"

"We ask the questions here," Austin said. "Who turned you? Who was your sire?"

"We don't know his name," Chris said in a sulky tone.

He was telling the truth, and I read the rest of it in their minds. "They found a notice on a bulletin board at school advertising a seminar on how to become rich and powerful and went to it."

"A bulletin board?" Austin repeated incredulously.

Yeah, it appeared the opposition was advertising now.

"What did they tell you?" Austin demanded.

The guys wanted to keep quiet in the face of Austin's anger but couldn't hide from me, so I told Austin what I'd learned. "Their sire told them they could kick sand in the bullies' faces and take whatever they wanted, then turned the three Cs, saying they could join their army after they made their first kill."

Austin shook his head. "Stupid."

WATCH OUT, Fang warned.

Chunky Charlie tried to surge up off the ground, but I slammed Lola into all three of them so they were nothing more than drooling love slaves. Sickening.

"Be still," I told them, and they had to comply. I rose to my feet, and Austin and Fang followed leisurely. Shaking my head, I added, "I'm not sure if they're meant as bait, cannon fodder, or if the vamp who turned them really thinks he can turn them into soldiers."

The guys looked appalled. I added with some heat, "This isn't some stupid cosplay at a comic convention where everyone believes you are what you pretend to be. And becoming vampire won't make you super soldiers or super lovers. It only makes you more of what you already are." Super geeks.

They glanced at each other, horror dawning in their eyes.

I glanced at Austin. "They haven't actually been able to bring themselves to bite anyone yet. Not even one of the zoo animals. For three nights." Austin nodded as he obviously got the message—they were pretty much starving.

"So you think they're salvageable?"

"Probably." All three were outcasts, from their homes and their families. They just wanted to find a place where they could fit in the world. I could relate.

Austin sighed heavily. "Okay, here's the deal. You agree to join the New Blood Movement, and we'll forget this happened."

"Movement? What's that?" Chris asked.

That was new. Before, the rogues were careful to tell their fledglings *not* to contact the Movement. Seemed they'd changed their strategy. So as to not tempt the newbies to the straight and narrow? Or to weed out the weaker ones?

Austin scowled down at him. "In the New Blood Movement, we don't attack people or animals. We don't take blood without permission, and we definitely don't hunt and kill innocents."

Carlos looked puzzled. "But . . . don't we need blood to survive?"

"Yes," Austin said. "But you get it from the blood banks we operate."

The three exchanged glances and seemed reluctant. Going to a blood bank didn't seem nearly as sexy as being a badass soldier. Hiding a smirk, I added, "As an added bonus, you'll have access to safe houses with others of your kind, meaningful work to do, and Austin here will teach you how to fight and defend yourselves."

That last one interested them more than all the others combined. They gave each other doubtful looks.

"This way, you can be heroes, ridding the world of evil rogue vampires," I confided. They seemed to like that.

"And if you don't," I said cheerfully, "we stake you right now and leave you for the sun to turn your ass to ash." I whipped out a stake and twirled it playfully, raising my eyebrows at them.

"I'm in," Carlos said hastily.

"Me, too," Chris chimed in.

Charlie looked mulish, so I raised my stake over his heart. He must be the ringleader in this little band of misfits.

"Okay, okay," he said, raising his hands defensively.

Austin glared at them. "Belonging to the New Blood Movement is a lifetime commitment. We'll feed you, house you, and train you as long as you follow our ways. But change your mind and hurt an innocent, and we take your life. Deal?"

They all gulped but nodded. "Deal," they said in unison.

Lola released her hold on their chakras, and they scrambled to their feet.

Austin pulled out his wallet and handed each of the guys a card. "Here, this has the addresses of the blood banks around town. Get yourself something to eat. Tell 'em Austin sent you."

The guys nodded and hurried off, apparently before we changed our minds.

Austin shook his head. "Three more fledglings to sponsor. And you wonder why we need more space?"

"Why the sudden increase in the undead population?"

"The rogues are getting out of control. They keep turning gullible idiots, then dumping them out on their own to survive or perish. We try to catch them and convert them before they can do much damage, but it's a never-ending battle." He gave me a rueful smile. "Sorry, this wasn't as fun as I'd planned."

"Hey, we added some new vamps to the good side. It's a win-win. I like that."

WELL, I DON'T, Fang complained. I WANTED TO BITE MORE VAMPIRE BUTT.

"There might be more vampires lurking in the park," Austin said. "There have been a number of clumsy attacks in this area. I get the idea the new ones get steered in this direction."

But before we could scout the area, my phone vibrated. I checked the screen. "It's Micah." My boss in the Demon Underground didn't call me often, but when he did, it was probably important.

"You'd better take it, then," Austin said.

I nodded and answered the phone. "Hi, Micah. What's up?"

"It's Shade," he said without preamble. "He ditched Tessa, and we think he's gone to the blood demon's former house. Can you check it out?"

I glanced at Austin, uncertain. After all, this was supposed to be a date.

He'd obviously heard both sides of the conversation—vamp hearing and all—and nodded. "Might as well," Austin conceded.

"What exactly do you want me to do?" I asked Micah. "I can force him to leave, but he'll be right back there tomorrow. Unless you want me to . . . ?" I trailed off, leaving the rest for him to fill in.

Micah sighed. "Does Austin have the amulet with him?"

"Yes."

"Then you can use it if you absolutely have to in order to make him stop this unhealthy, unsafe obsession, but only then. Got it?"

"Yes, sir."

"Good," he said. "Oh, and I have another request to ask of you."

"What?" I asked warily. I hadn't had to use my role as Paladin yet, except to babysit Shade, and I really wasn't sure I wanted to go there.

"We have a visiting demon—Ivy Weiss—and I wondered if you could put her up for a little while in Gwen's old room."

"I guess," I said reluctantly. After all, Shade wasn't using it anymore. "What kind of demon is she?"

"A rock demon. The Sedona Underground calls her a gemstone whisperer—she can read stones and rocks and learn about their owners. Call me when you get home, and I'll bring her by."

A ROCK HEAD?

Don't be rude, I admonished him. "Okay," I told Micah and hung up.

"Shall we go?" Austin asked, gesturing toward the car.

OH, GREAT, Fang grumbled. WE GET TO BABYSIT SHADE. AGAIN. SHEESH—HE NEEDS MORE SUPERVISION THAN THE HELLPUPPIES.

Chapter Two

Val

WHEN WE ARRIVED at the blood mansion and I got out of the car, Fang sighed. I'M TIRED OF DEALING WITH MR. DARK AND BROODY. YOU TWO CAN HANDLE THIS, RIGHT?

I could sympathize. I didn't want to do this, either. After my mother had kicked me out of the house six months ago, all I wanted was a place to belong. I had kinda sorta found that place with the Demon Underground, and I just wanted people to accept me—demon, warts, and all. Was that too much to ask? Apparently it was. Fitting in with the rest of the crowd was hard when I had to play the bad guy enforcer all the time. Especially when they feared me.

HEY, I LOVE YA, BABE, Fang said, nuzzling my leg.

I smiled down at him. *Thanks.* I did appreciate that, but I wanted more. Hell, I wanted it all.

"What's wrong?" Austin asked when I hesitated.

I sighed. "I'm just tired of Shade's drama. So is Fang. I wish someone else would deal with him." I looked at Austin hopefully, but he shook his head.

"You're the Paladin, darlin'. Micah can either count on you or he can't. Which is it?"

Yeah, well, sometimes responsibility sucked. I became Paladin because I believed in what Micah was trying to accomplish with the DU. And since I also believed in fighting for what was important to me, that meant doing what Micah asked, sucky or not.

I glanced down at Fang. *If I have to go in and confront Shade, so do you.*

He heaved an aggrieved sigh. FINE. LET'S GET IT OVER WITH.

"Okay," I told Austin and hitched my backpack up on one shoulder as I headed for the entrance. The new wooden doors looked a lot like the ones at Alejandro's main mansion and were probably just as sturdy. We'd broken down the previous oak doors the last time we'd been here and busted through the windows to take Emmanuel, the blood demon, by surprise. Though we'd whupped his butt good, we'd trashed the place in the process. Looked like Alejandro had gotten the doors and windows repaired.

"Looks good," I said. "Is the rest of the house cleaned up, too?"

He shrugged. "Partially. We're still working on it."

Austin let us into the house and flipped on the lights. Thank goodness someone had cleaned this area. No blood on the marble floor, no stray demon heads leaking nasty fluids over the grand curving staircase.

I could see Shade partway up the stairs, dark ribbons swirling everywhere to obscure his features—the price of being one-eighth shadow demon and cycling through hundreds of dimensions all the time.

He stood in exactly the same location where his twin sister Sharra had gotten sucked through the portal to the demon world where she'd died. I knew Shade was obsessed with getting her body back, but what did he imagine he could do here? He couldn't go through a portal he'd created—he had to remain on one side to keep it open. And there was no one else who could create one for him.

What's he thinking? I asked Fang.

DUNNO, Fang said, sounding surprised. I CAN'T HEAR HIS THOUGHTS FOR SOME REASON.

That was new—and troubling. Because it sure looked like Shade was trying *something*—he had his arms outstretched toward the left side of the staircase and hadn't even acknowledged our entrance.

"What's he doing?" Austin asked, frowning. He moved to the foot of the staircase, body tensed and ready for action, looking ready to take Shade down if necessary.

Since the crystal was so near, in Austin's pocket, I could use it to see Shade's expression. I connected with the amulet, then took a peek. Yep, his tortured expression was a pretty good clue he was trying to create a door into another world, and his lips were moving in soundless words. Cursing or praying, I didn't know which. "Trying to create a portal, evidently," I told Austin. Though I couldn't figure out why it wasn't working—no spooky green lightning cloud anywhere, though I could *feel* something trying to come into being.

"Shade, stop," I called out. This obsession of his was not only morbid, but dangerous. He couldn't go through one of his own portals, but what if there were demons waiting on the other side to invade our happy homes?

His brow furrowed even more, and his lips moved faster.

"I can take him down," Austin said, looking eager to do just that.

I understood his frustration, but I shook my head. "No, better not. He's generating a lot of energy—I don't know what will happen to it if you touch him." Would the lightning Shade generated in the cloud go through Austin?

FRIED VAMP. NOT A GOOD IDEA.

Yeah. I made a sudden decision. "I'm gonna need the crystal."

Austin frowned. "You can stop him without it."

"I can, yes." Lola could make Shade do anything. "Temporarily. But I want to stop him permanently." Only commands given using the crystal would last beyond my presence.

When Austin hesitated, I added, "So we won't have to do this ever again. Micah said it was okay, remember?"

Austin narrowed his gaze at me, and I gazed calmly back. "I'll give it right back to you, I promise." I understood that I had to prove to them all I could live without the crystal and its pull on me, but the amulet came in awfully convenient at times.

TOO CONVENIENT, MAYBE? Fang asked.

I ignored him.

Austin pulled the amulet out of his front pocket and handed it to me slowly, obviously still reluctant.

Sighing, I went slowly up the stairs toward Shade, who was still paying no attention to us, his eyes closed, arms outstretched, and mouth moving to form words I couldn't hear. When I got close enough, I tried Austin's way first, without the amulet to amp my power. "Stop it, Shade."

He ignored me and continued, looking even more desperate.

And this proved why I needed the crystal. "Shade, stop it now," I commanded, using the amulet to force him to obey.

He halted but stared at me with sadness in his eyes, as if I'd just killed his puppies. I felt for him, I really did, but couldn't let him endanger us or the rest of the world. "What were you thinking, trying to create a portal without backup?"

"I was *thinking* to rescue my sister," he said without heat.

"She's dead, Shade," I reminded him gently. "You can't rescue her, ever."

He sighed. "I know, but I can at least retrieve her body. We owe her that much."

I shook my head. "You don't even know if she'll still be there."

"I have to try, Val."

Feeling sorry down to my bones, I said softly, "No, you don't.

Micah doesn't want you to." Who knew what horde of demons he might let in from the other side? Clutching the crystal firmly in my hand, I said, "You will never open a portal to another world again without Micah's permission." I felt the command settle within him and take root.

His eyes widened, and he yelled, "No!" Snatching the crystal from my hand, he hurled it to the marble stair and stomped on it with his booted foot.

I felt the crystal shatter with a screeching high-pitched whine that pierced through my mind like shards of needle-tipped ice. Searing light flashed through the foyer, accompanied by a soundless shockwave that knocked us all on our butts. Blinded and deaf, I lay stunned at the bottom of the stairs for a few long moments, fear clogging my throat. I closed my eyes in disbelief. Was this loss of my senses permanent? *Please, don't let it be permanent,* I begged any gods who might be listening as I clutched at my aching head, which pounded with an unholy migraine.

WHOA. THAT WAS INTENSE.

An understatement. At least I knew Fang was okay.

Someone helped me to my feet. "Val, are you all right?"

Austin's voice. I could hear!

"No," I moaned and opened my eyes cautiously to blackness. "I can't see," I said, trying to hold back the panic.

"The shockwave overloaded the circuits," he told me, giving me a comforting squeeze. "I think it tripped some breakers."

"Oh." I wasn't blind—the lights were out. I glanced around, but it was too dark to see anything. I groped around on the floor.

"What are you looking for?" Austin asked.

"My backpack. I have a flashlight in it." It must have come off my shoulder when I was tossed on my butt.

"Here," Austin said and thrust it at me.

Thank heavens for vampire sight. I fumbled around in the pack until I found the flashlight by feel and switched it on. Pale yellow light illuminated the foyer. I sighed in relief. My vision was still intact, and the headache was receding. I played the light around the room, looking for Fang. He stood near Austin, shaking his head. *Are you hurt, Fang?*

I'LL LIVE. HOW ABOUT SHADE?

That's right—Shade had been at the epicenter of the blast. Weird. At one point, I would've worried about him first. Guess I was well and truly over him. But . . . was he all right?

Yes, he was sitting up on the cold marble floor, rubbing the back of his head with one hand. "You okay, Shade?"

"Yeah," he said. "Just bumped my head on the newel post when I fell. Remind me not to do that again," he said wryly.

He must be okay—that was the first time I'd heard him use anything resembling humor since Sharra died. Annoyed by the loss of the crystal, I snapped, "Was it worth it?"

He paused for a moment. "No—your command is still in place."

"Permanently, now," I reminded him sharply. "Since I can't use the amulet to remove it."

"I know." His tone was flat, saddened. Too bad I could no longer see his face. Unless, of course, I touched his skin, and I wasn't willing to do that right now.

I poked at one of the bigger crystal shards, wondering if it had retained any of the power of its larger self. Nope—it felt inert, dead. But, just in case, I picked up a few of the larger pieces and stuck them in my vest pocket.

SO, THAT'S IT? Fang asked. ONE BOOM AND IT'S GONE?

Yeah, it did seem kind of anticlimactic, after all the grief I'd been given about the thing.

"Why did it explode?" Austin asked.

I shrugged, my head pounding a little less now. "I have no idea. I don't have much experience with magickal objects. Ask Shade—he's the one researching stuff."

"I don't know, either," Shade said. "Does it matter?"

"I guess not," Austin said as Shade got to his feet.

Is he telling the truth? I asked Fang. *Can you hear him now?*

NOPE. ZERO, ZILCH, NADA.

"Why can't Fang hear you anymore?" I asked Shade.

Shade brushed the bits of crystal from his clothes. "Because I don't want him to. I found a way to keep him—and everyone else—out of my thoughts."

"Why?" Austin asked, his gaze narrowed suspiciously.

"Privacy," Shade said curtly. "I know it's a strange concept in your world, but I want to keep my thoughts to myself, without everyone picking over them."

WELL, EXCUUUUUSE ME, Fang said.

I rolled my eyes. *Shade can't hear you. Besides, he has a point.* We had kind of been all over him the past couple of weeks. "Sorry," I told Shade, meaning it.

Shade sighed. "And please don't ask how I did it—I don't want anyone poking around in my psyche under some misguided idea they're helping me."

"You got it," I said. After all, I'd just stopped him from doing the one thing Micah most feared—forever. I could afford to be generous.

"Thank you," Shade said and left without another word.

Austin gave me a raised eyebrow. "That was interesting."

I shrugged. "I just hobbled his powers, permanently." Not to mention taking away his only chance at recovering his sister's body. "I know what that's like, so I figure I can cut him some slack."

YEAH, Fang cheered. NO MORE BABYSITTING.

I shined my flashlight around the room. "We should probably clean this up. Do you know where the cleaning supplies are? Surely they left some. And maybe we could find the breaker box?"

"No clue on the cleaning supplies, but I can find out." He pulled out his phone, but before he could punch any buttons, a couple of young guys came running in, then stopped dead when they saw us. They couldn't be more than twenty or so and bore a strong resemblance to each other—both slight, blond, and, at the moment, slack-jawed.

VAMPIRES, Fang warned.

"Who are you?" Austin asked.

He didn't know them? Alarmed, I pulled out a stake, and Fang growled, bristling.

The vamps glanced at my stake. The taller of the two visibly gulped. "Are you the Slayer?"

"Yeah," I said and let Lola come out a little, just enough to make my eyes shine purple and creep them out. "Answer him. Who are you?"

The two glanced at each other, as if hoping the other would speak, then the taller guy said, "I-I'm Mike. He's Ike."

"Mike and Ike? Seriously?"

HOW . . . ORIGINAL.

"We're twins," Ike said, frowning. "Our mother named us," he said belligerently, as if daring us to make something of it.

"I don't know you," Austin said, narrowing his gaze. "Who's your sponsor?"

Mike and Ike exchanged wary glances. Ike nodded at Mike who said, "L-Luis. We're new." He gulped, looking nervous.

Well, heck, if Austin glared at me that way, I'd be nervous, too.

Austin relaxed a little. "What are you doing here?"

They did that thing again, where they each tried to mind meld with the other. Mike apparently won the right to speak. "We heard a noise and came in to see what it was."

"A crystal broke," Austin said, leaving out so much more they didn't need to know about. "But what I meant was, why were you here to begin with?"

Glancing down at the floor, Mike shrugged. "Uh, Luis asked us to help clean up. He's . . . outside."

"Good," Austin said and stuck his phone back in his pocket. "You can start with this mess. And turn the lights back on."

Ike and Mike exchanged another glance, then nodded and hurried off to do Austin's bidding.

"That was odd," I said, returning my stake to my back waistband.

Austin nodded thoughtfully. "Yes, it was. Supervising cleanup is usually Rosa's job." He shook his head and grinned at me. "But this mansion suits Luis's notion of what he's due in life. He must be eager to move in."

Yeah, this place was even grander than the other mansion. The lights came back on then, and Fang whined. A LITTLE HELP HERE?

"What's wrong, Fang?"

He glanced at the floor. TINY SHARP OBJECTS . . . NO SHOES?

Oh, of course. Sorry. "I just need to get Fang away from the shards," I explained to Austin. "Poor little baby doesn't want to cut his itsy bitsy little feetsies." Picking Fang up, I carried him to the front door, out of range of the broken crystal.

VERY FUNNY. NOW PUT ME DOWN.

Fang tried to sound stern, but it was difficult for the fuzzy mutt to look serious when I was cradling him like a little baby.

I grinned, and Austin opened the door for me so I could set Fang down.

Fang's feet hit the ground, and I could tell he was about to blast me with withering sarcasm but was interrupted by a voice from the right side of the stairs. "What are you doing here?" Luis demanded.

Austin raised an eyebrow at Luis's tone. "Taking care of errant shadow demons," he said briefly. "And you?"

"I'm supposed to meet Alejandro and Vincent here." He strode toward us, then paused when his shoes crunched on the crystal shards and looked down. "What's this?"

"Broken crystal," Austin said curtly. "Errant shadow demon, remember?"

Luis shook his head. "Irrelevant. Where's Alejandro?"

"Not my day to watch him," Austin drawled.

Luis's eyes narrowed at Austin's tone. "While you were out on a *date*, Alejandro and I actually had real business to attend to."

"What business?"

Luis sighed, sounding put-upon. "I was supposed to meet him here fifteen minutes ago." He consulted an old-fashioned pocket watch. "He's late."

Sheesh—who used pocket watches these days?

STUCK-UP VAMPIRES WHO ARE STUCK IN THE GLORY OF THEIR PAST? Fang suggested.

Good point.

Austin's look of annoyance vanished, replaced by puzzlement. "He's never late."

"Exactly," Luis said in exasperation. "So where the hell is he?"

"What's the big deal?" I asked. "Maybe he got held up in traffic or something."

Luis checked his phone, the modern device looking odd in his hands. "Not without sending a message or calling."

They frowned at each other, and tension rose in the silent room.

UH-OH. I HAVE A BAD FEELING ABOUT THIS, Fang said.

Yeah, me too.

Chapter Three

Austin

AUSTIN SCOWLED and tried not to let his annoyance show. Why did Luis always have to make everything a competition? "Maybe something came up." He pulled out his cell and speed-dialed Alejandro. No answer. "It went to voicemail," he said, frowning.

"You see," Luis insisted. "There *is* something wrong."

"Maybe." But Austin didn't want to buy into his fellow lieutenant's paranoia. "Or maybe an emergency came up," he repeated.

"Where exactly were you supposed to meet him?" Val asked.

"None of your business," Luis snapped.

"Well, aren't you just a little ball of sunshine," Val said, her eyebrow lifted at Austin as if to ask, "What burr got up his butt?"

Austin shrugged. It was Luis's default state these days. And he suspected Luis was just a tad jealous of Alejandro's interest in Val. "Be Teflon, Val," he said softly, knowing stuck-in-the-past Luis wouldn't get the reference. "Let it slide." Lately, Luis seemed to be looking for any opportunity to indulge the anger that seemed to simmer constantly below the surface. Not that Austin didn't want to see Val put him in his place, but this wasn't the time or place.

Luis narrowed his eyes at her. "This is none of your business. You may leave."

"Well, thanks soooo much for the permission," Val said, "but I think I'll stay. Just in case Austin needs me."

Luis snorted and began to say, "You—" but Austin cut him off.

"Thank you, Val. I'm sure Alejandro would appreciate the assistance of one of our staunchest allies." He glared at Luis, daring the jerkwad to contradict him. "Where were you supposed to meet him in the house?"

Luis scowled. "He said to meet in the kitchen, but he wasn't there."

"Let's give him some more time before we panic."

Before Luis could interrupt with some other rude comment, Austin asked, "What were you meeting here for?" Rosa was in charge of cleaning up the place and making it usable, not Luis. His arena was politics. Then again, Luis was constantly jockeying to be number one amongst the three lieutenants, trying to make himself indispensable. But Alejandro never showed favoritism, preferring to rotate the second-in-command position between the three. "Maybe he started without you," Austin suggested. Hell, he would do without Luis, given the chance.

Luis shot a glance at Val, but she was leaning down to pet Fang, acting as if she wasn't listening to the conversation.

"We're looking for Emmanuel's blood," Luis said shortly.

"You think he stored some of it?" That explained why they planned to meet in the kitchen.

Luis nodded. "Since he could use it to compel anyone to do his bidding, Vincent suddenly realized Emmanuel might have kept some on ice."

That made sense—the blood demon would have wanted to have it available whenever he needed it, especially if he wanted to control a larger number of people.

"What do *you* want it for?" Val asked suspiciously.

"Don't be an idiot," Luis snapped back. "Only Emmanuel could compel people using his blood."

Fang snarled, but Val let it slide, inhaling deeply and murmuring, "Be the Teflon."

"Remember, he also used his blood to heal people—your precious humans," Luis told her. "Vincent suggested we study it to see if we can duplicate its effects."

Austin understood why Vincent, the former EMT and current lab/clinic manager, would be interested. But Luis wasn't exactly altruistic. Not when it came to full humans, anyway.

Val asked the question for him. "Why?"

"Good public relations," Luis said.

That explained Luis's involvement—it was a political move, to get the humans on their side when the time was right to make their presence known in the world. At least, that's how Luis would see it.

"Sounds a bit self-serving," Val said. "But hey, if it helps people, I'm all for it."

"We don't need your approval," Luis bit out.

Val rolled her eyes. "You know, I think I'll go find something to sweep up the crystal." She headed off toward the kitchen.

Luis waited until she had gone, then said, "I don't understand what you see in her. She's a child."

"She's had a lot of life crammed into her eighteen years. More than most three times her age ever experience." Though she was unseasoned and impulsive, that would improve over time. But he wouldn't admit that to Luis. And, knowing Luis resented Val because Alejandro respected the "child" as much as he did his lieutenants, Austin couldn't resist needling the guy. "Besides, she's one of the best people I know."

"Best?" Luis repeated in disbelief. "You equate her with those such as Alejandro?"

"I do. Think about it. As a succubus, she has the power to compel any man to do her bidding—at any time. And how does she use it?"

Luis sneered. "To mesmerize you with lustful cravings, evidently."

Austin heard Fang growl from the doorway. Apparently, Luis had forgotten that the hellhound could understand everything they were saying—and probably relay it to Val. "No. She deliberately keeps her ability suppressed and uses it only when it's necessary to do her job or save someone's life."

"Or compel truthfulness," Luis spat out.

So that still stung, did it? Luis hated to feel as if he'd lost control of anything, and when Alejandro had Val force all of the vamps in the Movement to declare where their loyalties lay, Luis had resented the hell out of it—and her. "She didn't want to do that," Austin reminded him. "And she agreed only at Alejandro's request. Are you questioning Alejandro's decisions now?"

Luis glared at him but didn't answer.

"Besides, the soothsayer told Alejandro that he'd succeed with Val by his side." And Alejandro put all his time and energy into working on legislation to protect vampires belonging to the Movement while criminalizing those who didn't.

"If you believe the soothsayer was telling the truth," Luis snarled.

Austin narrowed his eyes. "Why wouldn't you want to do anything that furthers the Movement's agenda? Are you saying you're no longer on board with Alejandro's vision?"

Luis made a cutting gesture with his hand. "Don't be ridiculous. I just don't think partnering with a pack of demons is the way to do it. Or have you forgotten what the blood demon did?"

"Have you forgotten how that 'pack of demons' has helped us over the past few months—including with the blood demon?" Austin countered. "And Val is the reason for that."

"But if it wasn't for her demon friends, the blood demon wouldn't even—"

"Boys, boys," a woman protested from the open doorway. "Please, no fighting."

Austin glanced her way in surprise. He hadn't heard her come in. It was Lisette, the leader of the New Blood Movement in Austin, accompanied by two of her guards—matching blonds as always, chosen more for looks than brawn, and certainly not brain. Austin's eyebrows rose. She looked dressed for seduction in an emerald green dress that clung to her curves, her long red hair framing a plunging neckline that was guaranteed to compel the attention of all men in the room. "What are you doing here?" he asked abruptly.

Val came back in then, carrying a broom and dustpan. Ignoring the tension in the room, she started sweeping up the mess, either so Fang could come inside or because she didn't want to be in the middle of a vampire dust-up. The hellhound had wisely moved out of Lisette's way but couldn't advance any farther until the shards were gone.

"Ah, *mon ami*," Lisette exclaimed, pouting. "Are you upset with me? But I have permission to be here. Alejandro is expecting me."

Austin glanced at Luis, who nodded. "I suggested this blood research be a joint effort between the two groups. Alejandro agreed."

"So," she said, slinking in and eyeing Austin as if he were a particularly tasty bite. "I am here. Where is Guillaume?"

"Guillaume?" Luis repeated with a frown.

"I send him on ahead, to check the place first. He is here, no?"

Luis glanced at Austin, who shook his head. "Haven't seen him."

Lisette frowned. "Where is your master?"

Master? Alejandro didn't like to be called that, and she knew it. Austin wondered if it was worth it to correct her, but Luis spoke first.

"I don't know where he is," Luis said, his expression softening in Lisette's presence. "I was just planning to look for him when Austin distracted me."

Val set the broom and dustpan aside, the floor now free of debris. "Well, if you're so concerned, why don't we all look for him now?" she suggested.

It was a reasonable suggestion, and though Luis scowled, he said nothing.

"He's not in the kitchen," Val volunteered. "I was just there."

"And I just came from the right of the stairs," Luis said. He pointed at Lisette's guards. "You two, check downstairs. Austin, you and the

Slayer take upstairs. Lisette and I will search to the left. If you find him, send someone to let us know."

Austin didn't care for Luis's assumption of authority, but he let him have his little moment of dictatorship and motioned to Val. "Shall we?"

"Sure," she said, rolling her eyes.

They headed up the stairs together, Fang following behind.

Val chuckled.

"Care to share the joke?" Austin asked.

"Oh, nothing. Fang just made a comment about Luis, comparing him to Hitler."

Austin gave a wry grin. The hellhound wasn't far off. Luis deplored modern egalitarian society and wished they could return to the old feudal ways.

They turned left at the top of the stairs and started searching the bedrooms there. The cleaning crew hadn't made it this far yet—the rooms looked as though Emmanuel's followers had been so wrapped up in their charismatic leader that they hadn't bothered with simple hygiene or anything as unimportant as cleanliness.

Luckily, they didn't have to actually touch the disgusting mattresses or wads of clothing to know that Alejandro wasn't among them.

When they came to a bathroom, Val gave him a wary sidelong glance. "Uh, I think I'll pass."

Austin grinned. He could imagine what—

A scream from below scrambled his thoughts, and he and Val didn't even hesitate. They bolted downstairs toward the sound, Fang scrabbling after. That had to be Lisette. What would make her scream in such rage?

Following the sound of incoherent French invective, Austin and Val rushed to the room at the left of the stairs, followed closely by Lisette's guards. They burst into the altar room and found Lisette babbling in French at Luis, waving her arms like a crazed windmill.

"What's wrong?" Val and Austin asked in unison.

Lisette went suddenly silent and pointed a shaky finger at the floor behind the altar. "Guillaume. *Là-bas.*"

Austin rushed around the altar to see what had her so upset. There, lying face up on the floor, was the missing Guillaume with a dagger sticking out of his heart.

Chapter Four

Val

CONTRARY TO POPULAR belief, it wasn't just wood in the heart that would kill a vampire. Anything pointy would do. Poor Guillaume was definitely dead.

His body explained Lisette's scream, and I relaxed a little when I didn't see any immediate threat, though I remained on guard as Austin and Luis swiftly checked the hidden recesses in the rest of the room.

They found nothing, but I was still uneasy. This room would give anyone the creeps—black-shrouded walls, a roughhewn stone altar holding a tarnished silver cup and multiple knives, and unidentifiable icky stains decorating multiple surfaces. This was where Emmanuel had force-fed his followers his own blood, to compel them to treat him like the second coming. Major bad vibes here.

Especially for Guillaume.

WHICH ONE IS THAT? Fang asked, staring at the body. TWEEDLEDEE, TWEEDLEDUM, OR TWEEDLEDUMBER? LOOKS LIKE THEY LEFT TWEE AT HOME.

What? Oh, yeah, my nicknames for Lisette's showy male harem. *I don't remember which is which—they all look alike to me.* All tall, blond, buff, and totally subservient to Lisette. Pretty, but more decorative than useful, I suspected. And, I remembered, she wanted to add Austin to their number.

Fang snorted. FAT CHANCE. HE'S NO BOOTLICKER.

Yeah, definitely too butch to join their team.

Lisette let out another spate of French, then shook her head and spoke in English. "Who did this?" She looked at me, her eyes narrowed. "You—you are the Slayer, yes? You killed Guillaume?"

"No, of course not," I answered quickly. I didn't like the way she and the other two tweedles were looking at me. "I don't go around killing random vampires. Only the bad ones. And I didn't kill this guy. I would've used a stake, not a dagger." Cheaper and easier to leave behind.

"It's true," Austin said, standing up for me. "She is a friend of the New Blood Movement. And she was with me except for the few minutes she went to get a broom."

Even Luis had to agree. "We would have heard something if the Slayer had accosted Guillaume. But what of that 'errant shadow demon' you spoke of earlier?" he asked with a smarmy look I wanted to wipe off his face.

"Shade?" I snorted. "Yeah, right. It's not as if he could overpower a vampire." His skills ran only to opening portals and healing people, not great strength and dexterity.

"He may have witnessed something, though," Austin said.

True. "I'll ask him if he saw or heard anything." I called his cell, but there was no answer. Shrugging, I said, "I'll ask him later."

"And where is Alejandro?" Lisette demanded, her eyes narrowed.

"Alejandro didn't do this," Austin said with certainty. "He's missing, too."

Luis gave him a shrewd glance. "You think whoever did this killed Alejandro and Vincent?"

"Maybe," Austin said. "Did you find any other bodies?"

He sounded tense, but I wasn't sure if it was because he was ticked off at Luis or because Alejandro might have met with foul play. Probably both.

"No other bodies," Luis said.

YEAH, Fang agreed. I ONLY SMELL THE ONE DEAD UNDEAD.

The oxymoron ought to confuse me, but I knew what he meant.

"Then we need to find him before whoever found Guillaume does," Austin said, sharing a grim look with Luis.

I glanced around. "Well, there are so many people here, we've probably destroyed any evidence that might help us do that."

Luis snorted. "And who would need that evidence? We are not calling the police."

I'd had about enough of his surly behavior. Forget Teflon. "Oh, I don't know. Maybe one of us? You do intend to investigate, don't you?" Or was he too caught up in playing dominance games to think straight?

"Of course. And we don't need your help."

Ignoring him, I glanced down at the body. "Well, since Lisette sent him on ahead, we know he had to have been killed before we got here, or you would have heard something, right?"

Austin nodded, so I continued. "We got here about three fifteen. How about you, Luis?"

He frowned but answered anyway. "I arrived about three thirty, just as the lights went out. That's when Alejandro was supposed to meet me."

"Does he sometimes arrive early?"

"Frequently," Austin said.

I turned to Lisette. "Do you know what time Guillaume arrived?"

She gave an elegant shrug but seemed to believe I was one of the good guys—for now. "Perhaps around two thirty," she said, "to ensure that all was safe for my arrival. I was to meet Alejandro at three thirty as well."

And she'd shown up fashionably late, of course.

"Why were you late?" Luis asked, frowning.

"I was waiting for Guillaume to give the all clear first. But when I heard the two of you arguing, I came in." She glanced down at his body. Guess we knew why he didn't.

"Then it must have happened before we all got here," I said.

One of the tweedles leaned down to remove the dagger, but I said, "Wait—don't touch it. Is that one of Emmanuel's?"

He pulled his hand back, frowning.

"Does it matter?" Luis asked.

Austin's gaze swept the altar. "Looks like the others," he confirmed.

"Really?" I asked Luis in disbelief. "You left dangerous weapons around where anyone could use them?"

"We were waiting for Alejandro and Vincent to look at them first." He sneered. "Again, does it matter?"

"Maybe . . . if the knife was an athame and held magick." Though an altar usually only had one athame, not a collection of them. Then again, who knew what a blood demon's rituals needed?

"And maybe it isn't a ritual knife," Luis said. "He wasn't Wiccan, just a demon."

"How would we know if it's an athame or not?" Austin asked.

Uh, now that he mentioned it, I didn't have a clue. "A Wiccan would probably know." I stepped forward to peer at the dagger buried to the hilt in Guillaume's heart. The crossguard curved up in a flourish, and a green stone with red flecks was set in the pommel.

Austin peered at it, too. "Bloodstone," he pronounced.

FIGURES.

Stone . . . that reminded me. "There's a new demon in town," I told them. "Micah said she's a gemstone whisperer. Maybe she can get this stone to tell us something."

Everyone looked skeptical, even Austin. Come to think of it, it did sound kind of odd. But until a few months ago, I didn't even know other demons existed, much less what skills they had. And Micah would have no reason to lie to me about that. "I'm not sure how her ability works, but maybe she can tell us who touched it last—if we keep our hands off it."

Well, whaddaya know? They actually seemed to agree with me for a change. Before they could change their minds, I said, "Let me call Micah and see if she can come."

I called my boss, told him what had happened, and asked him to bring the gemstone whisperer by to see if she could learn anything from the bloodstone in the hilt.

YOU KNOW, Fang drawled. IF YOU ALL LEAVE THE ROOM, I MIGHT BE ABLE TO SMELL SOMETHING.

Good idea. I told the rest of them what he'd said. "Let's clear out."

They left the room, and Fang sniffed around the entire creepy place. "What do you smell?" I asked.

Fang roamed the room, nose to ground. LOTS OF PEOPLE—VAMPS, DEMONS, CRACKPOT RELIGIOUS FOLLOWERS . . .

"Any traces more recent than the others?" I didn't know if that was possible, but it was what we needed.

YEAH, IT'S POSSIBLE, Fang said. BESIDES THE DEAD TWEEDLE, I GET LOTS OF EAU DE BLOODSUCKER—SPECIFICALLY, ALEJANDRO, VINCENT, AND THOSE TWO CANDY VAMPS.

Candy vamps?

YOU KNOW—MIKE AND IKE.

Ah. I repeated the conversation for the others.

"Mike and Ike?" Luis asked.

"The two we sent to turn the lights back on and clean up the crystal," Austin said, looking thoughtful.

"I switched on the breaker," Luis said.

"And I cleaned up." So what had happened to Mike and Ike?

Austin and I exchanged glances. "They said you sent them here to clean up," Austin told Luis. "That you were their sponsor."

"I don't know of any vampires by those names," Luis said.

In unison, he and Austin said, "Rogues."

Oh, crap. They'd played us.

"Why would they kill Guillaume and take Alejandro?" Lisette asked.

Duh. "Because they want to be the only game in town?" I suggested.

"Then why not simply kill Alejandro and this Vincent as well?" she asked.

It was a reasonable question. "Blackmail?" I suggested. "Maybe they're going to send a ransom demand or something, demanding that you disband the Movement." After all, the Movement threatened the rogues' objective of fanging anyone they wanted.

"Entirely possible," Austin said thoughtfully.

"Or perhaps they took Alejandro and Vincent to torture them, obtain confidential information about the Movement," Luis suggested.

"We aren't going to find out just standing here," Austin bit out.

"Where do you suggest we start looking?" Luis shot back.

Whoa. Testosterone overload much? "Can you follow Alejandro's scent?" I asked Fang so everyone could hear.

I CAN, BUT HE'S BEEN ALL OVER THE PLACE HERE. I'M NOT SURE IT'LL HELP.

Repeating what he said for the benefit of the others, I asked aloud, "How about Mike and Ike? Can you follow their scents?"

I'LL TRY.

Everyone watched as Fang sniffed around in circles, then headed toward the staircase, where we'd seen them earlier. We all followed like ducklings until Fang said, STOP WANDERING AROUND. YOU'RE MESSING UP THE SCENTS. I JUST WANT VAL WITH ME.

I passed on the message, and they all congregated in the foyer while Fang did his bloodhound thing and I followed. His path took him through the kitchen and out to the side entrance, then he halted.

THE TRAIL STOPS HERE, he told me. THEY MUST'VE GOTTEN IN A CAR AND LEFT.

I was afraid of that. I returned to the foyer to find Luis shoving his face into Austin's. "This is your fault," Luis said.

Austin's fists clenched, but he didn't back off. "The hell it is."

"You're responsible for assigning Alejandro's guards."

"I did," Austin said. "And Alejandro refused to have anyone but Vincent today."

"Vincent wasn't enough, obviously," Luis said, his voice dripping with sarcasm.

"Well, sorry," Austin said, "but my crystal ball was broken. How would I know Vincent wouldn't be enough?"

"Perhaps because you wanted him to be unguarded?" Luis suggested.

"What? Don't be an ass. I had nothing to do with his disappearance."

"We only have your doxy's word for that."

Doxy? I wasn't sure what that meant, but I was pretty sure it wasn't a compliment.

IT'S NOT, Fang confirmed. HE'S CALLING YOU A TRAMP.

Asswipe. I'll tramp him.

Austin wasn't taking any guff. "Val isn't a doxy. And I'd take her word over yours any day. How do we know *you* didn't kidnap him so you could take over the Movement?"

Luis looked ready to explode, but Lisette said, "Enough. This is not helping." She glanced at me. "Did the *chien* find anything?"

"No, the trail ended at the side door. They must have gotten in a car and driven away."

"Was Alejandro with them? And Vincent?" Austin asked.

"No way to know. Their scents are everywhere."

MICAH'S HERE, Fang told me.

When I turned to glance at the door, everyone else's head followed, and Lisette slinked into a pose like a model, giving him a come-hither smile. Looked like Micah's incubus was working just fine. One of the tweedles whispered in her ear, and she backed off, scowling. Too bad. I'd like to see her come up against Micah's incubus, figuratively speaking.

Micah moved into the house, and a petite blonde followed, obviously keeping her distance from the incubus whose close proximity could inspire lust in any woman—except for me, of course. The blonde was about my age, with short, spiky hair, wearing a pale pink hoodie and a ton of jewelry—gemstones on every finger, jewels studding her ears, and even one in her belly button below her cropped top. She held herself with the sort of self-confidence I'd usually seen only in mature women. I wished I could display that sort of assurance.

"Good evening," Micah said. "Is this a bad time?"

Seemed like the perfect time to me. "No, this is good. Are you the gemstone whisperer?" I asked the girl. She looked nothing like I imagined a rock demon would appear.

She nodded, smiling, and shook my hand. "Ivy Weiss."

"Nice to meet you. I'm Val Shapiro." I introduced her to the vamps in the room, all except the tweedles whose names I didn't know, then introduced Fang.

"A hellhound?" she said in delight. "I've never met one before. And he can speak in my head?"

WHOA, Fang said. I'M NOT THE ONLY ONE. I'VE NEVER HEARD SO MANY VOICES IN SOMEONE'S HEAD IN MY LIFE. WHAT ARE THEY, IF NOT HELLHOUNDS?

Ivy grinned ruefully. "It's the price of speaking to stones. They're quiet most of the time, but they're excited about this situation, so there's a lot of chatter. The only way to block them out is by covering my head with silk." She demonstrated by pulling the pink hoodie up over her head. "Like this."

I had enough problems with Fang in my head. I couldn't imagine a whole bunch of voices. I'd go mad. I glanced at Fang, anticipating his comeback.

NAW, IT'S TOO EASY. BESIDES, I'M NOT CRAZY ABOUT ALL THOSE VOICES, EITHER. THINK I'LL STAY OUT OF HER HEAD.

Ignoring Fang, I asked, "What's your range? To hear the stones, I mean."

She shrugged. "It varies. Usually within a few feet, unless I've established a link with one already, then it's much farther."

Okay, so she couldn't tell anything from here. "We have a stone we'd like you to take a look at. Can you tell who touched it last? Or if it's booby trapped with magick?"

She shrugged. "Maybe. Let's see."

I led her to the body. Her pale face seemed to go even whiter when she saw the dagger sticking in the vamp's heart. "I—I don't think I'll be able to tell you anything," she said, clutching her hood around her face.

"Why not?" Luis snarled.

"The vibes—"

"You haven't even tried," Luis said and yanked her hood down. "What do you sense?"

Ivy's face filled with horror. "Nooo," she moaned, clutching at her head, and crumpled to the floor.

Chapter Five

Val

AS MICAH AND I rushed to Ivy's side, Austin got into Luis's face. "What the hell do you think you're doing?"

"Getting answers," Luis spat. "Or don't you want to find Alejandro?"

Austin backed off, but his fists were clenched. "*He* wouldn't hurt anyone to get those answers."

"I don't care—"

"That's obvious," Austin retorted. "You only care about yourself."

Luis took a swing at him, but Austin blocked it and punched Luis square in the face, sending him stumbling into the altar.

GO, AUSTIN! Fang cheered.

Though I shared the sentiment, this small space was not the place for a brawl, especially with two powerful, destructive vampires moving at breakneck speed. Leaving Micah to care for Ivy, I jumped up as Luis leapt for Austin, blood in his eye. Throwing out my hands to thrust Lola into both of them, I yelled, "Stop!"

I'd been careful to keep Lola up to capacity, but it was even easier than I'd expected to grab them both and force their compliance, even without the amulet. They halted obediently.

But now that I had them, what was I going to do with them? Damn it, having to grab your date by the chakras and force him to your will was *not* exactly the way to a man's heart. That's how I'd alienated Shade.

THIS IS AUSTIN, NOT SHADE, Fang reminded me. HE UNDERSTANDS.

But it shouldn't be necessary, I whined to myself. Why'd he have to go all Terminator on Luis?

OH, I DON'T KNOW. BECAUSE HE'S A MAN . . . BECAUSE HE'S A VAMPIRE . . . BECAUSE HE'S NOT A WIMP? WOULD YOU RATHER HAVE A TOTAL WUSS FOR A BOYFRIEND?

Well, no, but if I had to use Lola on him too frequently, that wouldn't make for a great relationship, either. *He's not my boyfriend,* I shot back at Fang. Not yet, anyway.

BUT HE WANTS TO BE. AND YOU HAVE TO ADMIT LUIS HAD IT COMING.

Yeah.

Lisette was suddenly in my face, up close and way too personal. "Release them," she ordered with a hiss, her canines elongating to make her, er, point.

I'd had about enough of her I'm-better-than-you, my-poop-don't-stink attitude. Sheesh, she was like a human version of Princess. I narrowed my eyes at her. "Back off, or Micah will do the same to you."

The tweedles seemed to take exception to that and took a menacing step toward me—or maybe toward Micah, who had risen to his feet beside me. "You, too," I ordered as I flicked Lola over their chakras in warning.

They looked startled but backed away.

Fang said, YOU'RE SCARING THE GEMSTONE WHISPERER.

I glanced at Ivy, who had regained her equilibrium and was slowly coming to her feet. She winced, looking more pained than scared to me. It did remind me what was important here, though. I loosened my hold on the vampire lieutenants. "Sorry," I told Austin and Luis, figuring an apology wouldn't go amiss, "but fighting in this small space isn't a good idea right now. Can you save it until after we find Alejandro?"

I reined Lola in but retained a light hold on them, just in case. Austin gave me a stiff nod. "I apologize, Slayer. I won't initiate any more altercations."

I appreciated the sentiment, but if he was calling me Slayer now and going all formal on me, did that mean he saw me more as an enforcer than a date? Not what I was going for.

NAW. HE WAS PROBABLY JUST EMPHASIZING IT FOR LUIS'S SAKE.

I glanced at Luis, who stood quietly fuming. *Maybe.*

YOU'RE NOT GETTING AN APOLOGY FROM THAT ONE.

Don't I know it. But Luis did give me a curt nod as assurance he wouldn't start pounding on Austin. I released them completely, and the tension in the room noticeably plummeted.

"Wow," Ivy said from inside her hoodie, her attitude apparently restored, "that was impressive. What did you do?"

SHE'S A SUCCUBUS, Fang told Ivy. SHE GRABBED THEM BY THEIR LUST HANDLES AND MADE THEM HER SLAVES.

I stiffened, then realized Austin couldn't hear that. Good thing.

Fang snorted. HE ALREADY KNOWS. AND NOW YOU'RE IVY'S HERO.

"What happened?" I asked Ivy. "Are you okay?" She certainly looked all right now.

She gripped the sides of her hoodie to keep it firmly on her head as she glared at Luis. "The reason I said I wouldn't be able to tell anything is because the bloodstone is traumatized."

"The *stone* is traumatized?" Lisette repeated in disbelief. "No, *Guillaume* was traumatized. A stone is inert, dead."

"To you, yes," Ivy said more calmly than I would have. "But from the moment gemstones are cut, polished, and admired, they become self-aware."

Kind of like a hellhound, I thought.

NOT FUNNY. I AIN'T POLISHED.

You got that right, I said, grinning as I finally scored one on Fang.

"And that is helpful, how?" Luis asked sarcastically, his jaw tight and his fists clenched.

"Gemstones absorb the emotions of people around them," Ivy explained. "The longer they're around someone and the stronger the emotion, the more likely they are to have absorbed it."

"Again, how is that helpful?" Lisette asked with a disdainful sniff.

"They can communicate what they know and feel to rock demons. *I'm* a rock demon," Ivy added in simple words, as if implying the two of them might not understand that with their limited intelligence.

Before Luis or Lisette could blast her, Austin said gently, "We are unfamiliar with rock demons."

"Call her a gemstone whisperer," Micah suggested. "It's closer to what she actually does."

Austin nodded. "How do we know they will speak the truth?"

Ivy shrugged. "They don't know how to lie, so they always speak the truth. Well, the truth as they see it from their limited, self-centered perspective, anyway." At a questioning glance from Austin, she added, "They talk about what matters to them, not you, and they have a hard time handling strong feelings." She glanced at the dagger. "This one must have witnessed some pretty awful emotions. I didn't even ask it anything, and it wouldn't stop screaming."

"Did you get anything from it at all?" Austin asked gently.

"Besides the screech in my head?" Ivy asked in disbelief. At Austin's nod, she said, "No, just that it felt the death. That's why it's screaming."

"Could you tell if there was any magick on the blade or the stone?" I asked.

She looked surprised, then paused for a moment. "I didn't think about it before, but there was no magick. I would have sensed it."

Well, that was a relief. We knew we could touch it now without being blasted.

"Can you tell us who did it?" Austin asked.

As if a dam had released somewhere within him, Luis blurted out, "And if anyone else was in the room. Anyone else killed? Was there—"

Ivy held up a hand to stop him. "I won't know anything else until I have a chance to cleanse the stone. It's screaming nonstop, remember?"

"How do you do that?" Austin asked.

"How long will it take?" Luis demanded.

"I use a special solution, with water, salt, and other minerals," Ivy said. "As with most magickal tools, the mixture soothes and purifies them."

Lisette snapped her fingers at Tweedledee, and he rushed off to the kitchen.

"As for how long . . ." Ivy shrugged. "Maybe a couple of days, maybe longer."

"Not acceptable," Luis said.

"Sorry," Ivy said and gave him back glare for glare. "They work on their own timetable, not yours."

The tweedle rushed back in, carrying a salt shaker and a Tupperware container full of water. Ivy looked doubtful but said, "Thank you. That's a good start until I get the rest of my tools. Could you . . . ?" She gestured toward the dagger.

The tweedle glanced at Lisette and, at her nod, removed it carefully from Guillaume's heart and placed the bloody thing in the plastic tub.

I glanced around the room. "What about the marble on the floor or the altar stone?" I asked her. "Can they tell you anything?"

Ivy shook her head regretfully. "It has to be a gemstone, though some of the things we call gemstones don't hold awareness—those that come from a formerly living being, like coral, amber, and pearls."

Luis looked impatient at the geology lesson.

"Even if the marble and altar stone were aware, I get the impression they'd be shrieking, too," Ivy said, looking around in trepidation at the bleak room. "What *was* this place?"

"You don't want to know," I assured her.

Micah stepped forward. "Ivy and Val, why don't we go so we can get the proper solution to cleanse the bloodstone—and question Shade to see if he knows anything."

Austin nodded. "We'll finish searching the house." He slanted a gaze at Guillaume. "And take care of our own."

I sighed and shared a glance with Austin. Not exactly how I expected this date to end.

WHAT? Fang asked. YOU WERE HOPING TO SUCK FACE? MAYBE GET A LITTLE SOMETHIN' SOMETHIN'?

Again, I was soooo glad Austin couldn't hear my hellhound. *Shut up.* But as an ending to a first date, it kind of sucked.

As if he'd read my mind, Austin quirked a smile at me and said, "We'll try again."

I sighed and nodded back. Now, if our jobs would just let us. . . .

Chapter Six

Val

FANG AND I RODE in Micah's Lexus, which was a nice treat. Between his fancy car and the ones the vampires maintained, they'd kind of spoiled me, making me wonder if I should get something other than my Valkyrie motorcycle. Don't get me wrong, I loved my bike—it was fast, maneuverable, and gave me a sense of freedom. But it was also noisy, let in the weather, and wasn't exactly passenger-friendly. Except for Fang.

YEAH, I LOVE IT, BUT YOU GOTTA ADMIT A CAR WOULD'VE BEEN NICE DURING THE SLEET LAST MONTH. PLUS, YOU COULD GET MORE SLAYAGE EQUIPMENT IN A TRUNK.

Maybe I'll look for a car, I told him. I couldn't afford something as expensive as the guys had, and one this luxurious would just be ruined if I had to transport a slayed vamp, but protection from weather would be nice.

Sheesh—was I becoming a wimp?

Fang snorted. NO CHANCE, BABE. DON'T WORRY—I'LL WARN YA IF YOU START GETTING WUSSY.

Good to know.

Micah called Shade on his cell and arranged for us to go by his apartment.

In the front seat, Ivy yawned. "Do you guys always stay up all night?"

"Sorry," Micah said apologetically. "But with me working at Club Purgatory and Val's job as Paladin and her association with the vampires, we do tend to work at night and sleep during the day."

I wondered why she'd asked, then realized we were going to be roommates for a while. I hoped she wasn't too much of a day person, or we'd annoy each other with our opposite hours.

Ivy nodded. "Well, I'm a night person, too, so I get it. But I think this is the latest I've ever stayed up."

YOU'LL GET USED TO IT, Fang said.

Ivy gave him a strange look as if she wanted to say she didn't *want* to get used to it, but we'd arrived at Shade's apartment, so there was no time to discuss it further. Shade greeted us at the door with a puppy in his hands and Princess at his feet. Luckily, that grounded him in this world so he wasn't all swirly when he was introduced to the gemstone whisperer.

"How cute," Ivy exclaimed, reaching out to run a finger over the puppy's soft fur. She shot a glance at Fang. "She looks like you."

THAT'S ONE OF MY GIRLS, Fang said proudly. I could almost see his chest expanding with pride.

"What's her name?" Ivy asked.

"We're calling her Delta for now," Shade explained. "Hellhounds choose their own name when they're old enough."

"When will that be?"

He glanced with affection at the puppy. "I'm not sure. They're about a month old now, so . . . ?" He glanced down. "Ask Princess."

I wondered why we he didn't just ask her himself, then remembered he'd blocked the hellhounds' ability to communicate with him. Hmm, how would Princess feel about that?

SHE HATES IT, Fang said. AND SHE'S GIVING SHADE THE COLD SHOULDER TREATMENT UNTIL HE TALKS TO HER AGAIN.

Princess answered the question, even though Shade couldn't hear the answer. THEY WILL CHOOSE A NAME WHEN THEY CHOOSE A COMPANION, Princess said, looking suspiciously at Ivy. But THEY ARE TOO YOUNG TO LEAVE ME NOW. WE MUST WAIT UNTIL THEY'RE AT LEAST TWO MONTHS OLD.

Ivy glanced down at Princess in surprise, apparently at finding another dog who could speak to her.

Micah smiled. "We are blessed with an abundance of hellhounds."

I wasn't sure anyone would call Princess a blessing. . . .

"Aren't you beautiful?" Ivy said, bending down to look at the Cavalier King Charles Spaniel.

YES, I AM, Princess agreed. YOU MAY PET ME.

Ivy quirked a smile but did as Princess bid her. When Princess had enough, she pointedly ignored Shade and trotted back over to the other three puppies, who were tussling good-naturedly in the living room.

"Could I hold one?" Ivy asked.

"Sure," Shade said and handed her the puppy he'd been petting.

Of course, Shade went all swirly, the ribbons of gray light spiraling endlessly within the confines of his skin. Ivy looked startled.

I hurriedly explained. "Shade is a shadow demon. Interdimensional energies move through him constantly, unless he's grounded in a being from this world."

"Oh," Ivy said faintly. "I've never met a shadow demon before."

"And I've never met a rock demon," Shade said, humor in his voice. "I've read about your kind."

"You read about rock demons?" Ivy said in surprise. "Where?"

Shade and I slanted a glance at Micah, uncertain if we should mention the books. "You can trust her," he said.

"In the *Encyclopedia Magicka*," Shade explained. "How do you talk to them?"

Ivy shrugged. "Mostly, I experience the emotions they've absorbed from the people around them. Once they're clear of negative emotions, they will often communicate with me."

"I've seen some books that list properties each stone possesses," Shade continued. "Are those accurate?"

Ivy looked confused, as if wondering why Shade wanted to know.

"I've asked Shade to expand our knowledge in the encyclopedia," Micah explained. "It's important to know as much as we can so when someone needs help, we know how to assist them."

Ivy nodded. "A well-cared-for gemstone can enhance your health, well-being, and other characteristics. Most of the 'new age' books published about their properties are pretty accurate—I can tell you which ones to use if you like." Her gaze slid off his swirling face, as if she didn't know where to look.

"Sorry," Shade said. "I know I take some getting used to." He scooped another puppy off the floor, and we could see his face again, bearing a sad smile.

Ivy smiled down at Delta in her arms. "How cute. She's talking to me."

"She is?" I asked in surprise. They hadn't talked to me yet, and I had to admit to a bit of jealousy. "What's she saying? Goo goo ga ga?"

Ivy laughed. "No, more like 'nice lady, rub my belly, feed me.' "

Definitely Princess's child.

HEY, Fang exclaimed. WHADDAYA EXPECT? SHAKESPEARE? SHE'S ONLY A BABY.

Sorry.

"I'm sure you didn't come by just to introduce me to Ivy," Shade said to Micah. "What did you need?"

"Alejandro went missing tonight from the blood demon's house, just about the same time you were there. Do you remember seeing or hearing anything?"

Shade frowned as he stroked the puppy in Ivy's arms. "I heard some people wandering around in the other rooms, but I don't know who they were."

"You weren't curious?" Micah asked with a frown when Shade wouldn't meet his eyes.

"He was too busy muttering to himself while trying to open a portal," I drawled. He probably hadn't heard much.

Shade shot me an annoyed look. "Well, I won't be doing that anymore, will I?"

"You can with Micah's permission," I reminded him tartly.

Micah gave me a questioning glance, and I explained about the shattered crystal that had sealed in my last order to Shade.

Shade shrugged. "I was trying to avoid everyone there," he admitted. "Keep a low profile. I wish I could help, but I really don't know anything about Alejandro's disappearance."

"You didn't hear any screaming?" I asked. "Or anything else?"

He shook his head. "No screaming. It did sound like people were moving furniture around in that altar room, but that's it."

Moving furniture? Well, Guillaume was pretty much dead wood, but I wouldn't call him furniture. "Could it have been a scuffle you heard?"

"Could be. I don't know—I wasn't paying attention."

I sighed. "Okay, I guess I need to get the books back so I can see if I can find a spell that might help." Though I was the Keeper of the encyclopedia, I'd loaned the books to Shade to help with compiling everything we knew about demons and other nonhuman entities. With the mage demons defeated, we didn't have to worry as much about the encyclopedia being stolen—and the books tended to protect themselves from anyone else.

DO YOU REALLY WANT TO USE ANOTHER SPELL? Fang asked. YOU JUST GOT BACK UP TO SPEED WITH LOLA.

No, I didn't want to deplete the strides I'd gained with Lola, but it was imperative to find Alejandro. Not only because he was the leader of the New Blood Movement and my friend, but because I had a feeling his three lieutenants—Austin, Luis, and Rosa—would each want to step into the vacuum of power left in his absence. I didn't need that kind of vampire drama on my watch.

LOOK AT YOU, BEING ALL SMART AND ANALYTICAL, Fang said

admiringly. BUT I DOUBT ROSA HAS A CHANCE AGAINST THE OTHER TWO.

He was probably right. She was more the domestic type, if you could call a vampire domestic.

"You don't have a finder?" Ivy asked in surprise.

Facepalm moment. "Oh, yeah, we do." Duh.

Micah nodded. "I was already planning to contact Erica in the morning. She's probably sleeping right now."

"Good idea." Maybe this would be easier than I thought.

Micah thanked Shade and asked him to let me know if he remembered anything else, then we left. I took the encyclopedia with me anyway, just in case we needed it for something else. Though I usually felt its pull when I was away from it, it seemed to like being with Shade, so the pull wasn't as insistent when it was with him. And it wasn't as if I could carry around three heavy books in my backpack all the time anyway.

Ivy yawned, and Micah said, "Let's get Ivy to a bed. She left her car at your townhouse, so we can just head there."

Good idea. The gemstone whisperer looked beat. After we took her luggage into the townhouse and Micah left, I showed her to Gwen's former room. "You want to sleep now?"

She shook her head. "No, I need to get that bloodstone in a proper cleansing bath first."

"What do you need?"

"I have everything I need in my case." She picked up a soft-sided carry case like the type used by salesmen. Opening it, she pulled out a white ceramic dish, sea salt, and some herbs, then took them to the kitchen. She filled the dish with water, sprinkled in the salt and herbs while keeping her hoodie firmly over her head, then said, "Would you mind putting the athame in the cleansing bath?"

"Sure, no problem." Micah had put the Tupperware container on the kitchen table, so I pulled the dagger from the pink water. Even if the salt water hadn't helped the stone, it had at least rinsed off most of the blood. I ran it under the water in the sink to get rid of any residual blood—that couldn't be good for cleansing the stone—then slid it into the ceramic dish.

Ivy secured an elasticized silk cloth over the top, then removed her hoodie with a sigh. "Good. That's done. So, what's up with McSwirly?"

Surprised, I said, "Huh?"

She grimaced. "Sorry, I watch too much TV."

A WOMAN AFTER MY OWN HEART, Fang declared.

"I mean Shade," Ivy explained.

Was she interested in Shade?

MAYBE. SHE THINKS HE'S HOT BUT WONDERS ABOUT THE SADNESS IN HIS EYES.

Yeah, he was a total hottie, but he was kind of damaged right now, not exactly great boyfriend material. I should know. Aloud, I said, "He just lost his twin sister Sharra and has been trying to retrieve her body from the demon dimension."

"That sounds . . . dangerous."

"It is. That's why I stopped him."

She nodded. "So, are you two dating? I kind of sensed something going on between you."

So she *was* interested. "We were, but not anymore."

SHE'S DATING AUSTIN NOW, Fang told her.

"The vampire?" Ivy's eyes widened.

"Yeah." I understood her shock—I'd resisted dating a bloodsucker for a long time, but Austin was different. "How much do you know about vampires and the New Blood Movement?" I asked.

"There isn't a Movement in Sedona yet, but Micah explained it to me. I take it they're the good guys here?" She sounded doubtful.

"Yeah, they really are. Under Alejandro's leadership, they're trying to wipe out the rogue vampires and pass legislation to make it mandatory for all vampires to use blood banks instead of munching on people. That's why it's so important to find Alejandro." I grimaced. "Not to mention the fact that he keeps Luis in check."

Ivy grinned. "Looked like Austin was doing that quite well."

"Yeah, he was, wasn't he?"

Fang's jaw dropped in a doggie grin. WOW, IS THAT PRIDE I HEAR IN YOUR VOICE FOR YOUR MAN?

Bite me. Aloud, I said, "But having the two of them at each other's throats isn't good for the organization."

Ivy grinned. "I was impressed by the way you took control and forced them to obey you. Must be nice being a lust demon."

I squirmed. I wasn't really proud of what I had to do, and I still wasn't comfortable with using my powers to control men. "Not really. I can't get too close to any man without him getting sucked into Lola's energy field."

"Lola?"

"That's what I call the succubus part of me."

"But . . . having every man want you, that's gotta be good, right?"

Wrong. I grimaced. "Not if they only want me because Lola makes 'em feel good."

She nodded in understanding, and I added, "I use it only when absolutely necessary."

"That's what makes you a good Paladin."

"I guess." Uncomfortable with the conversation, I changed the subject. "So, why are you visiting San Antonio?"

"I've always wanted to come here, see the River Walk, do the tourist thing."

In March? Something didn't add up. "No, why are you *really* here?"

Her mouth gaped open a bit, and she darted a glance at Fang.

I DIDN'T SAY ANYTHING, he said, his jaw dropped in a doggie grin. VAL'S JUST SMART THAT WAY.

She shrugged sheepishly. "Okay, I admit we've heard some rumors about the strange things that have been happening here. And Patricia—she's the leader of the Underground in Sedona—asked me to check it out, talk to the local people and stones, see if we need to be worried. But I've been traveling to lots of cities, not just here."

YEP, SHE'S NOT HOLDING ANYTHING BACK, Fang confirmed.

Not that she could, with Fang reading her every thought and emotion. "Well, I don't know what would worry you, but we've had more than our share of weird happenings, as if San Antonio is a magnet for trouble or something."

"Kind of like the hellmouth in the Buffyverse?" she asked.

Now, that TV show I was familiar with. "Yeah, but nothing so . . . concrete, physical. I think it's more because of opposition to Alejandro's New Blood Movement and because the *Encyclopedia Magicka* is here." They'd both certainly attracted their share of psychos.

"Didn't I also hear something about an amulet that could enhance your abilities?"

Well, if Micah and Fang trusted her, I guess I could, too. "Yeah, but no longer. Remember I talked about Shade smashing a crystal earlier this evening? That was it." An idea occurred to me. "Hey, I kept some of the crystal shards. Do you think you could talk to them, see if I can still use them?"

"That depends on whether it was man-made or formed in the earth. I can't talk to man-made crystals."

"Well, this one must not have been man-made, because it talked to me."

"To you? Not possible," Ivy said firmly. "You're not a gemstone whisperer."

"But it did."

YEP, Fang said. I HEARD IT, TOO.

Ivy frowned, looking worried.

"What's wrong?"

"There's some lore about mage demons imprisoning other demons in crystals. So, this crystal not only talked to you but helped you enhance your powers?"

I nodded.

"Then it's possible it housed a demon."

Oh, crap. That couldn't be good.

I TOLD YOU THAT THING WAS BAD NEWS.

Ignoring him, I asked, "So, when it was shattered, what happened to the demon? Was the demon killed?" I gulped. "Or . . . released?" Just what I didn't need—another rogue demon on the loose.

"I don't know," Ivy said with a frown. "But let's find out. You have the shards in your pocket?"

How . . . ? Oh, she'd probably heard them or something. I nodded and pulled the pieces from my pocket.

She handled them thoughtfully.

"Are you getting anything?"

"Not really. It wasn't man-made, but the trauma of breaking has put them into shock. They're not screaming like the bloodstone, but they're not coherent, either. They need to be cleansed before I can get anything out of them."

She slid them into the cleansing solution with the athame.

"How long will it take?"

She shrugged. "I don't know—it takes as long as it takes. The more traumatized the stone, the longer we'll have to wait."

Oh, great. Not only did I have to rely on inanimate objects to give me information, but I had to wait until they were ready to talk. Slaying vampires suddenly seemed a whole lot easier.

Chapter Seven

Val

IVY SLEPT AS LONG as I did, thanks to room-darkening curtains, way into the afternoon. Micah made arrangements for Austin and me to meet with Erica Small, the finder, after sundown, since he knew that the best way to find Alejandro was to have an object or person that was closely associated with him present when she did her finding thing.

So, we puttered around the house and vegged. After we ate dinner, courtesy of Fang's favorite pizza delivery place, Ivy said, "I don't sense any gemstones at all here. You don't have any jewelry?"

"I'm not really the jewelry type," I admitted, then wondered if she'd been hoping to read me through any stones I might own.

PROBABLY, Fang said.

"Well, it certainly makes for a peaceful place," Ivy said with a smile. "And you have no idea how much I appreciate that. But if you'd like, I can recommend some stones to leave around the house, to increase the positive energy."

What could it hurt? "Sure," I said. "Speaking of stones, can you get anything from the bloodstone yet? Or the crystal shards?"

Ivy checked on the stones in her special solution. "As I expected, not ready to come out yet."

I nodded. It was nearing sundown, so I grabbed my backpack. "I'll let Austin know." There was a peculiar look on her face, so I asked, "What?"

"I was hoping I could go with you— get a feel for what you do and how you do it here in San Antonio."

I hesitated. I was beginning to suspect the Sedona demons thought I was a danger to demonkind everywhere. Was she spying on me?

SHE'S THINKING—

No, don't tell me. Leave her some privacy. I'll ask her if I really want to know. And, given Ivy's frankness, she'd probably even tell me the truth. Like her gemstones.

CHILL. THIS IS THE BEST WAY TO PROVE YOU'RE NOT DANGEROUS, Fang said.

Or that I *was.* Was this such a good idea?

"It's drizzling out there," Ivy said, obviously sensing my reluctance. "We can take my car."

AN EXCELLENT IDEA, OH GREAT ONE, Fang mocked me. BETTER THAN GETTING SOAKING WET ON YOUR BIKE.

Oh, all right. "Okay," I said out loud. "But you do realize we may run into danger?"

HECK, IT'S ALMOST A GIVEN, Fang said to both of us.

Ivy nodded. "It's okay. I can handle myself."

I wasn't sure how, but it was her hide to risk. I shrugged. "Let's go. First stop, the vampire mansion."

I stowed the books in a safe place, and we headed out into the drizzle to her car—a cute little MINI Cooper in bright yellow with black racing stripes across the hood and roof.

I hesitated—I hadn't noticed the color last night. "Wow. That's . . . bright."

Ivy grinned and opened the doors. "It's called the bumblebee. I couldn't resist."

COME ON, Fang said as he jumped in out of the wet. IT'LL BE FINE.

What the heck. I got in the front seat alongside Ivy, my nose wrinkling at the scent of eau de wet dog.

WELL, EXCUUUUUSE ME, Fang muttered. YOU DON'T HEAR IVY COMPLAINING—AND IT'S HER CAR.

Ignoring him, I gave Ivy directions to Alejandro's mansion. By the time we arrived, the sun had fully set, and I could see the vampires were awake, given that the sun-defying shutters had been rolled up to let in the night.

Ivy looked thoughtfully at the mansion. "How many vampires are in there?"

"It varies. But a lot of them live here. Others live in converted hotels above the blood banks." And maybe other places—I really didn't know.

She gave me a wry look. "I'll wait in the car."

SO WILL THE SMELLY WET DOG, Fang informed me.

I shrugged and got out of the car, then dashed through the rain to the front door and knocked. Rosa opened it, and her eyes widened. "You have news?"

Rosa was normally totally polished and put together—one hot

Latina. But today, her eyes were puffy with dark circles under them, her hair was listless, and it looked as though she hadn't slept in decades. Tension practically radiated from her. I'd long suspected Alejandro was her lover as well as her boss, and this did nothing to make me rethink that. "No, sorry, I don't. I came by to pick up Austin, as well as something of Alejandro's, to take to the finder."

She opened the door wider to let me in, and the tension I'd thought was coming from her was actually permeating the entire house. About a dozen sullen vampires glared at me through narrowed eyes. It looked as though I'd interrupted an argument of some sort, with two sets of vampires facing each other across the open expanse of the entryway in what appeared to be a showdown. Fangs at twenty paces?

Lola perked up. All that lovely male energy—she wanted a taste of that, and her tendrils surged toward the vamps. I pulled the tendrils back and suppressed her urges ruthlessly. This was not the time or the place, and I promised her that Austin would help us out in that area sometime soon. At least, I hoped so.

Rosa threw up her hands. "Take Austin, take whatever you need. If you could take Luis, too, that would be *fabuloso*."

"Uh, I'll pass," I said as diplomatically as I could.

She let out a torrent of Spanish and gestured imperiously at the bloodsuckers filling the foyer, as if she were trying to shoo them away like errant chickens.

Austin came down the staircase, looking harried and more than a bit pissed. "Disperse, now," he ordered.

Some of them moved, but others just looked stubborn. "What's going on?" I asked when he reached me.

"The idiots want us to choose one person to be in charge, and they're starting to take sides."

Surprised, I asked, "Didn't Alejandro designate a deputy?"

"No, it's only necessary when he's gone for an extended period of time, and then he rotates the duty amongst us." He raised his voice and glanced askance to ensure the lingering bloodsuckers would hear him. "He hasn't been gone long, and I refuse to believe he isn't coming back, so there's *no need* to choose a new leader."

"*Sí*," Rosa said emphatically. "Back to work, all of you. Or I will have the Slayer force you to."

I had to curb Lola's leap of hope as the last lingering vampires slunk off. Jeez, since when had I become the boogieman?

"The bloodstone isn't talking yet," I told him. "So we will still need to see the finder."

Austin nodded and led me to Alejandro's study. "Here," he said, removing the bust of Cortez from his desk. "He touches this a lot when he's thinking. Will it do?"

"It should," I said as I picked up the heavy thing. The brass was dull on the guy's head where Alejandro evidently petted it often. Glancing at Austin speculatively, I said, "This will probably be enough for the finder—you don't need to come if you're needed here."

Austin's lips thinned. "No, I won't stay and play into their power struggle to force a decision."

Vampire politics. Couldn't blame him. I didn't want to get involved, either.

Austin's lips twisted, and he ran a hand through his hair. "Sorry, I'd hoped to get to know each other better."

Lola let me know how very disappointed she was, but the stakes were so high, our fragile new relationship would have to wait. "Don't worry about it. Let's get Alejandro back first, then worry about . . ." Hmm, how should I finish that statement?

"Us?" Austin asked, quirking a grin at me.

I shrugged. Yeah, if there was an "us." Lola pushed, insisting I worry about it *very* soon—she really liked Austin. I was too embarrassed to admit that, so I said, "Come on. Ivy and Fang are waiting for us in her car."

Austin put on his hat and took the bust from me, then followed me out to the bumblebee, thoughtfully grabbing an umbrella from the stand by the door to cover me. He took one look at Ivy's car and came to an abrupt halt. "We are *not* riding in that."

I couldn't help but grin. "I don't know. I've been thinking of buying a car myself, and this is really cute."

He slanted a glance at me. "Maybe, but it's also rather conspicuous for what we do, and I'm not sure I'd fit."

I glanced at his long legs. He'd probably fit in the front, but that meant I'd have to squeeze into the miniscule back seat. "Fair enough. Want to take one of yours?"

He nodded. "And when it comes to buying a car, I'll help you."

My eyebrows rose. Seemed like cars were a guy thing no matter how old they were. But since I really had no idea what to look for, I'd welcome his help.

Austin turned to open one of Alejandro's dark luxury cars while I leaned down to Ivy's window. "We're taking one of the vampmobiles," I informed her. "So we can all fit. You can leave your car here—it'll be fine. Unless you want to go back to the townhouse?"

She didn't even hesitate. "I'm coming with you," she said firmly and moved her car off to the side.

By that time, Austin had a vampmobile ready and waiting to go, so Ivy, Fang, and I climbed in. We drove to Erica's, and, though she looked startled at seeing so many of us at her door, she graciously invited us in, now visibly pregnant.

After I introduced everyone, and she settled us down at the dining room table, she asked, "What is it you're trying to find?"

"It's not a what, it's a who," I told her. "We need to find Alejandro. I remember you said it's easier to find a man with something he owns and touches a lot, or someone who knows him, so I brought Austin and this." I nodded at the bust.

Erica took the bust and spread a map of San Antonio on the table, then brought out a chain with a spear of amethyst shaped like a chunky hexagon at the top and tapering to a point at the end.

Ivy smiled. "May I?" she asked, nodding at the pendulum.

"She's a gemstone whisperer," I explained.

Looking curious, Erica handed it to her.

Ivy stroked the thing and smiled. "It is a good stone. Happy to have such an important job, and it likes being with you. You might want to keep it in a silk pouch to keep it from retaining any negative feelings from your clients between readings. It will serve you better."

Erica's eyebrows rose, but she said, "Thank you. I will." She placed her left hand on the bust and held the pendulum lightly between her thumb and forefinger over the map, swinging it in a wide circle. I remembered that the amethyst would slowly spin in smaller, tighter circles until it stopped and landed on Alejandro's location.

I watched eagerly, but the pendulum continued to swing in wide revolutions, without zeroing in on the vampire leader's location.

Erica frowned. "Perhaps he is not in San Antonio," she said. "Let's widen the area."

She spread another map across the table, this one of the whole world. Sheesh—I sure hoped he was at least still in Texas.

Still, no luck.

WELL, HECK. IT'S NOT LIKE HE'S IN OUTER SPACE, Fang said. YOU THINK HER PREGNANCY IS INTERFERING WITH HER FINDING?

I don't know.

"You are certain this object is closely associated with him?" Erica asked.

"Positive," Austin said.

"Let's try using you instead," Erica suggested. "You know him well."

She held Austin's hand and told him to think of Alejandro, but there was still no luck. Crap. I didn't want to think about the implications.

"Maybe it doesn't work on vampires?" Ivy suggested.

"It should," Erica said doubtfully. Still holding Austin's hand, she said, "Think of another vampire, one whose location you know."

She held the pendulum over the map of San Antonio, and this time the pendulum swung in tighter and tighter circles until it suddenly jerked to a stop and fell on the map, pointing to the west side blood bank.

Austin nodded. "Yes, that's where Luis usually is."

Crap. That blew the pregnancy interfering idea. I decided to point out the elephant in the room. "Is it possible that you couldn't find him because he's . . . dead?"

Erica frowned. "No, if he's dead, it should find his body."

"Even if he's . . . ash?" I asked, wincing at the thought.

Erica looked stricken. "I'm sorry, I don't know."

Austin's face went blank, and Ivy touched Erica's hand gently. "Is it possible that there's something or someone deliberately interfering with your ability to find him? Like a spell?"

Good question—and one I hadn't thought of.

"I don't know," Erica admitted. "I suppose it's possible, though I've never had it happen before."

Well, at least that gave us some hope. Austin's face was so rigid, I hoped, for his sake, that Alejandro was still alive. "I'll check the encyclopedia," I promised. "See if I can figure out something."

Austin nodded curtly, and we thanked Erica and left with the bust.

Once we were seated in the car, Ivy said, "Okay, assuming Alejandro isn't dead, what other leads do we have?" She sounded as if she had the utmost confidence in our ability to find him.

SHE DOES, Fang confirmed.

"We need to follow up on Mike and Ike," Austin said. "They must be involved."

My thoughts exactly. "Any idea how to find them?"

He glanced at Erica's front door, then must have realized we didn't know them well enough for her to find them. "No—we don't have any idea where the rogues are headquartered . . . if they even have a headquarters."

"What about the three Cs?" I asked. At Austin's confused look, I added, "Those three newbies at the park—they were recently turned by the rogues. Think they might know?"

He nodded, his expression lightening. "Good idea. And if they visited a blood bank like I told them to, we might be able to find them."

We headed to the nearest blood bank on the east side. I hadn't been to this one before, but it was a converted hotel like the others, with the blood bank on the bottom floor and rooms upstairs for the Movement's vamps. As Ivy looked around curiously, Austin spoke to the girl at the desk, describing Charlie, Chris, and Carlos.

"Sorry, I don't remember them," she said. "Do you know what school they go to? If they're students, they probably went to one near their college."

"I don't know," Austin said. "Did you get that from them?" he asked me.

I thought for a moment. "No, but I got the feeling they didn't live far from the park. Brackenridge Park," I clarified for the receptionist.

The girl nodded. "Then they probably went to the midtown blood bank."

"Thanks," Austin said. "We'll check there."

When we got back in the car, Ivy had all kinds of questions about the vampire blood banks and how they operated. I answered them as best I could while Austin took a phone call.

He interrupted us abruptly. "Change of plans. We're going to a different blood bank, on the west side."

"Why?" I asked.

"Because Luis has been attacked there."

Chapter Eight

Austin

WHILE AUSTIN WAS grateful to Gwen for the heads-up, he wasn't sure why she'd called him. One part of him hoped Luis had been ganked permanently, but Austin knew he couldn't be that lucky. Besides, a threat to Luis was also a threat to the organization Alejandro had built—the organization that had become the family Austin had never known. And you had to watch out for your family, even if they *were* bullies and jerks.

He shouldn't let Luis get to him, but he did hate the "us versus them" attitude Luis was bringing into Alejandro's family. It was unnecessary and not exactly healthy, either. The last time that had happened. . . . He smiled wryly.

"What's so funny?" Val asked.

"I was just remembering the last time one of Alejandro's lieutenants tried to take over."

"Oh. That," Val responded flatly.

"What happened?" the curious gemstone whisperer asked.

When Val didn't respond, Austin said, "Val cut off her head."

Fang looked up at him from his place in Val's lap and snorted in what could only be canine amusement, but a glance in the rearview mirror showed Ivy's horrified expression. She obviously didn't get the humor.

"Gee, thanks," Val muttered and jabbed her left fist playfully into his ribs. "I had to," she told Ivy.

Val looked really annoyed, so Austin drawled, "Well, Lily did have it coming. She'd kidnapped Val's sister and stepfather—and Fang." Not to mention Val's cop ex-boyfriend, who'd also been Lily's former fiancé. "And Lily was about to kill all of them, then start on us and take over Alejandro's organization. Val really had no choice. Killing Lily saved us all."

"I see," Ivy said faintly.

She did appear to understand, though Austin was sorry he'd brought it up since it seemed to bother Val.

"You said the last time . . . is someone else trying to take over now?" Ivy asked, looking worried that decapitation might be on tonight's agenda.

"I hope not—Val didn't bring her sword," he drawled and blocked Val's next blow to his ribs as Fang snorted again. "Seriously, Alejandro's disappearance has thrown us into confusion. We have no clear line of succession—there are three lieutenants now—so one of the lieutenants is trying to force himself into the role."

"Luis," Val explained to Ivy. "The one who pulled off your hoodie."

Ivy made a face. "Hate to see him in charge of anything or anyone."

Ditto. "I don't know what happened at the blood bank, though, or who attacked Luis—I hope it was the rogues."

"Who else would it be?" Val asked in surprise as she petted Fang. "You don't think Rosa would—"

"No, I don't." She wouldn't do anything to admit Alejandro might be gone. Though, after the finder's inability to locate the vamp leader, Austin was beginning to wonder if his own belief in Alejandro's continued existence might be overoptimistic.

"Then who?"

"Misguided newbies who think they need to protect my honor."

Val stopped stroking Fang's ears. "Who in their right mind would follow Luis?" she asked incredulously.

"The old guard."

Val snorted. "You're not exactly a spring chicken. What are you? A hundred?"

Once again, he realized how ancient he must seem to her. "A bit more than that," he admitted. "But we consider the old guard to be those who have been with Alejandro since he came over with Cortez. Mainly those who share Luis's superior attitude."

"Cortez?" Ivy repeated in surprise. "*The* Cortez who conquered Mexico and destroyed the Aztec civilization? The one in this bust?"

"Yep."

"Wow," Val said. "I didn't realize they were that old." She glanced at him thoughtfully. "So the old guard approves of Luis's methods?" At his nod, she added, "What about your followers and Rosa's?"

"I've trained most of the newly converted over the past hundred years, so they tend to side with me, though I never asked them to." He shrugged. "Those who don't choose sides or stay neutral are essentially following Rosa."

"And you're afraid some of your supporters may have picked a fight? Tried to take Luis out for you?"

Trust Val to get to the heart of the matter. Austin nodded curtly. But he didn't need or want that, no matter what anyone might think.

They arrived at the blood bank, and though everything looked peaceful from the outside, Austin knew that appearances could be deceiving. Especially since the CLOSED sign hung on the door. He turned around to speak to Ivy. "You probably want to stay here. It might be dangerous in there."

Ivy's chin came up. "I can handle myself. Besides, my gemstones might be able to help."

Austin shrugged. He didn't know what talking to gemstones would do to protect her or assist in this situation, but he wasn't going to argue with her, either. "Suit yourself." To be honest, the streets outside this blood bank weren't all that safe, either.

Ivy, Val, and Fang followed Austin into the blood bank. It looked like a war zone, with chairs overturned, the juice bar smashed, blood splashed on the walls, and knots of people either sobbing quietly or bristling for a fight.

The sobbing ones were female humans who had come to donate and gotten more than they bargained for, along with a few men. Elspeth and Gwen, along with other vamps, were helping them, while five followers clustered protectively around Luis. He stood against one wall, disheveled and bruised, a bloody hole in his shirt.

One of Luis's followers—the bearded Tobias—caught sight of the group at the door, scowled, and took a menacing step toward Austin. "You," he said accusingly. "Did you do this?"

Austin raised an eyebrow. Logic was obviously not one of his strong suits. "I wasn't even here," he told the short, wiry man curtly.

Val and Fang came to stand beside him while Ivy slipped off, murmuring something about finding a way to help.

"You could have sent your minions after Luis," Tobias accused. "To take him out so you could take over."

Fang growled, and though Val shushed him, Austin was ridiculously pleased that the hellhound wanted to defend him. "Don't be an idiot, Tobias. I'm not the one who wants to take over."

One of Luis's hangers-on brandished a bloody crossbow bolt. "They shot him! Barely missed his heart."

Luis pushed his way through his minions, heedless of the hole in his chest—it would soon heal. "Someone needs to take charge, and *you* don't want that someone to be *me*."

Austin controlled his simmering anger. "Someone does *not* need to. We need to work together, not apart. We'll have enough problems fighting the rogues now that they know of Alejandro's disappearance—we don't need to be fighting internally as well. Have you forgotten what happened during the Spanish-American War?" Alejandro's men had split into violently opposed factions, one side supporting the United States, and the other insisting their native Spain was in the right. The resulting carnage had decimated their population until Alejandro was able to pull everyone back together under his neutral leadership. It had taken decades to recover their strength and cohesion. "Do you want a repeat of that?" Austin sure as hell didn't.

Luis paused for a moment, then said more calmly, "This is nothing like that. This is you, wanting me to believe rogues were responsible for the attack."

"Well, did you recognize any of your attackers? Were they members of the Movement? Truth, now."

Luis scowled. "No, but how do I know you aren't turning men in secret? Sending them to ambush me? You could have told them I was here, set me up."

Looked like reason had taken a holiday. Austin wasn't even sure how to defend against insanity.

Elspeth spoke up. "Do not be ridiculous, Luis. Everyone knows you come here every night at the same time. It would be easy for anyone to discover your habits."

"You'd say that, wouldn't you?" Luis asked. "You're one of his."

As Elspeth turned away, shaking her head, Val spoke to Luis. "I could force Austin to tell the truth. Would that convince you?"

Luis scowled at her. "You're on his side, too. Why would I believe anything you have to say, anything you do?"

Val opened her mouth to reply, then, at a glance from Austin, shrugged and shut her mouth, muttering something about Teflon. Good choice.

Austin decided to take a different tack. "Look, if I were responsible for this, why would I come here immediately after the attack to help you?"

"Ha," Luis said, as if he'd caught him out in a lie. "To see the results of your perfidy, to gloat at my dead body, and to pretend you had nothing to do with it—like now."

His followers looked as though they were believing this load of bull.

"I didn't do any of that," Austin snarled, unable to fight the anger building within him. "I don't want a repeat of the Spanish-American War—I want Alejandro back."

"You'd say that, wouldn't you?" Luis said, sneering. "Trying to be the hero, the savior of the Movement. Well, your lies won't work on me. You just want Alejandro's position for yourself."

No, he just didn't want Luis to have it. "I want *Alejandro* in Alejandro's position," Austin said. "What can I do to convince you of that?" Not that he wanted to placate Luis, but he did want this crap to be over.

"Meet me alone and tell me that." Luis's clenched fists and the pugnacious set to his jaw telegraphed exactly what he meant by that.

Austin resisted the urge to roll his eyes. Was this what they were reduced to? Schoolyard brawls? "I don't intend to fight you, Luis." The older vampire was more experienced, but Austin was more agile. In a fair fight, he didn't know who would win, and right now, he didn't intend to find out. "We don't need to show dissension in the ranks. Besides, you're injured." Blood still oozed from the hole in Luis's chest.

"Afraid?" Luis thrust his face into Austin's, obviously baiting him.

"No," Austin bit out, not letting Luis intimidate him or force him into doing something stupid.

Rosa was suddenly between them—when had she arrived? "Stop this," she ordered. "It will not help us find Alejandro."

Austin noticed that neither Val nor Fang defended him against Rosa. Probably because she was right. Austin shrugged and backed away.

Luis shot Austin a murderous glance. "*He* probably kidnapped him or killed him."

Rosa stomped her foot. "No, *estúpido*, I do not believe that, and neither do you."

"Don't tell me what I believe," Luis snarled.

Rosa glared back. "You two will not fight. Alejandro would not like it. We will stop you."

Luis glanced around. Gwen and Elspeth had pulled the humans out of range and calmed them, but more and more vampires had come to gawk and rubberneck. Austin studied their faces as Luis did, and it appeared Rosa had might on her side. Luis's hangers-on were outnumbered.

Following up on her advantage, Rosa told Luis, "You will think upon this, try to remember what happened, give Austin any details of what you remember of the attack."

Luis scowled. "I don't trust him."

"Then you will tell me," Rosa insisted. "The more who know what to look for, the easier it will be to find our leader."

Luis's chin jutted upward. "As you wish, but I will not share the mansion with a man I do not trust."

"Fine," Rosa said. "Both of you stay out. Luis, you can move into the rooms above and Austin into another blood bank. Take your followers with you."

Luis looked nonplussed for a moment—that obviously wasn't what he'd intended. But he couldn't really argue, since the mansion was obviously Rosa's territory. He recovered swiftly, though. "Very well," he said, snapping a curt bow in her direction. "We will move out now."

Evidently, Luis hadn't noticed Rosa had taken on the leadership role in this situation. But since Luis deferred to Rosa's authority over the house, it had worked to shut him up, and Austin wasn't going to complain at the results. As he left, Austin raised an eyebrow at Rosa. "It will make even more of a separation between us," he murmured.

"It will keep you from each other's throats," she countered. "Until Alejandro returns and brings everything back to normal."

True, and that couldn't happen soon enough for Austin.

"*If* he returns," Val said. "Our finder couldn't locate him."

Now she was the one who deserved the shot in the ribs. At Rosa's demanding look, Austin had to nod and assure her it was true.

Rosa looked stricken for a moment, then her expression hardened. "No, he is alive. I know this. You will find him."

Knowing how worried she must be about losing her lover and her leader, Austin said, "I'll do my best."

"Good," she said. Glaring around at the lookie-loos, she said, "Clean this up," and swept out.

Austin glanced around at those who were left. "Okay, let's do it, shall we?"

He set everyone to work, then saw that Val had gone to check on the humans. He followed her. "How are they?" he asked.

"All right," she said. "Gwen and Elspeth got them out of the line of fire, Gwen gave them a sedative, and Ivy used one of her stones to help heal their injuries."

Austin glanced at Ivy in surprise. So, talking to gemstones did have its benefits.

"What about their minds, their memories? Have we adjusted those?" he asked. There was more than one kind of trauma.

Gwen glanced at Elspeth. "She's working on that. She seems to have a knack for it."

Austin nodded. It made sense that the former Memory Eater would be skilled in adjusting memories.

"Yes, I have," Elspeth said. "But would you check my work? I want to ensure I have done it correctly."

He did and was impressed by how thorough she'd been—she didn't erase their memories, she just lessened their intensity, made the murderous altercation appear to be a minor tiff, and the injuries negligible . . . which they were now, with Gwen and Ivy's help. "Excellent work," he said. "Let's move them to the donation rooms so they'll be out of the way."

After they left the donors to sleep off the sedative, Austin led Gwen and Elspeth downstairs to talk privately. Val and Fang followed. "So, did either of you see what happened?" he asked.

Gwen shrugged. "We came to check on the clinic's stock and were just leaving when it happened," she said, sharing a wary glance with Elspeth.

Austin understood—they tried to avoid Luis whenever possible. He nodded encouragingly.

She continued. "Luis came in with a couple of his followers just as we were heading out the door. A small group of guys followed them in." She glanced at Elspeth. "Maybe five or six?"

"Yes," Elspeth confirmed. "There were five of them."

Gwen nodded. "We heard screams, so we ran back in to see what was happening. That's when we saw Luis with a bolt in his chest, vampires fighting, and the humans scrambling to get out of their way. When more vampires poured out of the rooms to help, the attackers ran away."

"Some tried to follow them," Elspeth added, "but they had a vehicle ready and were able to escape unscathed."

"Did you see what kind of car it was?" Val asked. "Get a license plate?"

Elspeth shook her head. "I'm sorry. All I know is that the vehicle was a dark color. I do not know the names."

Since she'd been insane most of her vampire life, starting in Inquisition times, Austin wasn't surprised she wasn't able to identify a modern car. "Did you recognize any of the attackers?" Austin asked, hoping none of his own would-be followers had been foolish enough to do something so stupid.

"No," Gwen and Elspeth said together.

"Can you describe any of them?" he persisted.

Gwen frowned, biting her lip. "I'm sorry—it all happened so fast. The only thing I remember is two of them looked a lot alike, like they were brothers."

"Slight, blond, in their early twenties?" Val asked.

"Yes."

Val glanced at Austin. "Sounds like the candy twins."

Just what Austin had been thinking. "Looks like all roads lead to Mike and Ike. We'd better find them."

Chapter Nine

Val

WE ARRIVED AT THE midtown blood bank, and I reflected on how weird my world would look to outsiders. If I'd been born fully human like my half-sister Jen, I'd be like other girls my age who were in college and spent their time going to class, studying, and hanging out with friends. Instead, I spent mine going to blood banks, fighting, and hanging out with vampires and demons.

And college students thought *their* lives were rough. Ha!

Luckily, the rain had stopped so Fang didn't get wet again as we all trooped inside. Austin approached the girl working the desk—her nameplate read Amanda—and said, "We're looking for three fledglings who probably came here last night. I gave them my card. Can you check?"

She gave him a perky smile. "Of course, sir. Do you know their names?"

He glanced at me, and I said, "Chris, Carlos, and Charlie. Three college-aged geeks with squeaky new leather jackets."

Amanda's grin turned wry. "I remember them—they hit on me."

OF COURSE THEY DID, Fang said with a mental smirk. THEY PROBABLY HIT ON ANYONE WITH BOOBS. WONDER WHAT THEIR SUCCESS RATE IS?

Ivy must have heard that, too, because she muttered, "From your description, I'd say the odds were slim."

I shot her a grin. "Yeah."

"They did come in last night and again about an hour ago," Amanda told us. "You just missed them."

Ah, good. They'd followed Austin's instructions.

"You didn't give them access to a special donation room, did you?" Austin asked.

"No, they gave me your card, and I could tell they were fledglings—bottle babies—so I passed them on to Tracy for orientation."

Austin nodded. "Is she here tonight?"

"Yes—in the conference room."

"Wait here," Austin told us. "I'll be right back."

Ivy, Fang, and I retreated to a corner opposite the juice station. "Why didn't he want them to use a room?" Ivy asked.

"The rooms are for the, uh, fang-to-neck kind of donation," I explained.

YEAH, Fang added. FOR THOSE HUMANS WHO LIKE THEIR DONATIONS SPICED UP WITH A LITTLE FANTASY. THEY HAVE ROOMS DECORATED LIKE VENETIAN BORDELLOS, WOODLAND BOWERS, AND DUNGEONS.

I grimaced. "Can you imagine giving three new geeky vampires access to that without restraint? No wonder they make them take their blood from a bottle to begin with."

"Pretty smart," Ivy said. "I imagine it also helps keep the new fledglings in the fold, with something to look forward to. Good recruiting tactic."

I hadn't even thought about that. And didn't really have time to, because Austin was returning, wearing a grin and looking all lean and sexy. Lola wanted.

Not the time. I pulled her back.

"Let's go," he said.

One of the women in the waiting area stood up. "Wait. You're leaving?" she asked with a pout. Though no one else probably noticed her mouth with all that flesh surging up over the neckline of her dress. Neckline? More like belly button line—it was that low-cut. "Can't you stay?"

Fang poked me playfully in the shin with his nose. BETCHA SHE WANTS TO TAKE HIM TO THAT BORDELLO ROOM.

Austin tipped his hat and winked at her. "Not tonight, ma'am."

Not any night if Lola had anything to say about it. I heaved a mental sigh. Too bad she didn't. He kept on walking, and I followed, wondering how much time he spent in those fantasy rooms.

He glanced down at me. "I don't use the rooms—just takeout," he assured me, as if he'd read my mind.

NO, HE READ YOUR EXPRESSION, Fang hooted. YOU DON'T EXACTLY HAVE A POKER FACE.

Well, crap. I'd have to work on that. Pretending as if it didn't matter, I asked, "You know where the three Cs are?"

"Yes—they share an apartment in student housing." He waved a piece of paper. "I have the address."

He drove to an apartment complex not far from the zoo, and we all got out to track down the fledglings. Austin consulted the note. "Number 213."

We followed the signs to the apartment, and as we got closer, we heard the deep bass beat of speakers cranked to the max. The song lyrics were indistinguishable because of the chatter of voices competing with the music, with people spilling out the front door and down the steps. Were the three Cs throwing that party?

Nope, their apartment was *across* from the party.

One couple looked up from a clinch as we squeezed past. The guy seemed to be all hands, but the girl didn't seem to be enjoying their embrace as much as he was. "Hey, cute dog," the girl yelled over the music and pulled away from him to kneel and pet Fang.

"Thanks," I said, happy to let Fang be her excuse as he wagged his plume of a tail and pretended to be an adorable normal dog.

I DON'T HAVE TO PRETEND TO BE ADORABLE, he informed me. IT COMES NATURALLY.

I rolled my eyes, then ignored him.

"Are Chris, Charlie, and Carlos here?" I asked them.

The guy sneered. "Those guys? Not the sort we want at our party."

Ooookay. Austin knocked on the door of 213, but there was no answer.

"Maybe they can't hear us," Ivy yelled.

NO ONE INSIDE, Fang said.

It made sense. The beauty quotient at the party was pretty darned high—everyone I could see was probably a jock or cheerleader or something similar. The three Cs had probably left to avoid having their faces rubbed in their social and physical awkwardness. If this party was typical of what they had to deal with on a daily basis, no wonder they'd wanted to be on the top of the pecking order for a change.

"Why are you looking for *those* guys?" the girl asked, standing as her gaze assessed the three of us.

None of us really looked like geeks, so I understood her confusion. "Chris is my cousin," I lied. "Do you know where we can find him?"

She shrugged and looked up at her date. He grimaced, obviously annoyed by their kissface interruptus, and took a swig of his beer before replying. "Probably at the comic book store. It's geek heaven—they hang out there a lot."

"Which one?" Austin asked.

"How would I know?" the guy asked. "Do I look like a geek to you?" He reached for the girl again, but she evaded him.

Annoyed, I said, "No, you look like a—"

But I didn't get a chance to finish that sentence, because Austin grabbed my arm and said, "Thank you. We'll check it out."

I shrugged him off, annoyed by the beer-sucking jock who sneered at us and treated the girl like property. I stepped closer to him, so he was just inside Lola's field. He backed away, wide-eyed, probably wondering why he was so overcome with lust for an average-looking girl who didn't come up to his standard of hotness.

When his back hit the wall, I smiled and licked Lola into him. "You do know where they go, don't you?" I said and grabbed him by his chakras so he had to obey me.

"Yes, they go to Big Bang Books and Comics," he babbled and even gave us the address.

"Thank you," I said. Then, because Lola had been deprived for so long, I let her snack on the idiot—just enough to pull the lust out of him and leave him depleted and limp. While Lola was all up in his chakras, I decided to test a theory. "You seem pretty free with your hands there. Tell us, how do you really feel about the girl you're with?" And, of course, I used Lola to force him to tell the truth.

"Well, she's not as hot as I like, but she's got a great bod—bet she's great in the sack." Once the words left his mouth, he looked as horrified as his would-be partner did.

Wow, that worked even better than I expected.

The girl looked at me, appearing shocked. "What did you do to him?"

I shrugged. "Took the lust out of him. Hypnotized him into telling the truth." Sort of—but it was something she might understand.

She looked bewildered, so I added, "You're too good for him. Why don't you find someone else?"

She glanced at the idiot who had slumped against the wall, almost drooling after Lola's snack attack on his pleasure centers. "Yeah, I think I will," she said and left the party.

"Well," Austin drawled, looking amused. "You've done your good deed for the day. Shall we go?"

This time, we were luckier. The bottle babies were at the store, perusing racks of brightly colored books.

Carlos caught sight of us first and backed away, holding up his hands. "We went to the—" He broke off, obviously noticing lots of humans in the store, and gulped. "To the place you told us to go, honest."

Chris and Charlie whipped around. "We really did," chunky Charlie said. "Ask Tracy."

"It's all right," Austin assured them. "I know you did. We just want to ask you a few questions."

"Hey, get that dog outta here," the guy behind the counter yelled. "This ain't no pet store."

Fang growled at him, but I let it go. We couldn't have this conversation here, anyway. "We're leaving," I told him, then turned to the three Cs. "There's a coffee shop next door. Can we talk there?"

They nodded, and we went into the coffee shop, everyone except Austin ordering frappes, lattes, and other fancy coffee drinks. The three Cs evidently hadn't lost their habit of consuming human food yet, even when it couldn't satisfy. I settled for a cup of chai. I didn't know if the owners noticed Fang, but if they did, they ignored him. Good enough.

Once we all had our orders and sat in a quiet corner so we wouldn't be overheard, Austin said, "We're looking for a couple of rogues named Mike and Ike. Do you know them?"

Charlie, obviously eager to be seen as the leader, said, "No, we didn't get names from most of the ones we met."

"They're blond, about Carlos's size, and brothers—fraternal twins. Do you remember meeting anyone like that?" I persisted.

The three exchanged glances but shook their heads in denial.

Crap. I'd hoped it would be easier than this.

"What do you remember?" Ivy asked.

"We dealt mainly with our . . ." Charlie glanced around to ensure no one was listening and lowered his voice. "Our sire and the recruiter."

They'd already proved they didn't remember their sire's name. "Tell us more about the recruiter," I urged.

Charlie shrugged. "Said his name was Alexander, as in Alexander the Great."

No ego problem, there. "What's he look like?" I asked.

"Tall white dude. Looks a lot like Liam Hemsworth."

BET THAT COMES IN HANDY WITH RECRUITING, Fang snarked.

Yeah.

"How did you meet him?" Austin asked.

Charlie exchanged wary glances with his buddies. "Well, we told you about the notice on the bulletin board . . ."

"Yes, and . . . ?" Austin prompted.

"It said to meet at a room on campus, so we did. Others showed up, but we were the only ones who stayed. That's when we learned about . . . this life."

"And this Alexander was the only one there?" Austin asked.

"No, our . . . sire came in at the end. They said once we passed the test at the park, they'd know and would initiate us into the rest of the group."

THEIR FINAL EXAM WAS TO FIND HUMANS AT THE PARK AND SUCK THEM DRY, Fang told Ivy.

Her ewww-like expression clearly showed her reaction.

BUT THEY COULDN'T BRING THEMSELVES TO DO IT.

"How were you supposed to contact them?" I asked eagerly. "How would they know if you passed the test or not?"

Charlie shrugged. "They didn't say. They just said they'd know."

Not real helpful.

"Probably because they'd find the bodies in the park," Austin said, his distaste obvious.

"So," Ivy said, "what did they say would happen to you if you *didn't* pass the test?"

Pure panic crossed Chris's face, and the other two didn't look much better. "They didn't say," Chris said and visibly swallowed. "You think they'll . . . do something to us?"

"Well, if you flunked the test, you can't be their flunkies," I said. "Would that piss them off? Or would they just give you up as a lost cause?"

They exchanged frantic, clueless looks. "Are we in danger?" Carlos asked, his voice quavering.

"Maybe," Austin said. "I don't know how the rogues operate, but they have attacked some members of the Movement. Right now, you're our best lead for finding and stopping them."

"But we don't know anything," Chris whined. "What if they come after us?"

"Didn't Tracy explain that you can live at one of our houses or blood banks?"

"Yes," Charlie said, "but we didn't want to give up our apartment. It's so close to the school."

I snorted. "Do you really think you'll be able to continue going to school? How many classes are actually at night?"

I could tell they had just begun to think about that. "Tell you what," I said. "Why don't you move in with Austin?" I glanced at him. "Which blood bank are you moving to?"

He thought for a moment. "The one downtown—it's bigger and has the best clinic."

I nodded. He might need a bigger house if his followers decided to move out of the mansion and in with him to show their support. And Gwen and Elspeth spent a lot of time there. Austin had taken on their protection as his pet project.

"Can you think of anything else that might help us find Alexander?" I asked. "Anything at all?"

They thought furiously, brows furrowed. Evidently, now that their undead lives were at stake, they were eager to help.

"No," Charlie said, "but he'll probably have another recruiting meeting—we got the impression ours wasn't the first or last. Check the bulletin board in the physics building."

"It's not open this time of night," Chris said. "But you can go there tomorrow." He gave us directions.

Austin nodded. "Thank you, you've been very helpful. Now, go immediately to the blood bank and settle in—you'll be safer there."

"What about our stuff?" Carlos asked.

"We'll send a crew to help you pick up what you need tomorrow night."

Chris and Carlos glanced at Charlie, who nodded decisively. "Okay. Will you be there? You promised to teach us how to fight."

"I'll be there later," Austin promised. "Now go."

They didn't need any further encouragement as they peeked out the door and rushed to their car.

I smiled. "Looks like you have some new assets in your fight with Luis."

Shaking his head, Austin said, "More like liabilities."

"So, are we going to break into the physics building so we can take a look at the bulletin boards?" Ivy asked.

I glanced at her in surprise. And here I'd thought she was a goody-goody.

YOU'RE CORRUPTING HER.

"Tomorrow is soon enough," Austin said. "I doubt they'll have a meeting this late at night. We can check it out right after sunset tomorrow."

"Why wait?" Ivy asked. "Val and I can check it out during the day. No breaking in required."

Austin frowned, but before he could say anything, I said, "Ivy's right. It'll save time. It's not like they're going to have a recruiting meeting during the day. The earliest it could be is tomorrow night."

Ivy nodded. "Then Val and I can attend the meeting as prospective converts." She raised an eyebrow at Austin. "I think Alexander would figure out what you are right away."

He gave her a sharp glance. "Yes, but do you think it's wise for the two of you to go?"

"Better than having a real human do it—it'd be more dangerous for them," I reminded him. "Besides, if he tries to suck demon blood, it'll make him crazy. And I can defend myself against any man."

Austin thought for a moment. "It's too risky. I can't let you do that for us."

"Really?" I raised an eyebrow. "And how do you propose to stop us?"

WOO-HOO, Fang exclaimed. THAT PUT HIM IN HIS PLACE!

Chapter Ten

Val

AUSTIN LOOKED sheepish. "I stand corrected."

Him being able to admit that made me like him all the more. Relaxing, I said, "You're probably in more danger than we are. After all, they've kidnapped Alejandro and tried to take out Luis. Looks like the rogues—or someone—is trying to remove the leadership of the New Blood Movement. You might be next."

"That had occurred to me," Austin drawled.

"Then I should be the one to protect *you*," I finished triumphantly. After all, the attackers so far had all been male, from what I could tell. And Lola could take care of them, no problem.

Austin gave me a slow grin. "Why, if I didn't know better, I'd think you were angling to spend more time with me . . . darlin'."

My face flushed, and I searched for a witty comeback, but embarrassment and girly hormones made me totally witty-*less*.

MAKE THAT WITLESS, Fang said with a chuckle.

"Or that *you* were angling to spend more time with *her*," Ivy told Austin. "After all, you suggested it first."

Support from an unexpected direction. How nice.

I LIKE HER, Fang said suddenly.

Yeah, me too.

A look of pure amusement on his face, Austin said, "That's no secret. Everyone knows I'm fond of Val."

And again, my cheeks flamed even hotter. "I-I just meant you should have backup," I stammered. "Make sure you're not alone—don't make yourself an easy target."

Taking pity on my witless state, Austin said, "Agreed. Let's head back to the mansion, and I'll get some help to move to the blood bank. Will that work for you, darlin'?"

Was he making fun of me now?

MAYBE JUST A TAD.

Ignoring that, I said, "Okay, and while you do that, I'll look in the encyclopedia to see if there's a spell that could help us find Alejandro."

Austin took us back to the mansion, but when I would have followed Ivy and Fang to her MINI, Austin stopped me with a hand on my arm. Softly, he said, "Hold on a moment."

I looked at him with a question in my eyes, and he leaned down to press his lips against mine in a gentle kiss, a promise of things to come.

Pleasure thrilled through me, unexpected but very welcome. His soft kiss ignited Lola's possessiveness, and I couldn't help myself—I gave in to her. I grabbed his shirtfront in my fist and leaned in for more. The second kiss was even better. Lola's lustful energy strands swirled through him, then back through me, catching us both in a feedback loop of pure pleasure. I wound my arms around his neck, and our kiss deepened until I felt he was plumbing my very depths. Lola ate up as much of his yummy sexual energy as she could get.

GET A ROOM, Fang said from the car, sounding both amused and disgusted at the same time. BEFORE HE STARTS HUMPING YOUR LEG.

I suddenly realized I was wrapped in Austin's arms so tightly, you couldn't get a molecule between the two of us. And that we had a very interested audience in Ivy, Fang, and a couple of vamps who had come outside to watch.

Mortified, I pulled away. "I'm so sorry," I said breathlessly. "Lola—"

"No need to apologize," Austin said, his eyes smoldering as he gazed down at me. "I definitely didn't mind, though I would prefer to continue this somewhere less public."

Me, too, though now was not an option, darn it. "Some other time?" I suggested, feeling rather bold and daring.

"Darlin', just name the time and the place."

His slow grin promised a lot more delights where those came from, and I couldn't help going all weak at the knees. I couldn't tear myself away from his gaze.

COME ON, VAL, Fang urged. STOP ACTING LIKE A ROMANCE HEROINE SO WE CAN HIT THE ROAD.

All right, all right. Gimme a break.

Reluctantly, I pulled my gaze from Austin's and walked over to Ivy's car. As I got in, she said, "Wow, he's really hot. So, why aren't you hitting that yet?"

I glanced at her in surprise, not knowing what to say.

WHAT MAKES YOU THINK SHE ISN'T? Fang asked Ivy.

Ivy shrugged and steered the car toward the gates. "Body language mostly. Is it because he's a vamp?"

I glanced at Austin—he was still standing beside the vampmobile, watching me with an intense look and a half smile. My heart leapt in response. Sheesh—could I be any more schoolgirlish?

"Sort of," I muttered. "It's complicated."

NOT REALLY.

Ignoring Fang, I said, "I like Austin, but sometimes it just feels . . . wrong, to have the hots for a bloodsucker."

"Yeah, I get that, but after seeing the way those 'bloodsuckers' leapt in to help the humans, I understand why you say they're the good guys. Gwen and Elspeth really seemed to care."

"They do, but that could be because Gwen was just recently turned against her will—she was an ER nurse before that. In fact, she used to be my roommate."

Ivy nodded. "Micah mentioned that. And Elspeth? You can't tell me she was turned recently."

"True," I conceded. I wasn't sure why I was saying this when I *wanted* Ivy to think they were the good guys.

"So, why not go after Austin with all barrels blazing?"

"I'm . . . new at this," I admitted. At her incredulous look, I added, "Look, I may be part succubus, but I've spent most of my life suppressing my powers so I won't accidentally suck men dry. It's only been the past couple of months where I've learned to make peace with the demon inside me." Then, before she could ask any more embarrassing questions, I asked one of my own. "So, who are *you* sucking face with?"

Fang snorted. YOU REALLY SURPRISED HER WITH THAT ONE.

Ivy sputtered out a laugh. "I guess I deserved that. But, the answer is, no one."

"Why not?"

"The pickings in Sedona are pretty slim. That's one of the reasons I came here for a long visit—seems like you have quite the thriving Demon Underground organization here in Texas."

I shrugged. "I wouldn't know—I've never been anywhere else."

"Really? Well, you'll have to come to Sedona sometime."

I smiled at her. "Thanks—I'd like that." It reminded me of my plans to grab Fang and just take off and drive through the Southwest . . . someday when there wasn't a crisis to take care of.

THINK THAT'LL EVER HAPPEN? Fang asked wistfully.

I hope so, I responded mentally, though I was a little surprised Fang wanted to do something that didn't involve chomping on the bad guys.

EVEN HELLHOUNDS AND PALADINS NEED A BREAK SOMETIME.

Amen to that. And maybe Ivy was right about Austin, too. I didn't know when I might be dead . . . or he might be. Why *not* act on this attraction between us?

When we arrived back at the townhouse, the door was unlocked. What the heck? Because I kept the encyclopedia inside, I always locked the door.

Holding out my hand to keep Fang and Ivy back, I asked Fang mentally, *Can you read anyone inside?*

NOPE. MUST NOT BE DEMONS.

I glanced down at Fang and his noisy nails—the intruder would clearly hear them on the hard floor inside. *Stay here until it's okay to broadcast your presence. Tell Ivy I'm going in quietly to see why they're here.*

Fang rolled his eyes, but since it wasn't like he could put slippers on, he agreed. Ivy nodded to me and followed me inside. Not exactly what I'd intended, but she might be useful as backup.

We tiptoed inside, and I heard a male voice murmuring from my bedroom. Crap. That's where I kept the books.

Wanting to hear what he was saying, I crept closer and stood outside the door, listening. I couldn't understand the words—just the tone, as if the guy had just asked a question. There was no answer, and after a minute or two, another question and more silence. Was he on the phone, maybe?

Curious, I peeked around the corner. Wait—I recognized that swirliness. Shade was sitting on my bed and had one of the books spread out in front of him. And since Fang couldn't "hear" him anymore, that explained why Fang thought he wasn't a demon. But I didn't see a phone. Who was he talking to?

I thrust the door open fully. "What are you doing?" I demanded.

Shade jumped and probably looked guilty as hell, though I couldn't see his expression. He slammed the book shut and scrambled off my bed. "Sorry. I was just . . . doing some research."

Fang appeared by my side. GEE, THAT'S NOT SUSPICIOUS AT ALL.

Annoyed, I said, "You came into my place without asking?"

"I tried to call you," Shade said. "But your phone went directly to voicemail."

Well, I did tend to turn it off when hunting vamps. Even human ears could hear the buzz of a vibrating phone. I turned on my phone and checked it. Sure enough, there were a few missed calls from Shade.

"I assumed you wouldn't mind," Shade said. "And I still have a key from when I had to stay here."

Okay, that seemed sort of reasonable, though I still felt irritated with him. "Who were you talking to? I don't see your phone."

Shade shrugged. "Just reading out loud. Don't worry—I don't say the final words to invoke the spells."

Crap—I really wished Fang could still read his mind.

HE'S PROBABLY LYING, Fang said.

"Not lying exactly," Ivy said. "Just not telling the whole truth."

I gave her the raised eyebrow, and she tapped one of the many stones on her right ear. "My sodalite can sometimes tell."

I glanced at Shade. "Want to elaborate on that answer?"

"Not really."

"I could force you to, but neither one of us wants that," I reminded him.

"Fine," he snapped and snatched up the books. "But let's do it in the other room."

I moved aside so he could pass me, and as he brushed past Fang, Shade's expression flickered briefly to show the annoyance on his face.

I sighed inwardly, wondering why dealing with people always had to be so difficult.

We followed him into the living room, where Shade set the book on the coffee table and plopped down on the couch. Fang jumped up next to him, nudging Shade to pet him so we could see the shadow demon's face. Shade started to pull away but must have noticed Ivy's relieved expression, because he laid his hand back on Fang's head. Shade's swirliness was a bit odd until you got used to it.

"So, you were going to explain?" I prompted Shade.

He nodded. "I was talking to the book."

I glanced at Ivy who nodded. Shade was telling the truth, but getting it out of him was like pulling splinters from a staked vampire. "Why?"

"I was asking questions."

"You mean you were asking it to give you a spell?" I thought it would only show spells to me, the Keeper of the *Encyclopedia Magicka.*

"Not exactly," he hedged.

I didn't need Ivy to tell me that wasn't the whole truth. "So, what then?" I said jokingly. "You were expecting it to talk back?" Not likely. Now that the mage demon who had inhabited the encyclopedia was gone, the books didn't talk to me anymore.

Shade glanced at Ivy, his lips thinning. "Yes."

AH, HELL, Fang said. LET'S CUT TO THE CHASE. THE TRUTH IS, HE

CAN TALK TO THE BOOKS, AND THEY TALK BACK.

I stared at Fang, then Shade. "The books talk back to you?" I repeated for Shade and Ivy's benefit.

Shade nodded, looking defiant.

I glared at Fang. "You knew this and didn't tell me?"

"It was his suggestion," Shade said, obviously pleased at being able to share my annoyance with the hellhound.

I DON'T TELL YOU EVERYTHING, Fang said. BESIDES, WHO CARES IF THE BOOKS TALK TO SOMEONE ELSE?

Obviously, I did, but I wasn't sure why. "Who else are they talking to?"

Fang sighed. NO ONE BUT YOU AND SHADE, SO FAR AS I KNOW. BUT THE BOOKS WERE WORRIED ABOUT THE AMULET CONTROLLING YOU, SO THEY WANTED A BACKUP KEEPER AND CHOSE SHADE.

So that was why Fang hadn't said anything—he'd been just as worried about the crystal. "You're a backup keeper?" I asked Shade.

He nodded. "They told me not to tell you until the amulet was gone."

Whoa. Stunned, I wasn't sure how I felt about this at all. Had the crystal really been that dangerous? Before Fang could respond, I told him, *Don't answer that.*

Ivy leaned forward. "What's really important here is, what were you talking to the book about?"

He shrugged. "Actually, I was just telling it that I destroyed the amulet, and it no longer has to worry about Val doing her job as keeper."

"But I also heard a question in your voice earlier. What did you ask it?" I persisted.

"I asked if it still wanted me to be an alternate keeper. It said yes."

I wasn't sure how I felt about that. I glanced at Ivy.

She nodded. "He's leaving something out but telling the truth."

Before I could ask, Shade said, "Some of it is research. The rest is none of your business."

"What else did you learn from the book?" I demanded. Then realization dawned. "Oh. That's how you're able to keep Fang out of your head—a spell, right?"

Shade nodded.

My eyes narrowed. "And you were trying to find a way to get Sharra's body back, weren't you?"

"Does it matter?" he asked, his voice bitter. "I can't anymore—you made sure of that."

Thank goodness for that. Sighing, I realized there was something else missing from what he said. "*How* are you talking to it?" Dumb question—I rephrased. "I mean, how is it talking back?"

"It showed me a spell to communicate," Shade said and opened a book to a blank page he had bookmarked. "Will you confirm that everything I told Val just now is the truth?"

Yes appeared on the page, then faded after I read it.

"What's the spell to get it to talk to me?" I asked eagerly. This seemed like a heck of a lot easier way to communicate with the book, rather than by asking random questions about what spells were available and hope it opened to the right one, or reading through all of the books trying to find one.

Shade frowned. "The spell lasts several weeks, but if you invoke it before it dissipates for me, the book won't talk to me anymore until I use the spell again and vice versa. We'd have to use the spell a lot."

"Oh. Crap."

Ivy asked, "Why is that crap?"

I answered her. "Because every time I use a spell in the book, that ability becomes stronger within me, but my succubus becomes weaker."

"And when I use it, my ability to heal others and open portals weakens," Shade added.

Ivy nodded. "I see. So it's better for just one person to use the spell at a time."

"Right." I glanced at Shade, wondering if I should insist on using the communication spell myself.

"I can ask anything you want to know," he said.

"Okay, can you ask if there's a spell that will help us find Alejandro?"

Dutifully, Shade asked the question, and the answer was very clear: *No.*

Well, there went that idea. Curious now, I told Shade, "Ask another question for me. Why does it want two keepers?"

He did, and the answer came swiftly. *The keeper's job as Paladin is dangerous, and she risks herself and us too often. The shadow demon does not.*

"So it's because you want to be able to have a backup quickly in case something happens to me?" I asked.

Shade repeated the question.

Yes, partially.

"Ask it to explain," I told Shade.

Shade nodded. "What's the rest of it? Please be specific."

The Keeper's job as Paladin gives her split loyalties. We might be better off with a different Keeper.

Astonished, I stared at the words even as they faded from the page. The *Encyclopedia Magicka* didn't want me anymore? Crap—what would I do without it?

Chapter Eleven

Austin

AS AUSTIN ENTERED the busy entryway of the mansion, he smiled to himself, remembering Val's wholehearted response to his kiss. Her enthusiasm had been unexpected and even seemed to surprise her. She couldn't blame it wholly on her lust demon nature—not this time—and he looked forward to the "next time" she'd promised.

Austin turned to Rosa, who seemed to be directing traffic. "I've come to pick up my things," he told her and noticed the presence of a number of people he'd come to think of as Swiss, because they didn't want to take sides—and therefore aligned with Rosa whether they realized it or not.

She nodded in distraction. "You there," she said, pointing a finger at a tall woman wearing a dark ponytail. "Catalina. That lamp does not belong to you—put it back."

Catalina glanced at the stained-glass pole lamp in her hand. "I thought it would brighten up my room at the blood bank. It's so plain there."

"Put it back," Rosa insisted. "It belongs here." She could be fierce in defending Alejandro and his possessions.

"It's in my room here," Catalina said peevishly. "Why can't I take it with me so it's in my room there?"

Rosa glared, and a few of her supporters started to move toward Catalina, but she held up her other hand in surrender. "All right. Sheesh, so kill me for wanting to make the place look pretty."

She headed up the stairs, and Austin's smile widened. He supported Rosa's unwillingness to let anything leave the mansion—for Luis's followers and his own. Maybe if they all had to make do with fewer amenities, they'd be more willing to make up and return home.

"What are you smiling about?" came the rude interruption to his thoughts. It was Tobias—Luis's number one fan, who tried to look more aristocratic by wearing a spade beard. It didn't work—it just succeeded in making him look like a thug. "Are you happy we are being kicked out of our home?" the man demanded.

Tobias was obviously spoiling for a fight, but Austin wouldn't go there. *When* they found Alejandro, he wouldn't have much of an organization to return to if he and Luis couldn't repair this schism. But Tobias didn't want to hear reason, and neither did Luis.

Deciding not to waste his breath, Austin shook his head and started to follow Catalina up the stairs.

"Hey, I'm talking to you," Tobias shouted after him.

Austin would have continued to ignore him, but another voice entered the fray. "We're being kicked out, too, you know."

Austin took his boot off the step and turned. Jeremy, a former linebacker who hadn't been turned all that long ago, thrust his face belligerently into Tobias's bearded mug.

Austin reined in his anger toward Tobias and the whole rotten situation. Jeremy wasn't afraid of anything or anyone, but he could be led. "That's enough, Jeremy," he said calmly. "Let's just get our things and go."

Neither Tobias nor Jeremy budged an inch. Tension and vampire testosterone filled the space, which suddenly seemed much smaller. At a gesture from Rosa, the "Swiss" vampires surrounded Tobias, pulling him away.

Tobias stared incredulously at Rosa. "You are on *his* side."

"No," she snapped. "I am on the side of any vampire who respects Alejandro and who does not want to cause damage to his mansion or pain to any member of the Movement." Her eyes sparked with anger, then narrowed. "Leave now. You are no longer welcome here while Alejandro is away."

"And what if he doesn't come back?" Tobias asked, struggling against his captors.

"He *will*," Rosa insisted, and if looks could kill, Tobias's ass would be ash. She stalked forward to help push him out the door.

"Well, maybe we won't wait," Tobias spat as he struggled in the grip of his captors.

Chills of dread raced through him, but Austin didn't let it show. "I don't think Luis would thank you for revealing that," he drawled. In fact, he'd be right pissed if he found out Tobias was giving away his plans. The thought of Luis challenging Alejandro gave him unwelcome flashbacks to the devastation wrought by the Spanish-American War.

Tobias suddenly stopped struggling, looking surprised, and the guards' grips loosened. Straightening his jacket, Tobias brushed unnecessarily at his sleeves. "Don't be ridiculous. As if Luis would do such a thing," he muttered. And, summoning his most imperious manner, he left without saying another word, ignoring Rosa as she shouted imprecations in Spanish at his back.

"Honorless scum," Jeremy muttered.

"I appreciate you trying to defend us," Austin said, "but we need to unite the Movement, not tear it apart. There is no honor in fighting allies." Too many of the new recruits were eager to show off their new skills, before they'd even learned their limits.

Jeremy scowled. "So when *do* we fight?"

"When it's necessary—when they are harming humans, animals, or other members of the Movement." Slapping Jeremy on the back, Austin grinned. "You can fight and take down all the rogues you want. Okay?"

"Damn straight."

And if he didn't have more experienced fighters to fall back on, he'd have to make use of new recruits like Jeremy, Chris, Charlie, and Carlos. Heaven help them. "Good. There's a sparring room at the blood bank where you can practice. Let's get our things and go."

The three Cs had also shown up at the blood bank and were hanging out in the penthouse, playing video games in the living room that was a geek's wet dream. A bunch of other "followers" had joined them and were lounging in the comfortable chairs, playing cards or other games, talking smack, and working themselves up to take on Luis and his supporters. A disproportionate share of those who chose to side with Austin were female, thanks to Luis's less than PC attitude, but most of them were doing their jobs elsewhere.

Austin dragged his belongings in—what little he had—along with Jeremy and stood with his hands on his hips as he surveyed the scene. "What is this? A clubhouse?"

They all stopped what they were doing and stared at him. "Naw," one said. "We were just waiting for you." He gestured at the three Cs. "They showed your card, said you sent them. They didn't cause any trouble, so we let them stay."

"Good, but lounging in the penthouse is a privilege you all need to earn."

There were a number of grumbles, and one guy asked, "How?"

"By doing your job, keeping your nose clean." Most of the women and some of the men had already returned to their normal duties, but the ones here seemed at a loss. They needed tasks. "We need to increase the patrols to look for more rogues. But instead of killing them, we need to find out what they know. Capture, restrain, but don't kill until we can question them and see what they know about Alejandro's kidnapping."

Questions came at him from all sides.

"How are we supposed to do that?"

"What about Luis and his men—what do we do about them?"

"Why don't we just take over? You're the best man for the job."

Austin wasn't sure who'd asked that last question, but he decided to tackle it first. "Alejandro is the leader of the organization and will remain that way until we discover he's dead. *If* that happens, we'll worry about who takes command."

"Why wait?" someone in the back asked.

Austin went rigid with fury. Because Alejandro's charisma held the organization together and presented a united face to the world, making him their best shot at finding a way to emerge from hiding as nonthreatening equals to the humans. Because Alejandro had saved Austin from death and brought him back to life in this new form. And because, damn it, Alejandro was his best friend. Austin didn't want to admit to worry, but he was beginning to fear something fatal had happened to the vampire leader.

But he didn't say any of that, not wanting to get into a fruitless discussion. "Because I order it," he snarled.

Strangely enough, that stopped the questions and even seemed to garner him more respect. He'd wanted to give them an opportunity to have a voice in the organization, make them feel a part of decisions, but there were times when he just needed to tell them what to do. Like now.

"Luis and his men are still our brothers in arms. You will not attack them or harm them in any way." Before they could raise the inevitable question, Austin added, "You can, of course, defend yourself, but you will *not* initiate a fight, nor will you do more than incapacitate them, if necessary. We are better than that. Once Alejandro returns, you will be living side by side with these men again, and we don't want there to be any bull crap about who attacked who that will damage the organization. Is that clear?"

This time, the majority of them said, "Yes, boss."

He answered the first of their questions. "As for how we're going to get information out of the rogues, we have a secret weapon—our friends in the Demon Underground. Between Val and Micah, we can force any man or woman you capture to tell us everything they know."

"Hell, I can do that," one said. "Just lemme at 'em."

The others laughed, and Austin let them release a little tension. "But with the succubus and incubus's help, we *know* they'll be telling the truth. Those of you who have felt the touch of the lust demon know that." Reluctant nods greeted this statement of fact.

"Then . . . you're just going to let the rogues go?" Jeremy asked in disbelieving tones.

"I didn't say that. We give them the same choice we give all the others—join the Movement and adhere to our principles, or die like the beasts they are. The demons will let us know if they're telling the truth about joining us."

They nodded, absorbing the idea that none of the real rogues could pretend well enough to fool Val or Micah. Those who lived for the thrill of the hunt and rejoiced in the fear and death of their victims would never be able to become a functioning part of their organization.

"We are better than them," Jeremy said slowly.

"Exactly."

Charlie raised his hand, like a student asking permission to speak.

Austin sighed inwardly. "What is it, Charlie?"

"What about us?"

"Good question." Austin glanced around, wondering whom he could put in charge of the newbies. Ah, Diego was here. Though his swarthy good looks made him a favorite of the ladies, Diego was also reliable and could be trusted with the bottle babies. "Diego will show you how to handle your new speed and strength and defend yourselves against the rogues. Diego, will you take our new members down to the sparring room?"

"Sure, boss."

That was the second time they'd called him boss. It annoyed Austin, but he let it go, knowing they meant it to show respect.

"As for the rest of you, start patrolling, see if we can catch us a few rogues."

They all grinned at that, except for Jeremy who asked, "What about you? If they kidnapped Alejandro and attacked Luis, you're probably next."

The others looked surprised, as if they hadn't thought of that. "I am aware," Austin said and grinned. "That's why we're going to set a trap."

Chapter Twelve

Val

LATE THE NEXT afternoon, Ivy and I checked the bulletin board in the physics building for notices that might be from the rogue vampires. Sure enough, there was a flyer offering a seminar that promised to make everyone who attended rich, healthy, and incredibly powerful—no cost, no obligation, no risk. Anyone who could read between the lines would know they were talking about fangbangers.

Fang snorted. AND PEOPLE BUY THIS CRAP?

Ivy shrugged. "Lots of people are looking for a get-rich-quick scheme. They'd rather take shortcuts than do the hard work."

Yeah, I could understand geeks like the three Cs wanting to be able to be on the top of the food chain for a change. I stared at the flyer, noting the date and time of the next seminar—tomorrow night.

I'd hoped there'd be some sort of clue we could pounce on right away.

LIKE NANCY DREW? Fang mocked.

I stared at him. "How do you know about Nancy Drew?" So far as I knew, he couldn't read.

TELEVISION, BABE. EVER HEARD OF IT?

Ivy laughed. "What now?"

I thought for a moment. "Let's go back to the townhouse—check on the stones."

Thirty minutes later, Ivy gingerly pulled the athame out of its healing bath. The bloodstone had barely slid out of the water when she immediately dropped it back inside. "Still gibbering in shock," she explained. "Though I got the impression it was more affected by how the blood demon used it than by Guillaume's death." She slanted me an apologetic glance. "I'm not sure it will give you any answers, even once it's healed."

"That's okay. It was a long shot, anyway. How about the crystal shards?"

She pulled them out of the solution and weighed them thoughtfully in her palm. "Though the shards were broken in an act of violence, they weren't as disturbed as the bloodstone, primarily because they didn't absorb as much negative emotion. They're no longer in shock."

"So, what can you tell about them?"

"They feel . . . empty."

"Because they're broken pieces of the original crystal?"

"Maybe." Ivy shook her head. "But it feels more as if they were imbued with some sort of consciousness that's no longer there."

Remembering what she'd said earlier, I asked, "You mean . . . like a mage demon had imprisoned another demon inside the crystal?"

"Yes, but the demon isn't there anymore."

Crap. "Where is it? Could it have gone into something else? Does it have anything to do with Alejandro's disappearance?" Or was some kind of free-floating entity roaming San Antonio?

"I don't know."

GEE, THAT'S NOT SCARY OR ANYTHING, Fang drawled.

Ignoring him, I asked, "Can you talk to them, ask them what happened?"

Ivy shook her head as she fingered the shards. "They're not really sentient anymore. I've never seen anything like it." She gave me another apologetic look. "Sorry, it looks like I'm no help at all."

"Sure you are. You ensured Shade told the truth yesterday, didn't you? And helped those people at the blood bank."

"I guess. Let me think on it some more, talk to my dad, see if he has any ideas."

"Okay." I glanced outside. The sun had set, so the vamps would be awake. "I'll call Austin, let him know what we learned."

After I told him about the flyer and the stones, Austin said, "Tomorrow night? I didn't think it would be so soon. I won't be able to go with you—we're setting a trap for the rogues in hopes of catching Ike and Mike."

"I thought we agreed Ivy and I could handle this on our own," I reminded him drily.

"Yes, I know, but who couldn't use backup? I was planning to stay outside, just in case you needed me."

I laughed. "I think I can handle a few male vamps."

His voice lowered as he drawled, "I know you can, darlin', but I worry about you."

And didn't that give me a case of the warm fuzzies. My heart rate shot up, and since Austin was nowhere near Lola, I couldn't even blame her. Unfortunately, I didn't have a clue how to respond to that. "I, uh . . . thank you?"

He chuckled softly and said, "Well, now, if you really want to thank me . . ."

His seductive tone made me feel warm all over. My first instinct was to run away, to deny what I was feeling. But the heck with that—life was short. I needed to grab it by the tail and hang on for a ride. Feeling suddenly bold, I said, "Do you have a suggestion?"

"Come on over, and I'll show you," he said, his voice low and sexy.

Whoa—adrenaline rush. "I-I . . . okay." Brilliant response. Just brilliant. I could hear Fang laughing in my head, but luckily he didn't say anything, or I probably would've popped him one.

IF YOU COULD CATCH ME.

"Good. I—" Austin broke off, and I heard a scuffling noise in the background. "Hold on."

After a few moments, he came back on. "Sorry about that."

"What's going on?" Whatever it was, it better not keep me from seeing him.

"We caught someone lurking around the blood bank—a rogue. He says he knows nothing about Alejandro's kidnapping or the attack on Luis. I, uh, promised my people the Slayer would question any rogues we caught, make them tell the truth. Would you mind testing him for us?"

"No problem. I'll be there soon," I said and hung up.

Ivy glanced at me. "What was that all about?"

VAL'S GONNA GET SOME, Fang said with glee.

Ivy grinned, and I felt my face flame hot. "I'm going to help question a rogue Austin caught," I told her.

AND SUCK FACE WITH AUSTIN. GO ON, YOU KNOW YOU WANT TO.

Ivy held up her hands. "Hey, no problem here. Good luck with that."

I glanced down at myself. Same old boring Val—jeans, long-sleeved T-shirt, and a vest. Should I change?

NAW, DON'T CHANGE YOUR CLOTHES. AUSTIN LIKES YOU JUST THE WAY YOU ARE.

"He's not wrong," Ivy said with a smile. "And you don't want to look like you're trying too hard."

She was probably right. "So, are you okay on your own?"

SHE WON'T BE ON HER OWN, Fang said. I'M STAYING HERE, TOO. YOU DON'T NEED ME TO QUESTION A ROGUE OR WATCH YOU BUMP

UGLIES WITH AUSTIN.

Sheesh, where did he learn these things? I might have to hide the remote from now on.

Fang craned his neck to look up at Ivy. HOW ABOUT YOU AND I GO VISIT PRINCESS AND MY KIDS? PRINCESS HAS GOTTA BE GOING NUTS ONLY BEING ABLE TO TALK TO THE HELLPUPPIES.

"Sounds good," Ivy said, her eyes laughing. "See? We'll be fine. Go have fun with Austin."

Feeling as though my face had probably turned permanently red, I headed to the blood bank and took the elevator up to the penthouse. I don't know why I felt so nervous. It wasn't as if Lola hadn't fed on Austin before. Then again, this time was different. This time, something . . . more . . . might happen. To tell the truth, the thought scared me about as much as it excited me.

Austin opened the door, and I felt suddenly shy. Luckily, he didn't give me one of his patented suggestive remarks, but just smiled and opened the door wide. "The rogue is in the kitchen," he said.

Grateful for his restraint, I followed him to the kitchen where a young-looking guy sat sullenly in a chair, guarded by two of Austin's followers. They all looked a bit worse for wear.

"Hi," I said cheerfully. "What's your name?"

He didn't look up, wouldn't even meet my eyes. Okay, I guess it was Lola's turn. Slowly, I sent out strands of lust to the guy in the chair, careful not to catch the two guards in her spell. The rogue's eyes widened, and his mouth went slack as I eased into his chakras and took control. "What's your name?" I repeated.

"Tim."

"Okay, Tim. Austin here is going to ask you some questions, and I want you to answer them fully and completely. Okay?"

"Sure," he said, his eyes glazing over, a little drool escaping from his lips. Gross.

Austin grabbed a chair, turned it around, and straddled it with his arms on the back so he was face-to-face with Tim. "What do you know about Alejandro's disappearance?"

"Who?"

"Alejandro, the leader of the New Blood Movement. What do you know about his kidnapping?"

"Nothin'. Don't know him."

Austin frowned. "Who are you working for?"

"No one."

Looking frustrated, Austin said, "So what were you doing skulking around the blood bank?"

"I was hungry. I heard you have blood here."

I stifled a grin. Made sense to me. Taking pity on them both, I said, "Did you by any chance happen to attend a seminar recently with a vampire called Alexander the Great?"

"Yes."

Austin glanced at me. "Great. Another newbie."

I continued, "Did he tell you that you had to kill someone to be accepted?"

"Yes."

"And did you?"

"No."

Austin leaned forward. "Why not?"

"I-I couldn't."

Right answer. "Looks like he was really just hungry," I told Austin.

He nodded, then told Tim how the New Blood Movement worked. "Is this a life you can embrace?"

"Yes."

Everyone looked relieved, except one of the guards who seemed a little disappointed that he wasn't going to be able to whup any more ass.

"Good," Austin said, then glared at the guy who looked disappointed. "One more for our side is always a plus, don't you think?"

The guy shrugged but seemed to get it.

"Okay," Austin said, standing. "You two take Tim downstairs, show him the ropes, get him some blood. Good job, guys."

I released Lola's hold on Tim, and he seemed to deflate in relief. "Thank you," he told me fervently.

I wasn't sure if he was thanking me for making them believe he was telling the truth, or because Lola made him feel so good. Ew. I didn't want to know.

"Sure thing, boss," one of the guards said, and the three of them left the penthouse, leaving us alone.

I smiled at Austin. "You're good at this, you know."

"What?"

"Leading others."

He ran a hand over his face. "Not you, too."

"Huh?"

"These guys keep bugging me to take Alejandro's place. I won't do that."

"Of course not," I said softly. "You wouldn't be you if you did." He looked confused, so I added, "Alejandro told me that vampires become more of what they were when they were alive. And he said you're the most honorable man he knows."

Austin had such an odd expression on his face, I couldn't interpret it. "Thank you for believing in me," he said and drew me into his arms.

There was nothing romantic about the hug—just Austin expressing his appreciation for my support . . . at first. Lola had other plans.

She surged into him in a wave of pure need. For once, I didn't want to stop her, but, feeling Austin's immediate response, I felt a little guilty. "Sorry," I said, reining her in.

"Why'd you stop?" he asked softly, his embrace turning into something far more intimate.

"I don't want to force you to . . ." *Feel lust for me* is what I wanted to say but couldn't get the words out. I wanted the desire to come naturally, from him. I buried my head on his shoulder, feeling out of my depth.

He held me away from him so he could look me in the eyes. "Darlin', did I or did I not invite you here to do just this?"

My face flamed hot, but I still couldn't meet his eyes. "I guess."

"And since I can't feel Lola's effect over the phone, you think maybe you might just believe me when I say I want this?"

"Yes," I said in a small voice while Lola whooped it up inside me.

"And do you—does Lola—need her reservoir filled?"

I nodded, feeling shy. She'd been subsisting on short rations for a long time, since I never let her fully fill my chakras. She needed this. *We* needed this.

He grinned. "Then let's go somewhere more comfortable."

He entwined his fingers with mine and led me to the bedroom. Oh, my. Was I ready for this?

"Don't worry, darlin'. We won't do anything you're not comfortable with." He toed off his boots, then lay down on the bed and patted the comforter. "Come, snuggle with me."

It was exactly the right thing to say. I couldn't help but smile inwardly at the thought of a vampire who wanted to cuddle.

I removed my shoes and joined him, letting him wrap me in an embrace, both of us fully clothed. I sighed—it felt so wonderful to be held in a strong man's arms, something I rarely felt since Lola had to keep her distance.

And, of course, Lola rose to the bait. There was no going slow this time. She surged into his chakras with the force of a wooden stake to the heart. I heard him gasp.

"Sorry—"

"It's all right," he said soothingly. "You just surprised me, that's all."

To tell the truth, it surprised me, too. Maybe it was because I hadn't used many spells lately, so I was able to keep most of my succubus mojo, or maybe it was because Lola was so greedy, but she seemed stronger than ever. I reined her in, not wanting to go too fast.

As Lola drew on Austin's sensuous energy, his hands skimmed slowly under my shirt, over my skin, skirting the sensitive bits. I wasn't sure if he was teasing or going slow for my sake.

It didn't matter. I released all my inhibitions and let Lola loose.

Chapter Thirteen

Val

FANG HOOTED AS I walked in the townhouse door late the next afternoon. LOOK WHO'S DOING THE WALK OF SHAME!

Oh, crap. I should've left Austin's place early this morning. Instead, I'd conked out and slept way too late. Now, Ivy and Fang were up and waiting for me . . . and Fang could read everything in my mind about what I had done last night. As I felt my face flame yet again, I wondered if he would broadcast my special night with Austin to the entire world.

Fang came over to nudge my shin. NAW. I HAVE SOME DISCRETION WHEN IT COMES TO PEOPLE I LOVE.

Awww. I leaned down to hug the fuzzy mutt. *Thank you.*

"So, how'd it go?" Ivy asked from the living room couch.

"Unfortunately, the rogue didn't know anything about Alejandro—he was a total newbie."

"That's not what I meant."

I flopped down on the couch beside her. "I know. It went great, but I really don't want to talk about it, okay?" I wanted to hold it close and shiny to myself for a while, not tarnish the newness of it all. I might be part lust demon, but that didn't mean I liked to talk about what happened when Lola came out to play.

Ivy looked disappointed but said, "Oookay, I'll change the subject. I've been wondering . . . since you're the Paladin for the San Antonio Demon Underground, why are you at the beck and call of the vampires?"

"I'm not, really, but there isn't much going on with the Underground that Micah can't handle right now, and he and I both choose to have me spend time helping our allies with their problems."

"Why do you bother?"

Ivy seemed more curious than judgmental, so I answered her truthfully. "The world is going to learn eventually that demons and vampires exist, whether we want them to or not. The New Blood Movement is working to make their coming out as peaceful and unthreatening as possible, plus have legislation in place to protect those of us who are the good guys. The rogues . . . we don't really know what they intend to accomplish except for using humans as a food source."

"You think laws will really stop them from doing that?"

Fang snorted, giving her the answer. But I responded anyway. "Not stop them, no, but it will allow people like the SCU—the Special Crimes Unit—to arrest the bad guys and stake them if necessary. Plus it helps protect the good guys like Alejandro's people and us."

Ivy nodded. "Is this New Blood Movement happening everywhere? Or just here in San Antonio?"

Good question. "I'm not sure. I know there's one in Austin, too—probably most of Texas. Beyond that, I have no idea. You'll have to ask Alejandro when we find him." And, for everyone's sake, I hoped we'd find him alive and well soon.

Ivy glanced at her phone. "That seminar starts in a couple of hours. What's our objective?"

I thought for a moment. "We want to find Ike and Mike or learn how to find them."

"How are we going to do that?"

"I'm not sure. We'll try to weave it into the conversation. If we can't do that, we need to get them to trust us, want to turn us so they'll take us into their confidence."

Ivy looked a little sick. "Turn us?"

"Don't worry—they can't turn you. If a vampire drinks a demon's blood, it'll make him insane long before he's able to turn you."

"That's *not* reassuring."

I grinned. "It won't come to that—you have me as your secret weapon." The strength spell I'd invoked to take care of the three Cs was still in place and working. "Not to mention those gemstones of yours. You think some of them might come in handy?"

"Maybe," she said doubtfully. "Can't you just force the vampires to tell you what you need to know?"

"I could, but I was hoping to be able to do this on the down low, so they don't get wind of our intentions and warn Ike and Mike. We'll just need to ensure we stay together, for your safety."

WE GOT YOUR BACK, Fang said.

Ivy glanced down at Fang then up at me. "You know, if Fang accompanies you, they might figure out who you are—I'd think word would have gotten around by now that the Slayer travels with a hellhound."

I'M FAMOUS? Fang's mouth opened in a doggie grin. WAIT, THAT'S NOT GOOD.

"No, it's not," Ivy said. "Val shouldn't be seen with you at the seminar."

YOU MEAN I SHOULD MISS OUT ON THE FUN?

Ivy gave him a strange look, so I explained, "He lives for taking down vampires. But she's right, Fang. The word is getting around. You can wait outside the lecture hall, within mental shouting distance, okay?"

IF I HAFTA.

You hafta.

"We should probably change into something else, blend in," Ivy suggested.

"Blend in?" I glanced down at my clothes. True, I needed to shower and change, but. . . . "Don't I look like a typical college student?"

"Yeah, too typical, maybe. And too *Val*—they might know what you look like by now. We should make you over, so they won't recognize you."

"How?" I asked in trepidation.

"I was thinking we should go Goth. You know, like the vampire subculture."

"Not a bad idea, but I don't really know how."

"No problem—I do. I have some friends who are into the lifestyle and sometimes go out with them. I have everything we need."

After I showered, I found that Ivy had laid out a small selection of clothing on my bed.

"I'm a bit taller and thinner than you are, but I think we can wear the same size." She sorted through a collection of dark clothing. "What do you think?"

She had three outfits to choose from—black leather pants with a fishnet top, a bustier with a long, flowing tulle skirt, and a short, tight vinyl dress with a strange studded leather belt that had chains hanging from it.

IT'S A BONDAGE BELT, Fang explained.

I didn't even want to know how he knew that. Or what a bondage belt was used for.

I glanced at Ivy. "Why do you have this stuff with you?" Let alone three full outfits.

She shrugged. "I didn't know what kind of organization you had here, and I wanted to be able to fit in. Besides, it's a great disguise. People don't notice the real you when you're wearing clothes like this—all they see is the Goth."

She had a point. But I didn't really care for the choices. "The black vinyl dress is out—I don't know how anyone could even move in that, let alone hide a stake or two."

Ivy nodded. "The leather pants are probably too long for you—and tight enough that you'd have the same problem hiding a stake. The skirt is elastic, and the bustier adjustable."

So, the bustier and tulle skirt it was. She helped me into the bustier, and I blushed at how the tight corset-like garment pushed my boobs up and out so it looked like I really had something there. The skirt was a lot more comfortable, but stakes would show above the waistband. I looked at myself in the mirror, feeling foolish and overly exposed. "You think I could wear a vest over this?" I asked.

"No," Ivy and Fang said simultaneously.

THAT WOULD LOOK DUMB. WHAT ABOUT YOUR BLACK LEATHER JACKET?

I pulled my motorcycle jacket from the closet and tried it on over the bustier. "Not bad," Ivy said. "Let's go with that. Do you have black boots?"

Now, those I had. While I added boots to my ensemble, Ivy dressed in the leather pants and strategically-ripped fishnet blouse, wearing a black bra underneath. With her spiky hair, multiple piercings, and the addition of a couple of wide black leather studded bracelets, she looked like a real badass Goth.

Me, not so much. "I look like a wannabe," I complained.

"Wait—I'm not done with you," Ivy said. "We haven't put the makeup on yet."

"Makeup? I'm not real good with that."

"That's okay, I am." She pulled out a makeup kit and went to work on me, then painted my nails black. She glanced at me and nodded in satisfaction. "One more thing. Hold on, and don't look at yourself yet."

As I waved my hands to help the polish dry, she ran into the other room and came back with a wig. "Don't screw up your nail polish. Let me do this for you." She pinned my unruly hair ruthlessly on top of my head, then snugged the wig down over it and stepped back to admire her handiwork. "There. I defy even your family to recognize you now."

Doubtfully, I turned to look in the mirror. Holy crap—she was right. With white foundation, red and black eye shadow lined in the blackest liner, dark lipstick, and a midnight-blue wig cut in a bob with severe bangs straight across my forehead, even I didn't recognize me.

"You like?" Ivy asked.

I wouldn't say "like" precisely—it wasn't a look I'd wear often. "It's effective," I managed.

IT'S BANGING, Fang exclaimed. I WANNA DRESS UP, TOO.

Ivy grinned. "I can do that. Hold on." She ran to her room again and came back with a black leather collar with silver spikes. "Here. This is adjustable." She put it on Fang, and he immediately ran to the full-length mirror.

WOO-HOO. I LOOK BADASS.

Ivy laughed. "Yes, you do. Let me do my own makeup, then we'll be ready to go." She glanced at me, still grinning. "You look uncomfortable. Why don't you walk around in that for a while, get comfortable, so you don't feel like an imposter?"

Good idea. I wandered around the townhouse, picking things up, putting them down, feeling stupid, and watched Fang as he pranced around joyfully in his new collar.

When she was finished, Ivy just looked like an edgier version of herself, unlike the total transformation I'd gone through. I felt somehow as if things had spun out of my control, but I knew one way of getting them back. "You know, arriving in your bumblebee might give us away. How about we take my motorcycle? It's more in keeping with the look, don't you think?"

"I guess," Ivy said doubtfully. "But will all three of us fit?"

SURE, Fang said. I'M SMALL AND DON'T TAKE UP MUCH ROOM. WE CAN MAKE IT WORK. LET'S GO.

We arrived at the college a few minutes before the starting time. Unfortunately, black showed reddish-blond dog hair only too well, and with Fang sandwiched between us on the Valkyrie, we were both covered in it. "No problem," I told Ivy when she glanced down at herself in dismay. "I've learned to carry a lint roller."

HEY, I CAN'T HELP IT, Fang said defensively.

"It's okay," Ivy assured him as she ran the lint roller over my back. "I just didn't want our disguise to be compromised."

Once we were relatively dog hair-free, we headed to the lecture hall, Fang staying outside in the bushes where he wouldn't be seen but could still reach us mentally. It was a large room, but there were only about a dozen people scattered around in the stadium-style seats—all guys. Most of them looked a lot like the three Cs, but a couple of them were dressed like us. Thank goodness, or I would've really felt out of place.

"Remember," I murmured. "We don't want to tip our hand."

The seminar "leader" arrived fashionably late and burst into the lecture area with his arms held wide. "Welcome, welcome!" He spoke as if the hall were full of adoring fans. The few people here probably would be soon. He could've been the dictionary definition of tall, dark, and handsome, with artfully rumpled hair and a sexy beard stubble. He did look a bit like Liam Hemsworth, only shorter and thinner. No wonder they used him to recruit—women would want to be with him, and men would want to *be* him.

"I am Alexander," he said dramatically. "My friends call me Alexander the Great. And do you know why?"

"No," everyone murmured, including Ivy.

"Because I am! And you can be too!"

What the heck? Ivy looked totally enthralled. Duh. She probably was—they all were, by him. Another reason to use Alexander to recruit, if he was that good at mind control. He almost had me doing it as well.

Talk to Ivy, I told Fang. *Break this thrall.*

YOU GOT IT, BABE.

Ivy jerked and gave me a wide-eyed look, then mouthed, "Thanks."

I nodded, and she fingered one of the gemstone studs in her left ear with a frown. Maybe she had her own way of blocking the thrall now that she knew what was going on.

I tuned back in to what Alexander "the Great" was saying. He was touting the benefits of becoming a vampire, not making any pretense at being anything else. I frowned. I half expected some of the audience members to leave in disbelief, but he had them right where he wanted them and wasn't about to let them go.

Why was he being so forthcoming? Probably because he was planning to wipe their minds clear of the memories if they didn't agree to convert.

OR WORSE, Fang suggested.

Maybe, though I didn't see how killing everyone who elected not to join could possibly help their recruiting efforts. It was bound to be noticed by campus authorities. I made a mental note to have the SCU contact them and shut down any future seminars.

After about half an hour of talking at us and expounding the numerous benefits of becoming a fangbanger, Alexander the Great finally said, "Let's take a break. Come on down and have some refreshments, mingle, ask me questions."

He gestured at a table loaded with tempting snacks.

"He—" Ivy started to say, but I interrupted her.

"He's fabulous, isn't he?" Silently, I asked Fang to relay messages between us and remind her that vampires had incredibly good hearing.

YOU GOT IT. After a moment, he added, IVY WANTS TO LET YOU KNOW THAT HE'S TONED DOWN THE THRALL, PROBABLY BECAUSE HE WANTS TO SEE REAL REACTIONS.

Ivy nodded at me meaningfully. "Yes, he is wonderful. Let's go meet him."

As the students descended on the bounty like locusts, Ivy and I made our way down to talk to Alexander.

"Wow, you are such a good speaker," Ivy gushed as he held her hand and gazed down at her with a smarmy smile.

LAYING IT ON A BIT THICK, AREN'T YOU? Fang said.

Not from the way Alexander reacted—he expected adoration and apparently forced it when it wasn't freely given.

"We love what you had to say about the benefits," I said.

His attention turned to me. Or rather, to the flesh bulging above the bustier. Just as well—that way he couldn't see the disgust in my eyes.

"But there is one particular benefit we're really interested in," I said, forcing a smile I hoped was enticing and seductive.

"What's that?"

"Well, there are these two hot guys we met—blond twins. Do you think you could possibly tell us how to find them?"

GOOD PLAY, Fang said approvingly.

Alexander's smile turned brittle. "If you join us, you'll meet them, no problem."

I exchanged a disappointed glance with Ivy. "But we were hoping to meet them tonight." Feeling like an idiot, I ran a finger across my cleavage and pouted. "Can't you tell us where to find them?"

His eyes narrowed. "No."

Fang cracked up. WOW, I NEVER THOUGHT I'D SEE THE DAY WHEN VAL SHAPIRO TRIED TO ACT SEXY. EPIC FAIL.

Shut up. This was embarrassing enough as it was without his commentary.

Alexander's face hardened. "I'm sorry, but you two ladies are not what we're looking for. We want to build an army, not a harem."

Asshole.

"Wait over there, please," he said and pointed to a corner of the lecture hall, reinforcing it with a nudge from his mind power that even I felt.

Ivy and I obediently went to the corner while he went to talk to the others.

IVY WANTS TO KNOW WHAT WE'RE GOING TO DO NOW, Fang said.

Crap. *I don't know. It doesn't look like we can get the information out of him without using Lola.*

THEN LOLA HIM ALREADY.

I don't know. Maybe we can follow him, find their base of operations.

YOU REALLY THINK THAT'LL WORK? AS IVY POINTED OUT, YOU'RE NOT EXACTLY INCONSPICUOUS, AND HE KNOWS YOU TWO NOW.

I chewed my lip indecisively as I watched Alexander talk to each person separately. He sent a few more culls to join us in the corner and left the rest at the table full of food. "Congratulations," he told the chosen ones. "You will join us tonight." He glanced at those of us in the corner. "As for the rest of you, you won't remember a thing . . . and you won't ever return."

He stalked toward us, the smile fading from his lips as he looked like the predator he was. His fangs elongated, and I saw him eye my cleavage lasciviously. Realization dawned. Crap. He was going to feed on the culls before wiping our memories, then force the chosen ones into becoming vampires tonight—without giving them a choice as to whether they wanted it or not. That's undoubtedly what had happened to all the new recruits, and he'd altered their memories to make them believe they'd asked for it.

Well, I wasn't going to let that happen again tonight. Forget the down low. I was going in up high. Totally pissed, I let Lola loose and slammed her into his chakras. "Stop," I ordered.

He paused in midstep, looking surprised that he was doing my bidding. Crap, this was not going at all like I'd planned. "Tell every man here to forget what happened this evening, then release your mind control."

From the puzzled expressions on the guys' faces, I gathered he'd done as I ordered. Unfortunately, I'd forgotten to have him to tell them to leave. No problem. Since Lola had topped off with Austin, I had plenty of mojo to control them, too. Sliding Lola into each and every one of them, I said, "Nothing to see here. Go home." And, looking confused, they left.

Turning my attention back to Alexander, I said, "What have you done with Alejandro?"

"Nothing."

"Someone in your organization knows something about what happened. Who?"

"Ike and Mike were sent to kill him."

"Did they succeed?"

"No."

Relieved but frustrated, I asked, "What happened?"

"I don't know. You'd have to ask them."

Okay, back to square one. "Where can I find them now?"

"I don't know."

Ivy nudged me. "He may be taking you too literally. Ask him where they hang out, where they live."

I did, and Alexander answered, "They are in a different cell, so I don't know where they live. You can probably find them at Club Gothick most nights, when they're not working."

"Thank you," I said, then felt silly for thanking the murderous bloodsucker.

NOW WHAT ARE YOU GOING TO DO WITH HIM? Fang asked.

"Good question," Ivy murmured. "Can you force him to forget this conversation?"

"I could if I still had the amulet," I answered. But I didn't. Maybe I could take him to the prison cells under Club Purgatory, let Austin and Micah figure out what to with him.

"Are any more vampires going to show up here tonight?" I asked him.

"No. Except for the one who just arrived."

What?

WATCH OUT, Fang yelled.

Ivy screamed, and a vamp slammed into my side as Fang came charging in.

It surprised me so much that I let Lola slip, and I suddenly had two vamps on top of me on the floor, snarling and slavering for my blood. Not that it would do them any good.

Unfortunately, the vamp who'd tagged in was female, and Lola wouldn't work on her. I mustered my strength and threw them off. Wow—that worked better than I expected, even with the strength spell still in place. I scrambled to my feet and instinctively grabbed the two stakes from the back of my waistband. As they came at me, I was perfectly positioned to slam both stakes into their black hearts.

Bam—down they went, well and truly dead.

WELL, THAT WAS IMPRESSIVE, Fang said, staring down at the bodies.

Yeah, but not exactly low-key as I'd planned.

Ivy looked a little shell-shocked. "Are you all right?" I asked.

"Yeah," she said slowly. "But how are we going to get rid of their bodies?"

Fang laughed. OH, YEAH. SHE'LL DO.

Chapter Fourteen

Val

AFTER THE SPECIAL Crimes Unit picked up the dead undead in their "ambulance," I told Ivy, "I've been to Club Gothick once before on an investigation. We're actually dressed for it. It's getting kind of late, but want to see if the bar is still open so we can find Ike and Mike?"

Ivy glanced at me. "Sure. Your makeup isn't even messed up."

No doubt—I just hoped the Kabuki crap would come off when I wanted it to. But I was kind of surprised by her wanting to go along with us.

SHE BELIEVES YOU NOW WHEN YOU SAY YOU CAN TAKE CARE OF A COUPLE OF VAMPS, Fang confided.

It wasn't long before I brought the Valkyrie to a stop outside Club Gothick. Ivy glanced up at the over-the-top bar sign—a horror movie font dripping with fake blood. "You've got to be kidding me."

"Subtle, they're not," I said, shaking my head. "Fang should probably stay out here."

NO PROBLEM, he said, flopping down under a window and curling up with his head on his paws. I DOUBT YOU'LL FIND THEM INSIDE ANYWAY.

"Real vampires hang out here?" Ivy asked. "Isn't it a bit on the nose?"

I grinned. "Last time I was here, it was all fakers and wannabes, but maybe the candy twins figure they'll blend in better or gather groupies."

"Maybe even do some recruiting among people who are predisposed to like the lifestyle," Ivy suggested.

"Exactly. You ready?"

At Ivy's nod, I entered the door where the band was playing some creepy, dirge-like music. There were a few Goth-type characters sitting around and drinking, but I didn't see Ike and Mike. Then again, if they put on makeup and Goth clothes, I'm not sure I would recognize them.

I walked up to the bartender, who looked almost normal in a black ripped wifebeater showing off his muscles and tats. "We're looking for Mike and Ike. Do you know them?"

"Yeah," he said, sounding bored.

"Know where they are?"

He nodded to a doorway. "They were in the party room earlier. Don't know if they're still there."

I nodded my thanks, and Ivy ordered a couple of glasses of club soda. "We'll blend in more if we have something in our hands," she explained as the bartender squirted soda into two glasses.

True. And we weren't old enough to drink anything stronger, yet.

We took our drinks to the party door, and I opened it, trying to look as if I belonged. One chick who looked like Sally in *The Nightmare Before Christmas* looked us up and down. "Who are you?"

Until now, I'd felt pretty rocked-out Goth, but the proliferation of facial studs, partially shaved heads, and metal overload in the room made me feel like the faker I was. I hesitated for a moment, but Ivy, who fit in much better, intervened. "Mike and Ike invited us."

The girl rolled her eyes but let us in, then completely ignored us, strolling away with complete indifference.

"Wow, I really feel welcomed," I muttered.

"Try to look bored or depressed," Ivy suggested. "You'll fit in better."

Trying to look as though I were about to commit suicide, I glanced around the dark room, illuminated by sullen red lighting in isolated spots around the room. Couples of indeterminate gender made out in the dark corners or sucked on each other's necks.

I headed toward one small round table where a guy sat alone, looking more approachable in a romantic Goth look with lots of frothy lace at his neck and wrists under a dark jacket. At least, I thought it was a guy. With his/her/its long black hair and more stark makeup than I wore, it was hard to tell. Ivy followed, but I let her take the lead when we reached the table.

"Hi," Ivy said. "I'm Ivory. This is . . . Valentina. Can we join you?"

I heard Fang's mental snort from outside. SO, YOU HAVE GOTH NAMES NOW.

Yeah, I'm sure she'll give you one, too, if you ask nicely.

MINE'S ALREADY GOTH ENOUGH.

True.

"Sure. I'm Dante." Judging by the name, the low voice, and the way Dante was checking out my cleavage, I was going with "guy." When

Lola reacted to his proximity, I knew for sure he was really a he.

We plunked our butts down on the uncomfortable metal bar stools and looked around.

"I haven't seen you two here before," Dante said, sipping his blood red wine and trying to look sexy. Doing a pretty good job of it, too.

"New in town," Ivy explained. "Just looking for some guys we met before who told us to look them up."

He looked disappointed. "Who's that?"

"Mike and Ike," I told him, though I wasn't sure if they used different names here.

"Sure," Dante said. "The twins. I know them."

"Are they here tonight?"

"Not now. They were earlier."

Shoot—I was hoping this would be easier. "What do you know about them?" I asked casually.

When he gave me a cautious look, I added, "We hooked up with them yesterday and want to see them again, but they left before we could give them our numbers."

He shook his head. "I don't get why you chicks like them so much. So not Goth."

I shrugged. "They're hot . . . different."

"Yeah," he said and gave us significant looks. "Real different. Dangerous different."

"So you know what they really are?" Ivy asked.

"Yeah. Do you?" he challenged.

"Vampires," Ivy whispered on a hiss.

"I'm talking the real thing," Dante said, sounding intense.

"Me, too," Ivy said. "And we have the puncture marks to prove it."

Where was she going with this? He glanced at our necks, free of fang marks.

"Not there," Ivy said. "There are other veins to sink fangs into."

He glanced down at her lap, and I realized what she meant—the femoral artery near the groin. I felt myself flushing but hoped he wouldn't be able to see it beneath the white makeup.

"No," Ivy said. "We're not going to show you. You'll just have to take our word for it."

He shrugged, trying to appear indifferent. "Your funeral."

I entered the conversation. "So, if you know so much about them, maybe you can tell us where they went tonight after they left here?"

"I don't keep track."

I smiled and sent Lola into him, just a little. It wasn't as if he needed much encouragement. "But you know anyway, don't you?" His expression turned dreamy as Lola stroked his chakras. "And you want to tell us everything you know." I reinforced the suggestion with Lola, but it didn't take much. He was very eager.

"Mmm. They're okay, except for hogging all the chicks and boring us with talk about the Movement."

"What do they say about the Movement?"

"How it sucks, how it's ruining their lives, how they're going to take it down."

Now we were getting somewhere. "How are they going to take it down?"

"By killing the leaders." His mouth twisted in a wry grin. "But they haven't been very successful so far. They talk big, though."

"What was the talk tonight? Did they say where they were going?"

"Yeah, they were going to go after one of the leaders again."

"Which one?" Ivy asked when my throat closed up.

"Don't know his name."

"What do you know about him?" I asked, finally getting my voice back.

"The cowboy, they called him."

Oh, crap. They were going after Austin tonight.

AUSTIN CAN TAKE CARE OF HIMSELF, Fang reminded me.

"Did they say how?" I persisted. "Or where?"

"With crossbows and a lot of friends. At the downtown blood bank."

Oh, crap. Crossbows were a whole lot harder to dodge than mere fists and fangs. I exchanged glances with Ivy as we both slid off the barstools. "Thanks, Dante. Appreciate the info."

"No problem," he said with a leer at my cleavage. "Come on back anytime. With or without your friend."

Rolling my eyes, I pulled Lola out of him—he was enjoying it way too much.

Outside, I said, "Hold on. Let me call Austin and warn him." If it wasn't too late.

I pulled my phone out of my skirt pocket and dialed Austin. The phone rang once, twice, three times, my heart rate doubling each time. Finally, he answered on the fourth ring.

"Austin—" I began.

"Not Austin," a man said on the other end. "Who's this?"

"It's Val. Val Shapiro."

"The Slayer?"

"Yes. Where's Austin? Why didn't he answer the phone?" I asked, my heart in my throat.

"Get here quick. We've been attacked." And without another word, he hung up.

Chapter Fifteen

Austin

AUSTIN NEVER understood why some men found glory in battle—the aftermath was so agonizing. He glanced around the blood bank, now smeared with the life fluid this building was designed to collect, and sighed in frustration. Though their trap hadn't worked, they'd won the battle . . . but at what cost?

Three of the rogues had been killed, and, in trying to shield the humans from harm, two of Austin's followers had been slain, a dozen injured, and several humans wounded despite their best efforts to shield them. Most of the vampire wounded would heal in time, but he was worried about Jeremy, who had taken a bolt in the eye.

Hearing a commotion at the door, he glanced up from the wounded vampire he and Gwen had been trying to help. What now? He leapt to his feet and readied himself for whatever was coming.

Not necessary. This time it was two Goth girls trying to force their way in, along with a dog.

Wait—he knew that dog.

"Come on, you know me," one of the girls protested.

Austin realized he knew that voice as well . . . though it definitely didn't go with the way she was dressed. He raised his eyebrows along with his voice. "Let them in."

Val turned her head toward him—black lipstick and dark eye shadow stark against the paleness of her face—and he could see the horror in it even from across the room.

"Austin," she said on a gasp. "Are you hurt?"

He glanced down at his denim shirt, red with the blood of the fallen. "I'm fine. The blood isn't mine."

"Oh, thank the gods," she said and flew into his arms.

Austin grabbed hold of her and hung on tight, grateful for her presence and the fact that she was coming to care for him. He'd expected some awkwardness in Val after their night together, but fear trumped awkwardness apparently, and she was fine. At least there was one good thing to come from this night.

He pulled away far enough so he could look down into her face. Fingering the dramatic blue-black wig, he asked, "What's with the get-up?"

"Oh, I forgot. Ivy said we'd fit in better at the seminar if we dressed like this."

He nodded, realizing the other Goth girl must be Ivy. She'd gone to help the humans on the other side of the room, just as she had before.

"But never mind that," Val said. "What happened here?"

"Remember I told you we set a trap to try and lure Mike and Ike in so we could capture them?"

She nodded.

"It didn't work."

Fang, down by her side, snorted in what sounded like amusement.

Yeah, kind of obvious. "We put out the word that I was going to be here tonight at midnight, hoping to catch them off-guard. Unfortunately, they showed up early, and in much greater force than we anticipated. We'd planned to keep all the violence outside, away from the donors, but they brought it inside." Luckily, there were only a few donors this time of night.

"Was it the rogues?" she asked.

"Yes, definitely," Austin confirmed.

"You should have seen Austin," Charlie gushed from behind him. "He was faster and stronger than anyone else here—he took down twice as many as anyone else. He was like . . . like all supervamp and everything."

Austin winced, hoping no one else had heard that—he'd never live it down. "Looks like they need help over there," he said, nodding toward the far side of the room, and Charlie went eagerly on his way.

"You're really okay?" Val asked, and he could see worry in her eyes. "I was afraid that Lola might have . . . drained you last night."

He squeezed her reassuringly then let her go. "You don't have to worry about that with me. A little restorative sleep, and with my healing and recuperative powers, I was back up to normal in no time at all."

Val grinned in what looked like relief. "Actually, if what Charlie said is true, it sounds like you were better than normal. Or did he exaggerate just a tad?"

"Well, actually, he didn't. I was faster and stronger than I've ever been in my life."

"Why? You don't think Lola had anything to do with it?"

"No, I don't know why I was suddenly more powerful." But he'd felt almost like a berserker. He gestured at his shirt. "If it wasn't for Jeremy, this blood might be mine."

He glanced down at the former football player who was being tended by Gwen and Amanda. Val's gaze followed his, and she gasped when she saw the vampire with the bolt in his eye. "Is he still alive?"

"Yes," Austin said. "He took a bolt meant for me."

"Can he heal from that?" Val asked in disbelief.

"Yes," Austin said. "But the bolt has to come out soon, or he'll heal around it."

"So why haven't you taken it out yet?"

Gwen looked up. "We don't know if his brain has been damaged beyond the point where even accelerated vampire healing would help. I'm afraid we'll injure him more unless we can pull it straight out. But I can't keep him still, and Austin is afraid he'll crush his head if he tries to hold him motionless. Shade is on his way, but we need to get the bolt out first."

"I can help with that," Val said. Taking one of Jeremy's hands in hers, she must have done her mojo with Jeremy, because Austin could see the wounded vampire visibly relax. "Close your eyes, be perfectly still, and let us take care of you," he heard her murmur.

"Oh, thank you," Amanda breathed as Jeremy relaxed.

Her tear-streaked face just made Austin feel more guilty. The human receptionist had volunteered to man the desk here tonight, and, while she hadn't been injured, she shouldn't have had to witness such mayhem.

"Take it out straight," Gwen whispered. "Fast."

Austin nodded and, feeling as if he was performing a delicate operation with brute force, pulled the bolt straight out of Jeremy's eye.

Despite Val's control over him, Jeremy screamed and thrashed.

"Keep him still," Gwen said urgently.

"Shh, shh," Val said. "Relax," she said and placed her hands on him. Good—even if the man was brain-damaged and unable to understand her, Lola should work on him at a subconscious level.

"Can you put him to sleep?" Austin asked Val.

"I can, but Shade will want to get his permission before he heals him. He'll need to be awake for that." She must have seen the worry in his expression, because she added, "But I can keep him calm now that the bolt is out." She glanced toward the door. "Fang says Shade just arrived."

Austin looked in that direction. A man in a motorcycle helmet stood in the doorway, talking to the guard he'd posted. Austin raised his voice. "Let him in. Over here, Shade." He'd never been so glad to see the shadow demon.

Shade approached them slowly and paused to apparently take in the scene. "What happened here?"

"Mayhem," Val said curtly.

The helmet turned toward her. "Val?" he asked in disbelief. "Why are you dressed like that?"

"I'll explain later," she said impatiently. "Can you fix him?"

Shade knelt down beside Jeremy.

Gwen placed her hand on his. "He took a bolt in the eye. Can you heal him, please? I'm afraid there will be brain damage if we let him heal on his own."

Shade took off his helmet, and Austin saw the interdimensional whirling for only an instant before Gwen touched him again to bring him back into focus.

"He has to agree," Shade said, "and I'll need a template."

"Jeremy?" Austin said, hoping the wounded man's brain wouldn't be too scrambled so he could agree to the healing.

"I felt him respond to your voice," Val said softly. "Go ahead and ask."

"Do you agree to let the shadow demon heal you?" he asked.

Jeremy looked confused and in pain.

"Hold on," Val said. "I've never done this before, but I think I can find a chakra. . . . There." She sighed. "I found out how to block his pain. Ask him again."

This time, Jeremy breathed a "yes" in reply to Austin's question.

"And the template?" Shade asked.

Austin glanced around, wondering whom he could conscript. "Not Val," he said. "We need her to keep him calm. Ivy, maybe?" He glanced to where she was busy wrapping bandages around a human's hand.

He didn't know the gemstone whisperer very well, and this might be too much to ask.

"What's a template?" Amanda asked.

Shade responded. "To heal Jeremy, I'll need to use a person with a whole eye and brain as a template to repair Jeremy's and to provide energy for the healing. It can't be a vampire."

They'd learned that when they'd tried to use Elspeth as a template and failed—something about being undead made it impossible for the shadow demon to use them as a template.

Shade turned to Val. "Do you want to ask Ivy?"

"No, use me," Amanda said.

"Are you sure?" Austin asked, frowning. "What they didn't say is that you may also share very intimate details about your life and your feelings."

She blushed but lifted her chin in defiance. "I don't care. Jeremy has always been very nice to me, and I knew him before . . ."

Before the rogues had turned him into one of the undead. Austin nodded encouragingly.

She shrugged. "He's so brave. I want to do this."

"I can put him to sleep," Val suggested. "That should lessen the exchange of memories."

"Okay, do it," Shade said.

As Val told Jeremy to sleep, Amanda asked nervously, "What do I need to do?"

Shade sat next to Jeremy on the floor and placed a hand on his head. "Just lie here on the other side of me," he said gently to the frightened girl, "and let me place my hand on your head."

Austin pulled off his jacket and made it into a pillow for Amanda's head. "Thank you for doing this," he said. Definitely above and beyond the call of duty.

"It's okay," she said with a tremulous smile.

"It will be," Val assured her. "Don't worry. I've done this a couple of times myself, and everything turned out just fine."

"Okay," Shade said, "close your eyes. I'm ready to start." He glanced at Austin. "This may take longer if there's a lot of damage."

Austin nodded in comprehension. He just hoped the shadow demon would be able to help the man who'd thrown himself between Austin and the crossbow bolt.

Shade placed his other hand on Amanda's head, and they both closed their eyes. His head thrown back and teeth bared in concentration, Shade flickered in and out of focus as he pulled on another dimension's healing energy. Harsh streaks of violet lightning pulsed through him, flashing from Amanda to Jeremy. It looked as though a storm was raging inside the shadow demon.

Much faster than Austin had expected, it was over, and Jeremy's eye was completely restored. Shade let go of Amanda and Jeremy and slumped back against the wall.

"Are you all right?" Austin asked Shade in concern.

Fang lay down next to the shadow demon and rested his head on Shade's arm, bringing his face into view. He looked pale and drained.

"I'm okay," Shade said. "I just need some rest."

Val glanced down at the hellhound. "Fang says this was much quicker than any other healing you've done before. He's right. Are you sure Jeremy's brain will be okay?"

Shade ran a hand over his face. "It should be—I felt it being repaired at a cellular level. He might lose some memories, but he should function just fine."

"When—" Austin began, but was interrupted by Diego.

"Hey, boss, what should we do about the two guys we captured? I'm not sure how long they can hold them without killing them."

Jeremy was in Gwen's capable hands, so Austin glanced at Val. "Can you . . . ?"

"Of course," she said.

Grateful for her understanding and willingness to help, Austin led her to the room where six of his men had two rogues cornered. The conference room had definitely seen better days—the tables were smashed, the chairs ripped apart, and dents decorated all four walls. Thank goodness they'd reinforced this room with more than just drywall. The vampires had seen better days, too. The two rogues rushed the door, attempting to escape, but his people piled on them, until he could see nothing but flying arms and legs.

"Stop," Val yelled, her arms outstretched.

All eight of the combatants stopped immediately, frozen in a bizarre statuelike lump of bodies.

"Stand up," she said.

All eight followed her orders.

"Okay," she said to Austin. "Which ones do you want to question?"

Austin pointed out the two rogues, and Val released the six who'd kept them under control. "Good work, guys," Austin said. "You can stand down now."

They all retreated to the walls, leaving the rogues in the center of the room—one short and blond, one tall and dark. His people made no move to leave, and Austin let them stay, figuring they deserved a chance to see what their efforts wrought.

"Still no Ike or Mike," Val muttered in disappointment.

Austin nodded. "They were here, though. I remember seeing them."

"Okay," Val said. "Which one of you two knows most about this attack?"

They exchanged glances, and the shorter one of the two said, "I do."

"Then tell us why you attacked this blood bank," Val said.

"We were ordered to kill the lieutenant known as Austin," he said.

Obviously. "Why?" Austin asked.

When Val ordered him to answer Austin's questions as well as her own, the guy replied, "Because we need to eliminate opposition to our plans."

"What are your plans?"

"To take over the city."

"And how do you plan to do that?" Austin persisted.

"By taking out the leaders of the Movement first, then sowing discord and fear among the human population."

"Did you kill Alejandro?" Val asked.

"No."

Austin rephrased her question, in case they were being too literal. "Did anyone kill Alejandro, like Mike and Ike?"

"Not that I know of."

Relief filled him, followed by frustration. "Then where is he?"

"We don't know."

"Do Mike and Ike know?" Val persisted.

"Maybe," the vamp conceded. "But they told an unbelievable story about what happened."

"What was the story?" Austin asked impatiently. Any leads would be good about now.

"We don't know. We just heard that it was bogus, not the details."

Damn. Looked like it came back to the candy twins again. "Where can we find them?"

"At the training camp."

Now they were getting somewhere. "Where's the training camp?"

"I-I—" the vamp began, then stopped.

Val looked annoyed. "Both of you—tell us where the camp is. Immediately."

The two of them made grinding motions with their jaws, then went into spasms.

What the heck?

"Oh, crap," Val said, glancing down at the hellhound. "They've just swallowed demon blood—Fang felt it hit their bloodstream."

Damn it. Demon blood made vamps go insane. "Now we'll never get anything out of them."

The rogues went berserk, and his followers united to stake the rogues.

"What happened?" Val asked after they were both down. "How'd the blood get into their systems?"

Austin leaned down and opened the short guy's mouth. Just as he expected. "A hollow tooth. They must have been implanted with a command to destroy themselves rather than reveal the location of their camp." Now they had two dead rogues and no answers.

Ordering his men to clean up, Austin went back into the other room to check on the progress of the cleanup. Gwen must have taken Jeremy to the clinic downstairs, and it looked as though the rest of the cleanup was well in hand.

Ivy approached them, and Austin noted how the Goth look suited her so much better than it did Val. Not that he was complaining about the unexpected cleavage Val displayed.

"Did you get any answers?" Ivy asked.

Austin shook his head. "Nothing helpful. How about you two? Did you learn anything at the seminar?"

Val grimaced. "Not really. I ended up having to stake the recruiters."

"But we did learn one of the twins' hangouts," Ivy said. "Club Gothick—we tried to find them there."

"Did you learn anything?" Austin asked.

Val shook her head. "Just that they planned to attack you here tonight. But maybe we can stake out the club, wait for them to show up."

"It's worth a shot," Austin said. "Right now, it's the only lead we have."

"I don't know," Ivy said. "If they learn we were there asking about them, they might not show up again."

She was right. "And if they figure out you've been doing the questioning," he told Val, "you are probably one of their targets now, too." *Damn it.* He didn't want to put her in any more danger, but with Val, there was no choice. It was one of things he admired most about her, even as he hated the fact that helping him put her in danger. "I worry about you. Especially since your powers—"

He broke off, glancing at Ivy, unsure how much she knew.

"You can trust her," Val said. "With my powers diminished, you mean."

Val and Ivy both glanced down at Fang.

He knew what that meant by now. "What'd he say?" Austin asked.

"He's not so sure my powers *are* diminished," Val said slowly. "Earlier, I felt so much stronger than I have before—and the bruises don't seem to bother me as much. Maybe my powers are coming back." She glanced down at the hellhound again, apparently in mental conversation. "You also said you were stronger and faster than before, and Shade was able to heal Jeremy in record time."

"Yes. Does that mean something?"

"I think it does," Ivy said excitedly. "I talked to my dad a little bit ago. He said it's possible the demon inside the crystal fractured when the amulet did, and pieces of the demon went into the people present."

"I have a demon inside me?" Austin asked. "Does that mean I'm going to go insane, too?" Surely it would have happened by now.

Ivy shook her head. "I should have said that pieces of the demon's *power* went into the people present." She turned to Val. "You said the full crystal enhanced your natural abilities, so it follows that part of the crystal inside you would do the same thing."

It made sense.

"Who else was present when it broke?" Ivy asked.

"Just Shade, Austin, Fang, and me," Val said. She glanced at the hellhound. "You notice enhanced powers?"

She listened for a moment, then grinned at Austin. "He said maybe, but he's just always been that good."

"Luis was there, too," Austin reminded her. "In another room."

Ivy frowned. "I think the closer you were to the crystal, the more power you'd get. So Luis probably got a lesser amount."

"Any amount is too much," Val grumbled.

"Is it permanent?" Austin asked. He kind of wanted to know if he'd go all berserker every time they were attacked.

"I don't know," Ivy said. "I'll guess we'll see."

Unfortunately, they were no closer to finding Alejandro than they had been before, and Austin was beginning to worry that they never would.

Chapter Sixteen

Val

THE REST OF THE evening was a bust. No one knew anything about the attackers except that they were fast, lethal, and had no apparent leader. None they were able to identify during the attack, anyway. Not even Austin, since he was the focus of their attack and had way too many vampires focused on taking him down.

Leaving the vampires to finish cleaning up the mess, I headed home with Ivy and Fang. It was almost dawn, anyway, and I was really hungry.

Ivy offered to fix breakfast, and I let her—cooking was not one of my skills, and I hadn't improved since Gwen left.

Just as we were finishing eating, my phone rang. I checked the caller ID. Mom. I groaned and considered not answering it but knew she'd just continue calling if I didn't. "It's my mom," I told Ivy. "She gets up at this time and knows I'm about to go to bed."

Ivy nodded in understanding. She made as if to leave the table, but I waved her back down. No secrets here.

After the initial "how-are-you's" came the real reason she'd called. "You are coming to dinner the day after tomorrow, aren't you?"

"Day after tomorrow?" I didn't remember discussing this with her before.

"It's Jennifer's birthday, or had you forgotten?"

Oh, crap. I did remember her birth date, just not that it was coming up so soon. "No, I didn't forget. I just didn't know you'd scheduled a party."

"Oh, the party is next weekend—a pampered spa thing with all her girlfriends. This is just a family dinner—Jennifer would love to see you. You can bring that nice Shade if you want."

No other full humans besides my family, I noticed. Guess they didn't want the ugly secret of their demon daughter getting out.

WOW, BITTER MUCH? Fang asked.

Well, they had kicked me out of the house and their business because I wasn't a good role model for my sister, but I wasn't bitter, not really. *Guess I'm just tired.* "Shade and I aren't dating anymore," I told her.

"Oh, that's too bad. He was such a nice boy."

I rolled my eyes. "But I do have someone staying with me from out of town—from the Underground in Sedona. Can I bring her with me?"

"Really? I love Sedona."

Mom hesitated, and I realized she was wondering what kind of demon Ivy was and whether she'd play havoc in Mom's nice, neat world. "Ivy is a gemstone whisperer," I said, to head off the awkward questions. "She talks to gemstones, and she doesn't know anyone else here, so I'd like to bring her along." Plus having any kind of buffer between Mom and me had to be a good thing.

"Of course she can come," Mom said, sounding relieved that Ivy wasn't going to pose a threat.

"What should I get Jen for her birthday?" I asked. I didn't know much about her interests over the past few months.

"Oh, nothing. Your presence is enough."

Yeah, right. Like that would go over well with Jen.

"So, we can expect you at seven?" Mom asked.

"Okay," I said on a sigh. "We'll be there." And just hope there wasn't going to be any serious slayage needed during that time.

I hung up and glanced at Ivy. "My parents are having a birthday dinner for my sister Jen the day after tomorrow. You're invited if you want to go."

She smiled. "Sure. It will be nice to get to know more families in the Underground."

"Well, they're not." At her puzzled look, I explained, "My parents were divorced when I was a baby, and my mother remarried. My father was the one with demon blood, so when Mom had my sister, it was with Rick, her new husband. They're all fully human."

"Oh," Ivy said, looking surprised. "And your father?"

"He died when I was five." I didn't go into the whole suicide bit—I didn't know her well enough to reveal that much. "So, they're all human. They're kind of okay with me being part succubus—Rick and Jen much more so than Mom—but I don't like shoving their faces in it, even though they are new agey and kind of accepting."

"I'm sorry for your loss," she said, her Goth makeup making her look extremely sad.

"It was a long time ago," I said dismissively. "But what I really need to know is, what the heck am I going to get my sister for her birthday?

She's turning seventeen this year. Any ideas?"

"What does she like?" Ivy asked.

I shrugged. "I'm not sure—I haven't seen her in a while. Her tastes change a lot."

"Then . . . a gift card?" Ivy suggested. "Depending on how much allowance or money she earns, she'd probably appreciate being able to buy what she wants."

Mom would think it too impersonal, but Jen would love it. Okay, then—a gift card it was. I grinned. "Good idea—thanks." Easy, too. "Guess I'll get some sleep. Do I need anything special to get this gunk off my face?"

"I have something that will help with that," Ivy said, inviting me back to her bathroom with a wave of her hand. "Come on."

Fang announced his intention to go to bed and trotted off in that direction.

Soon, Ivy and I were both back to our makeup-free faces. Since we were feeling all girlfriend-like, I asked, "So, I guess this was a bit more dangerous than what you expected. What are you going to report back to Sedona about us?"

"Oh, I already told them not to worry. You guys have it under control."

Not exactly, but I appreciated her confidence in us. "What happens in San Antonio, stays in San Antonio?"

"Something like that." She sighed. "I love Sedona, but my parents are geologists, and when I turned eighteen, they sold the rock shop there and left to roam the world in search of rare stones and adventure. That's what they used to do before they had me, and now they're having the time of their lives traveling all around everywhere."

Strange, she didn't sound unhappy about it. "My parents kicked me out when I was eighteen, too. You're okay with it?"

"Oh, they didn't kick me out. I know they love me, and they knew I could make it on my own since I've been working in their shop since I was a kid. But now, there's nothing holding me in Sedona, so I wanted to visit other cities—bigger cities, see where I might want to live for a while, use my savings to open up my own rock shop. I checked out Phoenix, Albuquerque, and Dallas before I came here. For the Sedona Underground and myself."

"Where to next?" I kind of envied her the self-confidence to strike out on her own.

She shrugged. "I don't know if there is a next. I kind of like it here."

I stared at her, flabbergasted. "Even after the vampire attacks and everything?"

She grinned. "Maybe because of them. It's kind of exciting, and you guys are making a difference here. I think I can help, and I'd like to be a part of that."

Wow—not at all what I'd expected. "Well, great," I said. "And since Gwen moved out, I do need a roomie, so you can stay here."

"I hoped you'd say that," she said with a smile.

She hugged me—a quick thing, but it made me feel good. *I think I'm gonna like having her here.*

ME, TOO, came Fang's sleepy voice in my head. BUT CAN WE GO TO SLEEP NOW?

Grinning, I headed for bed. A new boyfriend, a new girlfriend, and a new roomie. Life was looking up.

WE GOT UP LATE the next afternoon, and I'd had a brainstorm, so I called Austin. "I set up an appointment with Lieutenant Ramirez," I told him. "To see if the SCU has heard anything about where the rogues might be concentrating."

"Good idea. What time?"

"I asked for seven. Will that work for you?"

"Yes. We'll come by and pick you up, okay?"

"We?"

"Yeah, my men won't let me go anywhere alone again," he said, sounding testy but resigned. "They insist I need backup."

"Okay. See you then."

The three of us were ready and waiting when Austin drove up in a dark nondescript luxury car—one exactly like it following along behind him. He had the vamps riding beside him move over to the other car so we could all fit.

They seemed a little paranoid, but Austin reassured them, saying, "I have the Slayer, the gemstone whisperer, and a hellhound with me, plus you'll be right behind me. I'll be fine."

They reluctantly agreed, and we drove to the SCU station, though we made them stay outside. It wasn't as if the rogues would attack us inside the police station.

I asked the desk sergeant for Lieutenant Ramirez, and he told me to go on back. As we walked down the long hallway, Austin rested his hand at the small of my back.

It was an odd sensation, almost as if he was claiming me as his, or showing affection—I wasn't sure which. Either way, I didn't mind. In fact, I kind of liked it. It made me feel warm and cherished. I hadn't had much of that in my life, ever.

We met Dan on the way into the lieutenant's office. He glanced pointedly at Austin's hand on my back and frowned. Too bad. He'd dumped me, so he had no say in whom I chose to date anymore.

BESIDES, AUSTIN IS THE BETTER MAN, Fang declared.

I wasn't going to argue with that.

We entered the lieutenant's office together, and I introduced Ivy to everyone. I didn't explain that she was part demon—that was her secret to tell, if she wished. But I could tell the lieutenant and Dan both wondered what kind of demon she was—they had to know she was one, or we wouldn't have brought her in.

Lieutenant Ramirez shook Ivy's hand, then waved us all to seats. "I asked Sullivan to join us since he's familiar with the background. So, what can we do for you?"

Austin explained about Alejandro's disappearance and what we'd discovered so far. He concluded by saying, "We were wondering if you've heard of Mike and Ike, have any more info on them, or if you're aware of this 'training camp' they have."

Dan shook his head. "I haven't heard of them or a camp. Do you know where it is?"

IF WE KNEW, WE'D HAVE TOLD HIM, Fang said, sounding exasperated.

I shook my head, and Ramirez said, "I don't know either."

"What about patterns?" I asked. "The rogues are gearing up to take over the city—have you seen an increase in murders or attacks?"

"Yes," Ramirez conceded. "But we didn't realize it was a concerted effort."

"Why didn't you tell us about this before now?" Dan demanded.

"Because we just learned it ourselves last night," I said, trying to be patient with him. "Have you noticed the attacks concentrated in any one part of the city?"

"I'll have to check through my notes," Dan said.

Ramirez nodded. "We haven't noticed a pattern, but we weren't looking for one."

"Could you provide us with the data?" Austin asked. "That way we can see if there appears to be any pattern we can discern."

Dan looked really reluctant.

I THINK HE DOESN'T WANT TO GIVE IT UP TO THE BLOODSUCKERS, Fang said.

Probably. He still wasn't convinced there was such a thing as a good vampire, except maybe for his sister Gwen who'd been turned into one against her will.

"Maybe you could provide the info to Micah?" I suggested, not wanting to see them get into a pissing contest. "He can combine it with the Underground's data and see if we can find a concentration of any attacks in any one area." Micah had watchers all over the city, collecting data and keeping an eye on the vamps. He was skilled at analysis, too.

"Yes," Ramirez said, staring sternly at Dan. "We can do that."

"And we'll continue to question any rogues we capture," Austin said.

"I just remembered something," Ivy said. She glanced at me as if for permission to speak, and when I nodded, she added, "Alexander—the vamp recruiter—said something about Mike and Ike being in a different cell. What do you know about that?"

That's right—he had. I'd forgotten that.

Ramirez scowled. "It's a type of organization, used by people like terrorists and insurgents. Usually, you only know the people who are in your cell, so that if you're captured, you can only reveal the identities of a few people. They'd know their higher-ups but wouldn't necessarily be aware of other personnel on their same level." I didn't think Ivy needed the explanation, but she let it slide. Ramirez added thoughtfully, "I didn't realize they were that organized."

Crap. That just made this all the harder.

Austin nodded. "And for those who do know more information, the rogues now have a strategy in effect to ensure they don't reveal important information—a false tooth with demon blood inside it."

Dan nodded. "Demon blood sends them batcrap crazy."

"Yeah," I said. "Essentially, suicide by demon blood. It will also make them unpredictable and harder to kill." I glanced at Ramirez. "You might want to warn the rest of the scuzzies. Don't ask the rogues questions unless you want them to go berserk."

"Yes," Austin added. "Now that we know the tooth is there, we can remove it before they can use it. If you capture any, call us."

Ramirez nodded grimly. "I will." He glanced at Austin. "Who's in charge while Alejandro is . . . missing?"

"No one," Austin said, his tone curt.

Ramirez raised an eyebrow. "I meant, who do I contact if we learn something?"

"All three lieutenants—Rosa, Luis, and Austin—are doing the jobs they normally do," I explained, to head off unnecessary explanations. "But for the purposes of this investigation, you can contact Austin."

Austin nodded, willing to accept that hierarchy. He stood and offered his hand to Ramirez. "Thank you. With your assistance, I hope we can not only find Alejandro, but shut down the rogues' operation for good."

As we headed for the exit, I said, "I'm sorry. I thought they could help."

"They still might," he conceded. "But I just wish we could catch a break."

Me, too. We were due for one—and soon.

Chapter Seventeen

Val

ONE MORE DAY had passed without getting any closer to finding Alejandro and Vincent. Frustrating. After I bought some gift cards at the mall, Ivy, Fang, and I headed to Club Gothick to stake it out before night fell. Austin had let us borrow a vampmobile so we wouldn't look so conspicuous, and we hung out for hours waiting for the candy twins to show up.

No luck in that arena so far, but I had learned a lot more about Ivy—and I liked what I learned. She was about a year older than I was but had a lot more self-confidence than I'd ever had. I envied her that, and she envied my strength and speed. We both liked each other's sense of humor. Fang fit right in, too.

YOU TWO ARE LIKE A REGULAR LOVE FEST, Fang snarked. DON'T TELL ANY GUYS, OR THEY'LL WANT TO WATCH YOU MAKE OUT OR SOMETHING.

"Really?" I shook my head. "Guys are so strange sometimes. You'd think they'd want to be in the middle of all the making out." At least, that was true from Lola's experience.

TRUST ME, Fang said. I WATCH TELEVISION.

Ivy shrugged. "I don't understand it either, but he's right." She glanced at me. "Not that I want to try it. I mean, I like you and all, but I'm totally into guys."

I laughed. "Me, too."

"Speaking of guys," Ivy said. "There's yours now." She nodded to a spot behind me, and I saw that Austin had arrived, along with a retinue of his followers, in a couple of vampmobiles.

I rolled down the window, and Austin sauntered over to our car. He leaned down into the driver's side window and gave me a smile as if I were the only person in the world. "Hello, darlin'."

And didn't that make my heart go pitty-pat? "Hi," I replied with a goofy smile.

YOU'VE GOT IT BAD, Fang said.

Oh, shut up. Do I have to remind you of how you were around Princess?

THAT WAS SURVIVAL OF THE SPECIES—YOU AIN'T GONNA PROCREATE WITH HIM.

I hadn't planned on "procreating" with anyone. And as for his excuse for dallying with Princess. . . . *Liar, liar, pants on fire.*

Fang turned his head away from me and didn't respond. Ha. Got him that time.

"I take it you haven't seen Mike or Ike?" Austin asked.

"Nope," Ivy responded. "No sign of them."

Austin nodded. "Lieutenant Ramirez called. Suggested we check out the area near New Braunfels."

"Really?" I asked in disbelief. Turning to Ivy, I explained, "It's a small town about forty minutes north of here—settled by Germans in the eighteen hundreds. Great food and a cool historical district. It always seemed so safe to me."

"It is," Austin confirmed. "But they've called in the SCU several times lately on some problems that sound like our guys. That's why it seems so unusual. Shall we check it out?"

"Sure."

"Okay, hold on a minute." He conferred with people in the two vampmobiles and came back to me. "Okay, I've given them a description of Mike and Ike. One vehicle will stay here to watch for them, and the other will follow us to New Braunfels. I'll drive."

I opened my mouth to protest, then realized not only was it his car, but he knew where we were going, and I didn't. I shrugged and got out of the car to move to the passenger seat while Fang got in the back. Ivy decided to pass, and since she'd left her bumblebee a couple of blocks over, we dropped her off so she could avoid the possible coming confrontation.

The drive didn't seem to take very long, but, just before we got there, Austin pulled over into a rest area with a gas station and parked.

"Potty break?" I asked, though I would have thought I'd have more need of that than he did.

"No," he said, "we're being followed."

"Followed?" I repeated and glanced over to stare at the entrance to the rest area where three other cars pulled in and parked, the windows tinted dark as the law would allow. That was a little suspicious this time of night when many people weren't around. "What do they want?"

"I don't know," Austin said. "Let's find out."

The other vampmobile pulled up beside us, and Austin rolled down his window. The others did the same. "How long have those cars been following us?" he asked.

"Since we left San Antonio," the vamp in the other car replied. "You want we should take 'em out?"

"No, let's wait and see what they do."

NOT DEMONS, Fang said. OR I'D BE ABLE TO READ THEM.

I passed on what he said, then added, "I'll get out, pretend we stopped here so I can use the facilities, and see what they do."

I COULD STAND TO TAKE A LEAK, Fang said.

I headed for the restrooms, and Austin got out of the car as if to guard me and stood gazing around at the beautiful, tree-lined area. And, incidentally, trying to get a look at what was going on with those three cars who'd followed us. All were identical, bland midsize sedans. Nothing that would stand out in any traffic.

Let us know if anything happens, I told Fang as I entered the restroom and left him watering the bushes outside.

WILL DO.

Since I was here, I went ahead and used the facilities. As I washed my hands, I asked Fang, *What's going on out there? Do we need to delay more?*

I DON'T THINK SO. NOTHING'S HAPPENING.

I opened the door and strolled outside. Austin stood there as if casually waiting for me, but I could sense the tension in every line of his body. "Let me have your keys," I said softly.

He gave them to me, and I went over to open the trunk of his car. I had stakes in my waistband like always but figured a crossbow might come in handy right about now, and I'd stashed a couple of them in the trunk before I left.

I pulled one out, along with a quiver of bolts, and walked toward the three cars parked at the other end of the lot. There was one other vehicle in the rest area, but when the humans saw my weapon, they got the hell out of there, fast.

"What are you going to do with that?" Austin asked.

"Whatever needs to be done."

"Val?" Austin asked, a hint of warning in his tone, but didn't try to stop me. He and Fang followed me and so did Austin's five followers in the next car.

Still no reaction from the three cars? Interesting.

When I got close enough to the nearest car, I took aim and shot bolts into two of the tires. There. They weren't going anywhere anytime soon.

I started to move around to do the same to the other two cars, but vamps came boiling out of the first car.

"Luis," Austin gritted out.

"What the hell did you do that for?" Luis demanded, glaring at me.

"Why are you following us?" Austin countered, stopping a few feet away from Luis.

Casually, I shot bolts into both front tires of the next car. Everyone emptied out of the remaining two vehicles then, and they all charged menacingly toward me. Pissed now, I shoved Lola at them and yelled, "Stop."

Everyone stopped except for the one woman in the group. I jerked up the crossbow and sighted it at her heart. "You, too, or I'll kill you now."

She halted, fuming.

"Enough, Catalina," Austin said. "We just want to know why you're following us."

Her lips thinned, but she jerked her chin up and refused to answer.

"Could you release Luis, please?" Austin asked me.

I frowned but did as he asked. If it were up to me, I'd force him to tell us what we wanted to know.

NAW, Fang said. AUSTIN'S RIGHT. YOU DON'T HUMILIATE YOUR PEERS . . . UNLESS YOU *WANT* TO TURN THEM INTO ENEMIES.

Well, that made sense. Sorta. I carefully released Luis while keeping the others enthralled and kept an eye on Catalina.

"Call her off," I told Luis.

Luis glared at me, unnecessarily straightened his jacket, and brushed invisible lint off his sleeves . . . as if I'd contaminated him or something. But he jerked his head toward Catalina, and she backed off, sending killing looks my way. I lowered the crossbow but kept it cocked . . . just in case.

"Why are you following us?" Austin asked Luis.

"When you left town, I knew you were up to something. You have Alejandro hidden out here somewhere, don't you?"

Sheesh—that again. The guy was like a broken record.

I THINK HIS BRAIN OSSIFIED SOMETIME IN THE LAST CENTURY, Fang drawled. HARD TO GET NEW THOUGHTS THROUGH ALL THAT ROCK.

Had to agree with him there.

"No," Austin said curtly. "We're following up on leads from the SCU—we believe the rogues might have a training camp out this way."

"Likely story," Luis said with a sneer.

"Very likely," I put in. "Because it's the truth."

"And that's why you need so much backup?" Luis countered.

"No, he needs it for the same reason you do—because the rogues attacked him last night, too. Only this time, they came in more force and did a lot more damage."

Luis shot a look at Austin, as if wondering if I were telling the truth.

"She's right," Austin said. "Just ask your flunky Christoph. He was there spying on us."

A flash of annoyance crossed Luis's face. Guess he didn't realize his spy had been discovered. I wondered which one had been Christoph and why Austin hadn't pointed him out to me.

PROBABLY WANTED THE GUY TO THINK HE HADN'T BEEN MADE, Fang suggested.

Luis snapped his fingers at Catalina. "Contact Christoph," he ordered, obviously more comfortable commanding the peasants than actually using something manufactured in this century.

She jumped to do his bidding, and her fingers flew over the screen on her phone. Texting, I guess. In a very short time, she said, "He confirms—rogues attacked Austin last night, too."

Luis glanced suspiciously at Austin. "How do I know you're not in league with the rogues? That you didn't stage the attack?"

"Don't be ridiculous," Austin spat out. "Do you really think I'd risk my people to stage an assault? I have way too many dead or injured."

Catalina texted again, then nodded at Luis. "Confirmed."

Luis scowled. "Then why didn't you contact me to help?"

I choked out a laugh. "Because you've been sooo helpful before?"

Austin shook his head at me, silently asking me to keep my mouth shut. Okay, I could take a hint.

"I wasn't sure how you'd react," Austin said.

"So, instead, you went off like a glory hound to rescue Alejandro on your own?"

Austin's jaw tightened, but he somehow managed to keep his tone level. "No, I'm following up on a lead that may or may not pan out. And you made it very clear that you don't want to work with me."

"No, I don't want to work *for* you," Luis said with a sneer. "But that's what you want, isn't it? Rescue Alejandro on your own, show yourself as his savior, and take over?"

"No, that's your agenda," Austin shot back. "You do your job, let me do mine, and we'll be fine."

Luis shook his head. "That won't work for long, and you know it. You won't yield to me, and I sure as hell won't yield to you. And our followers will fight amongst themselves unless the issue is decided. So, let's deal with this once and for all," Luis said, shoving his pointy goatee in Austin's face. "Duel with me—let's settle the issue of who's in charge."

"As I've told you before, *Alejandro* is in charge," Austin said. "And I'm not willing to give up on finding him so soon. Are you?"

"And what if we don't find him?" Luis asked insistently. "What then? We can't leave the Movement leaderless."

"What about Rosa?" Austin asked. "She's a lieutenant, too."

I wondered if anyone would remember that, and I was absolutely fascinated to hear Luis's response.

I CAN TELL YOU THAT, Fang drawled.

No need—Luis laid it out for us. "She's no leader—nothing but a housekeeper and a bed-warmer," he mocked. "She's smart enough to know that, and she doesn't want the job."

Chauvinist much?

"If we don't find Alejandro soon, I will consider 'settling' the matter," Austin said, his voice tight.

"When?" Luis demanded. "He's been missing for days now. When do you think it's 'appropriate' to ensure the Movement has a united leadership?"

Austin looked cornered—and pissed. "A couple more days at least."

"All right," Luis said. "If we don't find him in two days' time, we will meet in combat to decide leadership as set out in our ancient rules. But if you don't meet me on the field of honor then or, failing that, cede leadership to me, I will *take* it—and damn the consequences."

Total silence reigned as we all tried to absorb the impact of what that would mean for the Movement.

NOTHING GOOD.

That was for sure.

Austin broke the silence, giving Luis a hard stare. "I will agree to meet you only if you agree to work with me instead of against me until then."

Oh, crap. I couldn't believe Austin had just agreed to fight Luis for leadership of the Movement.

HE HAS NO CHOICE, Fang said.

Unfortunately, Fang was right. I worried my lip between my teeth. What did a duel involve? Pistols at high noon? Fangs at midnight? And how did they decide who won? Was the fight to the death? *Mano a mano?* Or a skirmish between the two factions?

Even more important, who would win in such a battle? I'd bet on Austin but didn't underestimate Luis's cunning and sneakiness.

Gulping, I realized we had to find Alejandro right away, before Austin and Luis took each other on.

Chapter Eighteen

Val

"WHY SHOULD I work with you?" Luis asked Austin.

"We both have the same goal—to find Alejandro, right?" Austin said that as if he wasn't sure Luis did, and I was beginning to wonder about that myself.

I was getting really tired of Luis's sneers, but he seemed to have an unending supply of them. "How are we to help you?" he demanded. "We have two vehicles out of commission."

"It's not like I blew them up," I reminded him. "Have you ever heard of spare tires? Between the three of those cars, I bet you'll have enough to fix one of them at least."

Luis scowled but snapped his fingers at one of his flunkies to get it done. "Call the auto club," he snapped at another.

"Benjamin," Austin said to a tall, skinny vamp in the other car, "could you bring the map, please?"

The difference between the two men was clear in just the way they treated their subordinates. The clash between Luis and Austin was more than just a struggle between the old guard and modern ways—it was a fight to shape the very values and principles of the organization for the future. Would Luis's entitled might-is-right dictator attitude prevail . . . or would it be Austin and Alejandro's more *laissez-faire*, inclusive approach?

WELL, LOOK AT YOU, MISS SMARTY-PANTS, Fang marveled.

Annoyed, I ignored him and concentrated on what Austin was doing.

Instead of a paper map, Benjamin brought up a map of the area on his tablet. Using Google Earth, he zoomed in to the area surrounding the farm where the local police had reported some problems. "One main house and two smaller outbuildings," Benjamin said. "Not too big."

Austin nodded and told Luis, "From one of the rogue recruiters, we've learned they're structured in cells." He explained the hollow tooth problem. "So, our first thought was that there probably aren't too many people there."

"Except the rogues called it a training camp," I reminded him.

Austin nodded. "They may have new recruits as well—no idea how many."

"We need to do some reconnaissance first," Luis said.

They agreed on a general strategy while some of Luis's guys replaced the tires I'd shot on one of the cars. Another stayed with the remaining car, which wasn't going anywhere, to wait for the auto service to show up. That left the other three stranded vamps to squeeze into the back seat of the other three vehicles. For some reason, they didn't want to share with Austin and me. Not that I was complaining.

Once we were about a quarter mile from the farm, we all pulled over to the side of the road where we could hide the cars in the dark trees. We'd go on foot from here, so as not to advertise our presence. But first, Austin and Luis sent out scouts to check out the area.

"Is it really possible to sneak up on a vampire?" I asked as I got out of the car.

Austin shrugged. "Yes. In a crowded city, people and noise are always around. We tend to tune them out most of the time, or we'd be constantly paranoid."

"And out here in the country? Will they be more alert?"

He shrugged again. "Depends on how many people they have coming and going—how many strangers. As a training camp, it probably has a good-sized turnover of unknowns, but since they operate in cells, there shouldn't be too many there at one time. We may not alert them right away." He glanced aside at me. "Besides, we have a secret weapon."

"What's that?"

He grinned. "You. We figure most of the rogues will be men—they don't seem to have a whole lot of female initiates that we've seen."

HA! CHAUVINISM WILL GET THEM EVERY TIME.

"So, if you don't mind using Lola to hold them in check so we can question them, we'll avoid a lot of bloodshed."

"Okay." I used to slay vampires to keep the lust and Lola in check, but I didn't need to do that anymore. So, I was happy to help in a way that would avoid bloodshed, especially for my allies.

One of Luis's men slipped in next to Austin and Luis. "No patrols—they must be confident no one can find them."

"How many?" Luis asked.

"Maybe twenty," the scout said. "Not sure. They all seem to be in the main house."

EIGHTEEN AGAINST TWENTY, Fang said. NOT BAD ODDS WHEN YOU CONSIDER YOU AND I COULD TAKE 'EM ALL ON.

That might be Fang's idea of fun, but it wasn't mine.

"Can you confirm that they're all in the main house before we go in?" Austin asked me.

I'd never thought about using Lola to do that. Then again, all I had to do was deploy Lola like a man-seeking missile, and she could find every single one.

"I should be able to," I told him.

Luis nodded, and we snuck up on the three buildings. Only the main one had any lights on, and the other two were dark. Lola verified there were no men in the smaller ones.

I let Lola out slowly, sending her lust-seeking tendrils through the main house. "Sixteen men," I whispered, knowing Austin and Luis would be able to hear me. The ones inside were partying too hard to hear anything anyway—whooping it up and having a good old time.

"Disgraceful," I heard Luis mutter. "No dignity."

Like there was anything dignified about sucking blood. "What do you want me to do?" I whispered.

"Can you hold them all?" Austin asked.

Fang snorted. OF COURSE SHE CAN.

"Sure."

Lola had just been gently testing their chakras, but at Austin's request, I thrust her into all of them so fast I felt most of them bow with the movement. "Got 'em."

A chorus of exclamations and "What was that?" followed.

"I thought you had them," Luis said in disapproval.

"I do, but I can't tell them what to do if they can't hear me." Idiot.

Austin nodded and strode toward the front door, me right behind him. Luis and the others followed more slowly, as if they didn't quite trust the demon in their midst—me.

Austin burst through the door and yanked on the cord attached to the stereo system. Good—relative silence. Before they could all pile on top of my boyfriend, I yelled, "Stop!"

THIS IS A RAID! Fang yelled, and I almost grinned. But since no one else here could hear him, I stifled it.

All the rogues obediently froze, and I stared around in disbelief. What the hell were they doing? Shirtless, with most of their chests covered in blood, they'd been jumping around like savages in front of the roaring fireplace as if they were rehearsing for *Lord of the Flies*. Bottles of booze and munchies lay everywhere. What the heck? They didn't eat human food.

NO, Fang said grimly, BUT THEY DO EAT HUMANS.

Oh, crap. "What's going on?" I whispered to Austin.

He didn't answer me—he just looked grim, his face as tough as granite and royal rage blooming in his eyes as he glanced around the room, apparently counting statuelike vamps. "Twelve. Where are the other four?"

"In other rooms," I said.

Luis sent his guys to find them, and Austin gave the others a quick hand signal. Suddenly, my view was blocked by three hulking bloodsuckers.

Annoyance filled me.

HE'S TRYING TO PROTECT YOU, Fang explained.

I don't need protection—Lola has a good hold on the rogues. I tried to push one guy aside, but he wouldn't move. Well, I knew how to *make* him move.

HE'S NOT TRYING TO PROTECT YOU FROM THE ROGUES. THEY KNOW YOU CAN HANDLE THAT. THEY'RE TRYING TO PROTECT YOU FROM WHAT YOU'LL *SEE*, Fang said, sounding as if he agreed with Austin. HELL, I'M NOT SURE I WANT TO SEE IT, EITHER. NOT IF WHAT I SMELL IS ANY INDICATION.

I stopped, appreciating Austin's consideration. But I was also a tad horrified, wondering if my imagination was conjuring up something worse than reality.

I'LL CHECK IT OUT.

Austin's voice came from the other side of the vamp wall in front of me. "Val, they're all here now." As if Lola didn't know. "Could you please ask them all to open their mouths?"

"Open your mouths and leave them open," I ordered.

"Thank you," Austin said.

I heard some shuffling around, then Luis said, "Only three have the false tooth. We removed them."

"They must be the leaders," Austin said. "The rest are probably trainees."

Benjamin came up behind me. "Hey, boss. We checked out the other two buildings—look like fight rings."

Was it possible the blood on their bodies came from each other?

NOT ALL OF IT, Fang said grimly from the other room.

Crap. I didn't feel any more men in the house. Were there other men here . . . dead? Or women, dead or alive? Lola wouldn't be able to feel them.

Fang trotted back to stand beside me. TRUST ME, BABE, YOU DON'T WANT TO KNOW WHAT'S BEEN GOING ON IN THOSE OTHER ROOMS.

"Thank you," Austin told Benjamin. "Val, if you could ask the three trainers to step outside?"

It took a moment to sort them out, but I did, and ordered them, "Answer any questions they ask you."

Austin led them and me outside onto the porch where the air felt a whole lot fresher and cleaner. Only Luis and Fang followed us, and Austin closed the door, probably to block my view of the scene inside. What the heck had happened in there?

"Who's in charge here?" Luis demanded of the three.

Their jaws moved back and forth laterally, but nothing happened. Good thing Austin had thought to remove the false teeth.

"Answer him," I ordered, reinforcing it with a surge of Lola's special brand of compulsion.

In unison, they said, "Zachary."

"Which one of you is Zachary?" Luis asked, jabbing his finger into the tallest one's chest.

"None of us."

"Is he inside?"

"No, he's not here."

"Where is he now?" Luis asked. "When will he be back?"

"I don't know."

"Where is Alejandro?" Austin asked.

"I don't know."

Broken record much? "What *do* you know about Alejandro and Vincent's whereabouts?" I asked, trying to get beyond three word answers.

"Mike and Ike were supposed to kill Alejandro. They said they didn't—he and the other guy disappeared."

"Disappeared where?" Luis asked.

DUH. IF THEY DISAPPEARED, HOW WOULD DUMB AND DUMBER HERE KNOW WHERE?

"I don't know."

"Where are Mike and Ike?" Austin asked. A much better question.

"Not here."

Obviously. "Do you know where they are now?" I asked.

"No."

"Where do they usually hang out?" I asked before Luis could twist one of their heads off in pure frustration.

"Club Gothick, and they often troll the parks, especially HemisFair Park."

"Is that where they're most likely to be?" I asked.

"No, they—"

But I didn't hear his answer as I felt one of Lola's strands abruptly recoil and snap back into me. A second and a third followed, almost giving me whiplash. I gasped. What the heck?

THEY'RE KILLING THEM, Fang told me. INSIDE THE HOUSE, LUIS'S PEOPLE ARE KILLING THE TRAINEES.

"What's wrong?" Austin asked.

"Stop," I said, gasping. "Tell them to stop killing."

"Why?" Luis demanded, a hard edge in his voice.

"Because they're hurting me each time they kill someone in my thrall," I bit out. "I'll lose control." Besides, it wasn't exactly sporting to kill a helpless victim.

Austin opened the door and yelled, "Stop. Cease what you're doing until we tell you otherwise." He turned back to me. "Are you okay now?"

I nodded shakily. It felt like three gaping holes in my psyche, but I'd live. The remaining thirteen lifelines were still intact.

"What'd they say about where the candy twins are mostly like to be?" I asked.

"They heard we've been asking around about them, so they've gone into hiding—somewhere Mike and Ike think we'll never look."

"We have what we need," Luis said. "Let's kill the rest and go."

"Kill the rest?" I repeated. "How do you know they're all bad?"

"We know," Austin said curtly.

TRUST ME, THEY DO, Fang agreed.

How? When he remained silent, I said, *Tell me. Or I'll go look myself.*

I . . . DAMN IT, VAL, Fang said, sounding as though he wanted to cry. DON'T GO. THEY VIOLATED THREE GIRLS . . . BEFORE AND AFTER THEY KILLED THEM. AND EVEN IF SOME OF THEM DIDN'T DO IT, THEY DIDN'T STOP IT EITHER.

Fang's distress was so great that he inadvertently shared his memory with me. I got a flash of blood-soaked sheets, sightless staring eyes, and mutilated bodies.

Quickly, he cut off the connection, but not before I got a very good glimpse of what had been done to those poor girls. I turned away, trying not to be sick.

Damn it, I'd forgotten this wasn't just a war between the good and bad vamps, between good and bad demons. I'd forgotten innocent humans were still in danger from the monsters. I'd forgotten just how damned important my job was. No one should have to suffer that kind of torture. No family should have to experience that kind of loss.

This had to stop. Now. I nodded curtly at Austin. "Do it."

"On my signal, please, Val," Austin said. He and Luis shoved the three men back into the house. "Heads up, boys," he called inside. Glancing at me, he said, "Let them go, please," then shut the door again, remaining outside with us and Luis.

DO IT, VAL.

I pulled a stake out of my back waistband, just in case, then pulled Lola free. There were a couple of moments of unholy noise inside, then it suddenly ceased. Our side had a head start, especially over the newly-turned vamps, so I had no doubt we'd won. The whole thing made me sick, but at least the monsters wouldn't be harming any more young girls.

Austin turned to Luis. "You'll take care of the gir—The bedrooms?"

Luis nodded briefly. "It will be my honor to see that they are cared for. Leave the rest of it alone—a lesson for Zachary and any who would try to harm people under our protection."

"Agreed," Austin said.

Well, I kind of liked Luis for saying that. "Is there anyone . . ." I started to say, then wondered if I really wanted to know the answer to that question.

"No one left alive," Austin said with a grim look.

I sighed. I was afraid of that.

"You can trust Luis to do what is right for the humans," Austin said.

I nodded, somewhat surprised, but glad to hear it. I'd been wondering how Austin and Luis could possibly be on the same side to work together in the Movement. In this, apparently, they were united.

"And I'll call Lieutenant Ramirez, let him know what happened so he can handle it," Austin said. He tossed me his keys. "Why don't you bring the car around? I'll make sure our guys are okay and that they clean themselves up."

He was obviously trying to get me away from the carnage. Well, I wanted to get away, too. I walked toward the car, Fang following.

This should feel like a victory. Instead, it made me feel heartsick and kind of scummy. Sixteen people had lost their lives in there tonight, and it was mostly because of me.

NINETEEN PEOPLE LOST THEIR LIVES, Fang corrected me. BUT TRUST ME, THOSE SIXTEEN VAMPS DESERVED EVERYTHING THEY GOT. AND YOU SAVED THE GOOD GUYS FROM GETTING HURT.

Maybe, but were there any good guys here? Really?

Chapter Nineteen

Val

A SEARCH OF IKE and Mike's favorite park hadn't yielded any results, so I went home disappointed. We'd thought they were individual rogues, maybe a gang of thugs. But their organization, training camp, and structure made it obvious they were a lot more organized than we'd expected. Which meant there was going to be a lot more violence and bloodshed before we were done.

That realization, combined with the earlier bloodbath, left me depressed, and I went to bed feeling out of sorts and annoyed with the world. When I woke up the next afternoon, I wasn't much better. Tonight, I had to go to Jen's birthday dinner, and I wasn't sure which one I'd rather do less—have dinner with Mom or set up vampires to be slaughtered en masse. Neither sounded fun.

Nevertheless, I'd promised, and Fang, Ivy, and I drove over to Mom and Rick's house in Ivy's little bumblebee.

"You said your family is fully human. How do they feel about other demons?" Ivy asked apprehensively.

I shrugged. "They love Shade and Micah. They don't seem to have a problem with anyone but me." I grimaced. "It was tough on Mom having a teenage daughter who's a succubus—she didn't know how to handle it." Still didn't, really. Rick was the one who'd helped me with that. "They think I'm a bad influence on my little sister."

Fang snorted. YOUR LITTLE SISTER DID STUPID ALL BY HERSELF.

Yeah, but Mom didn't see it that way.

"Because you hang out with vampires and demons?"

"Yeah, that, and because Jen thought she wanted to be like me for a while." I grimaced. "After she and Rick—my stepfather—were kidnapped and almost killed by rogue vampires, I think she got over that particular fixation."

Ivy looked sympathetic. "Yeah, I can see why your parents might have a bit of a problem with vampires."

It was strange knocking on the door to the house where I'd grown up, but I didn't feel welcome enough to barge right in. Mom opened the door, looking as wary as I felt. Would we be able to get through one evening without arguing?

GOOD LUCK WITH THAT, Fang said drily.

Well, I was tired of fighting, so I made a mental note to keep it light. "Hi, Mom," I said and reached out to give her a hug. It was a little awkward, but she was trying to be nice, too, so it was okay. "Something smells great." It really did—the aroma of garlic, onions, and tomato sauce scented the air, making my stomach rumble in anticipation.

"Jen," she called over her shoulder, "Val and Fang are here. Put your cat in the bedroom, please."

AH, THAT'S NO FUN, Fang protested halfheartedly.

After Jen took care of the cat, I introduced Ivy to Mom, Rick, and Jen. They looked a little taken aback at all her piercings and jewelry, but it didn't take long for Ivy to put them at ease. "Thank you so much for having me in your home," she said. "I don't know many people here, so it was so nice of you all to invite me."

Good manners was all it took to appeal to Rick, and we went into the living room and sat down to chat. Looking for something non-demonic to talk about, I said, "Here, Jen, I brought you something. Happy birthday."

She opened the birthday card and squealed in delight when she saw the gift cards I'd purchased. "These are my favorite stores. Thank you!"

Mom gave me a disappointed look, but I ignored her. Giving Jen what she wanted on her birthday was more important than pleasing Mom.

"This is so cool," Jen gushed. "Now I'll be able to get what I want." She cast a stricken look at Mom. "Not that I don't love the sweaters you gave me."

Mom grimaced. "You can return them tomorrow."

Jen grinned. "Thanks—and I really do love the new phone." She gave Rick a kiss on the forehead. I suppressed a smile. Guess I knew whose idea that was.

A ding sounded in the kitchen, and Mom said, "Dinner's ready." She glanced at Ivy. "Jen got to choose what she wanted to eat. I hope you like spaghetti and meatballs with garlic bread."

"Who doesn't?" Ivy said with a smile.

We sat down to dinner and chatted about little things—how the store was doing, how Jen was doing in school, and her new musical obsession—a group I'd never heard of.

WATCH OUT, Fang warned. YOU'RE NEXT.

I'm ahead of you. Mom didn't approve of me hunting vampires even though she knew it was necessary, so I didn't want to know what form her small talk would take. When Mom turned to me, I said, "Ivy is thinking of moving here permanently." There—give them someone else to focus on.

"Really?" Mom said to Ivy. "Val said you're from Sedona. I can't imagine why you'd want to leave."

Ivy shrugged and explained about her parents and the rock shop she'd sold there.

"Rock shop?" Jen repeated. "Is that why you have so many piercings?"

"Jen," Mom said in a censuring tone. "Don't be rude."

"No, it's okay," Ivy said. "I don't mind explaining." She glanced at me as if for permission, and I nodded.

"You see, I'm a gemstone whisperer," Ivy confided.

Sounded so much better than rock demon.

AND THAT'S WHY SHE USES IT, Fang said in amusement.

"If a gemstone is polished and cut, it retains some awareness—the bigger the gemstone, the more awareness it has."

"What do you do with that kind of ability?" Jen asked, looking fascinated.

"Well, since gemstones often take on the personalities of their owners, I can get a read on someone based on how their stone reacts, especially if they're in their owner's presence a lot. Plus, some have other properties, like healing, clarity, enhancing certain abilities, that kind of thing. Some stones are more powerful than others." She ran a finger along the piercings on her right ear. "That's why I wear so many of them. It's not a fashion choice—it's so I'll have the stone I need when I need it. Wearing them works better for me than carrying them jumbled in a purse or pocket."

"Really?" Mom asked, looking interested. "Can you look at a stone for me, tell me what you know?"

"Of course."

Mom went into the other room and came back carrying a turquoise nugget on a chain. "Someone gave this to me and told me it would help with meditation, but when I wear it . . ."

Ivy took it in her hands and nodded. "The person who owned it before is a bit of a negative Nelly—bitter and angry." She glanced apologetically at Mom. "That may not be the person who gave it to you, but the person who sold it."

"Both—the woman who gave it to me sells gemstones. And you nailed her personality perfectly. You can tell that from the stone?"

"Yes—gemstones attune to our energies, then absorb them and send them back out into the world."

"No wonder it didn't help with mediation," Mom said, frowning. "It jangles my nerves."

"Can you cleanse it for her?" I asked.

"Sure," Ivy said. "Many people who sell stones don't realize that a simple cleansing will release any negativity the stone has."

Mom and Rick exchanged one of those glances that couples do where they seem to read each other's minds. Mom nodded, and Rick said, "The person who gave that to her supplies the gemstones for our new age store. They haven't sold well at all, and we've been wondering why. Now we know. Is that cleansing something you can teach us?"

"Of course, no problem."

Another married couple glance, then they both smiled, and Mom said, "Are you serious about moving to San Antonio?"

"Yes—I like it here," Ivy said. "And Val has offered to let me be her roommate."

"Excellent," Rick said. "Are you looking for a place to set up shop?"

"I probably will. I kept some of the inventory."

"How about selling at our store?"

"What a great idea," Jen exclaimed.

Ivy looked taken aback, though I'd seen it coming. "You don't even know me," she protested.

"We've been thinking of expanding our inventory in that area," Rick said.

Mom nodded. "Metaphysical stones are very popular in jewelry-making these days."

"But why me?" Ivy protested.

"You just proved you understand gemstones and their properties far more than our current supplier," Rick pointed out. "Besides, Val trusts you. And we trust her assessment."

They did? News to me. Surprised and pleased, I asked, "You want her to be your supplier and cleanse your gemstones?" It wasn't the same as a store of her own, but it was a start.

"At the very least," Rick said. "You could label them with their properties, and we'd know they'd be clear of negative emotions. Or we could set aside a corner display case for you in the store where you could sell them yourself."

Ivy's eyes lit up. "That would be even better. I try to match people's personalities with the right stone so they'll be compatible, plus I design and repair jewelry."

"I'm sure our customers would love that," Mom said.

Ivy glanced at me, obviously wondering what I thought about it.

"Sounds like a great idea," I said. "If it will be big enough for you—the rock shop you had in Sedona was pretty big, wasn't it?"

"Yes, we had a lot of tourist traffic and did mail order. But I ran that with my parents, and it's too much work for one person. This would be perfect, and I assume I wouldn't have to be there all the time if I label the stones. Plus my parents are traveling the world collecting unique finds—they can help fill out the inventory."

Jen's eyes lit up. "You could teach me what you know, so I can sell them when you're not there. And I'd love to learn how to make jewelry."

I couldn't even be jealous that my little sister was looking at Ivy like she was her new hero. Making jewelry out of pretty rocks was better than trying to slay vampires.

YEAH, Fang said with a doggie grin. BUT HOW WILL YOUR MOM REACT WHEN YOUR BABY SISTER WANTS TO GET ALL THOSE PIERCINGS LIKE IVY?

That's their problem, I told him, suppressing a smile.

Mom smiled. "Not a bad idea. What do you say, Ivy? If you like the idea, you could come down to our shop tomorrow, take a look, and we can discuss consignment and sale options."

"Sure," Ivy said.

"Great," Mom said. "Val can show you where it is." Then, over birthday cake, she ambushed me. "How are you doing, Val? I'm so sorry you and Shade didn't work out. He was such a nice boy."

Crap. I thought I'd escaped the inquisition. But Mom had set the kindling and lit the bonfire before I even saw her coming.

SUCK IT UP AND FRY, Fang said.

I shrugged. "I'm okay." They wouldn't understand anything that had happened, and I didn't want to explain it to them. My new world was so far removed from this TV-perfect family that I didn't want it to spill over and spoil them any more than it already had.

"Are you seeing anyone else?" Rick asked.

I shoved a large bite of cake into my mouth so I could stall while I wondered what to say. They probably wouldn't understand why I was dating a vampire.

YA THINK?

After I swallowed, I lied, "Not really." I hoped Ivy wouldn't say anything. I should have thought to ask her not to mention Austin.

Luckily, her expression was very bland.

NAW, SHE'LL KEEP HER LIPS ZIPPED, Fang said. SHE UNDERSTANDS YOUR FAMILY MIGHT NOT BE COOL WITH YOU DATING A FANGBANGER.

I winced.

"Don't worry," Rick said, patting my hand. "You'll find someone someday. No need to be in a hurry."

I gave him a grateful smile and checked my watch before they could ask me anything else they really didn't want to hear the answers to. "Oh, is it that late? I'm sorry, but we need to go. We have a . . . thing."

WELL, THAT DOESN'T SOUND SUSPICIOUS AT ALL, Fang snarked.

"A meeting with Micah," Ivy lied smoothly. "An Underground thing. He's seeing us between sets at the club."

Why did the lie sound so much easier to believe coming from her?

YOU COULD LEARN FROM HER.

Yeah. We helped Mom clear the table, then I hugged everyone goodbye, wished Jen a happy birthday again, and we left.

Once we were in Ivy's car and heading away from there, she asked, "Are you okay? You seemed so quiet tonight. If you don't like the idea of me working with your parents, I'll just tell them I changed my mind."

"No, it's fine, really. I'm glad this can help you both out."

VAL'S TELLING THE TRUTH, Fang told Ivy. SHE HASN'T LEARNED TO LIE AS WELL AS YOU DO.

I thought Ivy would be offended by that, but Fang obviously knew her better than I did. "Only to help a friend," she said with a laugh. "It was obvious you were uncomfortable with your mom's questions and wanted to leave."

She cast me a curious glance, so I explained, "You've seen my life-style and theirs. Do you think the two are compatible in any way?"

"No, but they're your family."

"And that's why I want to keep them as far away from vampires and bloodshed as I can. They've already had enough anguish because of me." I wasn't sure Mom would ever forgive me. "Tonight, everything was going so well, I didn't want to spoil it." Shaking my head, I said, "I don't belong there anymore."

"It's more than that," Ivy said. "You've been quiet all day. Did something bad happen last night?"

YOU COULD SAY THAT, Fang said drily.

I shot him an annoyed glance. Now I couldn't even shrug it off and pretend everything was okay. "Kinda sorta."

"You want to elaborate?"

Not really, but I sighed and decided to explain before Fang gave his version of events. "It's just that there was more . . . bloodshed last night than I expected." Killing vamps one-on-one seemed fair, equitable, when I knew they were evil and deserved to die. But setting them up for slaughter didn't sit well with me, even when they clearly deserved it. It didn't seem sporting, somehow. It made me feel too much like a monster myself.

THEY DESERVED TO DIE, Fang said. EVEN AUSTIN AGREED.

"I know, but it was the way it was done that bothered me," I explained to Ivy. Her nonjudgmental silence gave the courage to add, "Sometimes . . . I feel like a monster myself. I mean, I know those guys deserved to die for what they did, but why did I have to be the executioner?"

"That's not what's really bothering you, is it?" Ivy asked softly.

"Partially." But she was right—there was more. A lot more. "Those girls . . . gods, that was horrible." The worst I'd ever seen, even if it was secondhand. "And when Austin asked me to hold those guys so they could slaughter them, I just *did* it, like it was perfectly normal. What kind of person does that?"

"It bothers you that he asked you to do it."

"Yeah, I guess. Though I understand why," I hurried to say. "I know no one means to treat me like their personal killing tool . . ." But Micah did it, too.

"But it turns out that way anyway, and it hurts."

Yeah, Ivy did understand.

Fang licked my hand and snuggled up against me. I DO, TOO.

I rubbed his scruffy ears. *Yeah, I know. Thanks.*

"He's not a bad person, you know," Ivy added. "And neither are you."

"I know. But what kind of existence is this for anyone?" Certainly not one I'd expected only six months ago. "Is it going to be this way the rest of my life? Wading in death, blood, and pain?" Would I get so used to it that it became normal? That I became like the monsters I slayed? I didn't think I could do it.

"They ask this of you because you can do what no one else can do nearly so well. You're special, Val. People need you, need your skills . . . your heart."

I looked at her in disbelief.

"No, really. Your family, Micah, Austin—they all love you and know you're the only one strong enough to take on the burdens you do. Your heart is big enough to take all this pain and death and sadness without turning dark yourself. Others don't understand that and may resent you for your specialness, but they all respect you."

"Really?" I wanted to believe her but wasn't sure I could.

SHE'S TELLING THE TRUTH, Fang assured me.

"Yes—you're giving everything you have to save your friends, people you don't know, and the whole city. They need you, Val. You're their hero."

She probably meant that to make me feel good, but instead, it made me feel inadequate, as if I were carrying everyone's hopes on my shoulders alone.

NOT ALONE, Fang reminded me with a nudge of his nose. I'LL HELP.

Thank heavens for that. I don't know what I'd do without you.

PROBABLY DIE A LONELY, HORRIBLE DEATH, Fang speculated privately.

He made me laugh, which was probably his intention.

"What's so funny?" Ivy asked.

"Oh, just Fang being Fang," I explained, then sighed.

I JUST WISH YOUR FAMILY WOULD TREAT YOU LIKE THE HERO YOU ARE, INSTEAD OF LIKE A CRIMINAL, Fang said, sounding testy, broadcasting to both of us again.

"Yeah, me, too."

SO WHY DO YOU KEEP RETURNING TO THE SCENE OF THE CRIME?

"Crime?" Ivy asked, looking confused.

THEIRS, Fang said. WHEN THEY KICKED HER OUT.

"They weren't so bad tonight." In fact, it had gone better than it had in months. Was it Ivy's influence? Then again, after what happened at the farmhouse, their actions didn't seem like all that much of a crime.

What Fang said suddenly registered. Wait. Was it possible that's what Mike and Ike had done? Returned to the scene of the crime?

Chapter Twenty

Austin

AUSTIN STROLLED through HemisFair Park, along with about twenty other members of the Movement, looking for any sight of the elusive candy twins, as Val called them, and warning humans it wasn't safe there this time of night. Most of the ones they warned weren't exactly innocents themselves, and though they might think they were badass, they wouldn't be able to defend themselves against the type of predators the rogues had turned into.

They'd rousted a few rogues, but not the ones they'd been looking for.

Austin felt his phone vibrate in his pocket and pulled it out. It wasn't a text message from one of the members of the Movement as he'd expected, but a call from Val.

"Hello, darlin'," he drawled and suppressed a grin. That particular greeting inevitably seemed to spark confusion in Val, and he loved seeing how a little affection turned the formidable Slayer into an adorable mass of conflicting hormones. It wasn't nearly as satisfying over the phone when he couldn't see the effect of his words, but he had an excellent imagination.

"Hi," Val said, shaking off his attempt at discombobulating her all too easily. He'd just have to find another way to keep her off balance—it was turning out to be quite fun.

"How'd the visit with your family go?" he asked, continuing to stroll while keeping a watchful eye out for any rogues.

"Fine," she said dismissively. "But something Fang said made me think. Did you leave anyone at the blood house in case Alejandro and Vincent came back?"

"No—we searched it thoroughly and found no sight of them. When they return, it's most likely to be at the main mansion."

"That's what I thought," Val said in satisfaction. "So why is Lola reading two men inside the blood house right now?"

Austin halted. "Two men? You're thinking vandals? Or more of Emmanuel's followers?"

"No. The rogues said Ike and Mike had gone to ground, someplace we'd never think of looking for them. What if they decided to return to the scene of the crime?"

It was just stupid enough to be possible. "You haven't gone in yet, have you?" he asked urgently.

"No, Ivy is with me, so we parked a few houses down from the blood house, and I sneaked up to check it out."

"Could I impose on you to wait until I get there before you go inside and tackle them on your own?" He knew she was perfectly capable of doing so, but this was one confrontation he wanted to be in on.

Val laughed. "Fang said you're learning—you didn't order me to wait for you."

He grinned. "I can be taught."

"Sure, I'll wait. That's why I called before doing anything. I figured you'd want to do the questioning."

"Thank you. I'll grab some backup and meet you there. Watch for my text."

She agreed, and Austin hung up. As he'd arranged before, he did a group text to all of his guys to meet in the parking lot and be prepared to withdraw. Luis's men could continue searching the park on their own, just in case the two trespassers weren't the candy twins. Austin debated with himself for a moment, then called Luis and left a voicemail, telling him they were following up on a hunch. If the technophobic Luis didn't get the message until too late, that was his problem.

Austin met his team in the parking lot and instructed the drivers of the other two cars to head to the mansion Val called the blood house.

Partway there, one of the drivers called to let him know they were being followed.

"By who?" Austin asked.

"Not sure, but I think it's Luis."

Austin pulled over into an empty parking lot just shy of the neighborhood and waited. Sure enough, Luis pulled up next to him.

Austin rolled down his window, and Luis did the same. "What's going on?" Luis asked suspiciously.

"Val said there are two men inside Emmanuel's former mansion. I'm going to check it out, see if it's the rogues we've been looking for."

"So why'd you stop here?" Luis asked, frowning.

To keep you from scaring them off, Austin thought to himself. But aloud, he said, "To coordinate a plan. We don't want to spook them, so let's park a few houses away, surround the place—quietly—and go in to find them."

Luis nodded curtly. "I'll take the front. You take the back, and we'll both station men on the sides in case they try to go out a window."

Luis just had to try to take control, didn't he? It wasn't worth it to argue, so Austin said, "Okay. I'll text you when my men are in place."

At Luis's annoyed look, Austin amended that. "I'll text Catalina." Did Luis even know how to text?

Luis nodded curtly and raised the window. Sighing, Austin set the car in gear again and called Val. "We're almost there. Luis is going in the front. Can you meet me at the back? We're going to make sure they can't escape."

Val hesitated. "I can do that all by myself, if you want."

"I know, but this is something we need to do—it'll make everyone feel better if they have a hand in finding Alejandro. I'd like to keep you in reserve, okay?"

"Okay," she said. "I'll meet you there." She paused, then added, "Hey, can you give me a ride home? Ivy wants to head home."

"Of course."

A short time later, Austin found Val and Fang waiting quietly in the backyard of the mansion. She pointed upstairs, to let him know where the two intruders were. He nodded, then unlocked the back door and texted Catalina to let Luis know everyone was in place.

Go, was her reply.

Hearing Luis's unsubtle entry into the house, Austin gave up all attempts at subterfuge. Bursting in through the door, he rushed through the kitchen and up the stairs, hearing Luis bark, "Fan out. Find them."

Luckily, he had his own homing system with him. "First door on the right at the top of the stairs," Val said, right on his heels.

But he didn't need to open the door, because they came out to meet him, snarling and fighting to get past. Ike and Mike, all right. Austin grabbed one of them and slammed him up against the wall. Jeremy, now almost healed from his injury, did the same with the other. He had a score to settle. With the help of the rest of his men, they subdued the twins as Luis came pounding up the stairs.

"Val?" Austin said.

That's all he needed to say, because she understood perfectly. "Freeze!" she yelled, and Fang growled for good measure.

Austin felt one of the twins stiffen against his hold, but he stopped fighting.

"I have them," Val said unnecessarily, probably for Luis's benefit.

"Check their mouths," Luis ordered.

Since Austin was already doing that, he decided not to respond, but nodded at Jeremy who had looked to him for permission.

Sure enough, the candy twin had the telltale blackness of the hollow teeth the rogues used. Austin yanked it out of the twin's mouth and ground it beneath his boot. Jeremy did the same.

"Are these the men you saw here the night Alejandro went missing?" Luis asked.

"Yes," Val said, then glared at the two men. "Answer Austin's questions," she ordered.

Luis gave her a scowl, but Austin was grateful that only one person would be interrogating them. Less confusing that way.

Austin allowed a bit of satisfaction to creep through him. Finally, they had the two men responsible for Alejandro's disappearance. Now he could put this ordeal to an end. "Which one are you?" he asked the guy he'd slammed up against the wall.

"Ike."

"Where's Alejandro, Ike?"

"I don't know."

What? Damn it, this could not *be happening.* "You have to know—you were there the night he went missing." He was so frustrated, he didn't know what to ask next.

Val came to his rescue. "You came here that night to assassinate Alejandro, didn't you?"

"Yes, those were our orders."

"Tell us what you know about that night in this place."

Ike spoke obediently. "We followed Alejandro and one of his men to this place and waited for them to go inside, then followed them in. We figured they'd be soft, easy to take, one-on-one."

"But there was a third man here, too," Austin said. "Guillaume."

"We didn't know he was here at first. He must have already been inside, waiting for them."

"What happened next?" Austin prompted.

"We followed them to that black room and heard them talking to Guillaume. We thought we might be able to take three of them since we had the element of surprise, so we rushed them. Guillaume was faster than we thought, and he had Mike pinned up against the altar in no time, so I went to my brother's rescue."

"Where was Alejandro at this time?" Luis barked.

Ike didn't reply, so Austin said, "Answer that question, Ike."

"Against the far wall. He couldn't get out the door because we were blocking the way. His man was trying to convince him to go out the window, trying to get him to safety," Ike said with barely concealed contempt.

Apparently, he had no respect for a leader who wouldn't fight his own fights, but Vincent had done the right thing—especially since it was obvious that Alejandro was their target. "What happened next?"

"I had to save my brother, so I grabbed a knife from the altar and stabbed Guillaume. When I turned around to get Alejandro next, he disappeared."

"Out the window?"

"No. One moment they were standing against the wall, the next, *poof*, they were gone. Vanished."

"That isn't possible," Luis snarled.

Austin had to agree. He glanced at Val. Were they still under her control?

"He's telling the truth," she said, frowning. "At least, as he sees it. Tell us the rest, and don't leave anything out."

"We searched behind the curtains and everywhere in the room and outside the window, but there was no sign of them. After a while, we felt some kind of shock wave, and all the lights went out. Thinking maybe they'd teleported using some kind of spell or something, we ran to check the rest of the house. When we heard your voices in the foyer, we thought it was them. That's when we ran into you guys. We pretended we worked for Luis and got the hell out of Dodge."

Val glared at Ike. "Did you hear or see anything else? Anything unusual, outside the norm?"

"I didn't, but Mike did. He was facing them before they vanished."

"What did you see?" Austin asked the other brother impatiently.

"A purple cloud, shot through with lightning. It, like, swallowed them."

Similar to the shadow demon's portal. Austin gave Val a sharp glance. Did Shade have more to do with this than they realized?

Hastily, Val said, "I think I know that spell." She shot him an imploring glance, as if asking him not to reveal Shade's potential part in this. For emphasis, Fang poked his leg and glared up at him.

Austin hesitated, then realized she was probably wise. If Luis thought Shade had something to do with it, he'd take the shadow demon apart. Austin nodded reassuringly at her. He wouldn't rat on Shade to Luis, but he wasn't letting the shadow demon off the hook, either.

"What does the spell do?" Luis asked.

Val frowned at him. "I don't want to say anything until I know for sure. Let me do some research in the encyclopedia and see what I can find out."

"Do it now," Luis said.

"I will, but it's at my house, and my ride left. I'll need Austin to take me there. It might take some time to find it," she said warningly, obviously trying to buy some time.

Knowing Luis had no patience for research and biding his time, Austin wasn't surprised when the Spaniard growled, "Let me know as soon as you find out anything." The man had major control issues.

Austin nodded in acknowledgment but refrained from promising anything. "Shall we go, Val?"

"Yeah. The sooner we figure this out, the sooner we can get on with our lives."

"Just one moment," Luis said, raising his chin as if he were the King of Spain. "Don't forget your promise to duel for the right to lead the Movement. We aren't much closer to finding Alejandro. Your time is up tomorrow night."

Damn it, he'd tried to forget about that. "If I'm not busy trying to find Alejandro," he snapped.

"Are you trying to back out on me?" Luis's tone implied Austin was a coward.

"No, I'm trying to find Alejandro. Tonight, I want to see what I can learn about this spell." Questioning Shade shouldn't take that long. "If we can't find him tonight, I will meet you on the dueling grounds tomorrow night at midnight."

The men around them shifted in response—eager or uneasy, Austin wasn't sure.

"I'll hold you to your word," Luis said sternly. "I'll set up the arrangements—"

"No," Austin said. He didn't trust Luis not to set a trap or lay things out to his advantage. "Rosa will make the arrangements." He could count on her to be impartially pissed at both of them.

Luis nodded curtly then glanced at Val. "Release them, Slayer, and we'll take care of them."

She hesitated for a moment then nodded. "As soon as I'm out the door."

They left, and just as they closed the front door behind them, Austin heard a commotion upstairs. He put an arm around her waist. "Lost your appetite for violence, have you?"

She seemed surprised by the physical contact but, after a moment's hesitation, rested her head briefly on his shoulder. He exulted in the feeling. She was finally coming to trust him.

"Pretty much, especially after last night." She raised her head. "Though I think I might make an exception for one shadow demon."

Austin nodded. "I thought it sounded like Shade might be responsible. But his portals are normally green, aren't they?"

Val strode away from him. "Yep. Come on. Let's go find out what really happened that night."

Chapter Twenty-One

Val

AUSTIN LED ME down the block to where he'd parked his car. "We're going to Shade's?" he asked.

WHAT ARE YOU GOING TO DO TO SHADE? Fang asked. FORCE LOLA DOWN HIS THROAT? THAT'LL GO OVER REAL WELL.

I'd forced Shade to do enough in the past few months. *If I have to,* I told Fang. But maybe I didn't.

"Yes," I said aloud to Austin. "But let me see if Ivy's available to come with us first. She can tell when Shade's lying."

Austin gave me a raised eyebrow but didn't say anything.

NAW, HE'S PRETTY BRIGHT. HE KNOWS WHY YOU'RE NOT GONNA USE LOLA ON SHADE.

I called her and asked, "Are you still up?"

"Yeah—I figured I'd wait until you came home to go to bed." She laughed. "Might as well match my sleep cycle to yours."

"Good. We think Shade may be responsible for Alejandro's disappearance. Can you come with us? Make sure he's telling the truth?"

She didn't answer, and I asked, "Ivy?"

"Sorry, I was trying to remember our first conversation with him. You never actually asked him if he had anything to do with the disappearance. Sure, I can help."

"Okay, great. We'll pick you up."

I checked the time. Micah should be closing the club right about now, so I called him next. "Hey, Micah, we think Shade knows more than he's saying about Alejandro's disappearance—the two vamps who tried to kidnap him said he vanished into a cloud that sounds remarkably like one of Shade's portals."

"And you believe them?"

"Yes—they were under Lola's influence at the time. Can you come with us to question him?"

Micah sighed. "What do you think I can do that you can't?"

"He respects you as leader of the Underground. If you ask him to tell us the whole truth, he probably will." And Micah should know why I didn't want to use Lola on Shade—ever since Dina had used him as her love slave, the poor guy had had enough succubi forcing him to do their bidding for a lifetime.

"Okay, hold on. Let me check something." I heard his keyboard clicking, then he said, "Shade is on watcher duty tonight. He's not far from your place. I'll ask him to meet us there."

"Works for me." I hung up and told Austin what Micah had said. "It'll be a few minutes yet."

My stomach growled, and Austin gave me a sideways grin. "Hungry?"

"I guess so." It had been a long night. "Can we stop and grab something to eat on the way?"

PIZZA? Fang asked hopefully.

I rolled my eyes. "Okay, pizza. There's a twenty-four hour grocery store not far from me."

We stopped there, and I grabbed Fang's favorite frozen brand, then we arrived back at my place the same time as Shade and Micah.

I let them all in, and Ivy looked surprised. "Change of plans," I told her. "We're doing this here."

She glanced down at the pizza box in my hands. I shrugged. "We got hungry."

Grinning, she took it from me. "I'll heat that up."

While Ivy messed about in the kitchen, I motioned the guys to take a seat in the living room.

I STILL CAN'T READ HIM, Fang told me and leaned up against Shade so we could at least see his expression.

The shadow demon looked apprehensive. "What's this about?"

"We're here about the night Alejandro went missing," Micah said. "And need your help."

"Okay," Shade said warily.

"Remember those two vamps who came running into the foyer after you smashed the crystal?" I asked.

"Yeah."

"Well, they were the ones who tried to kill Alejandro. But he disappeared before they could do anything."

"So?" He looked confused as Ivy slipped back into the room. She sat behind Shade so I could see her face, but Shade couldn't.

"So, they said he disappeared into a purple cloud. You know, like the kind you make when you're building a portal."

Annoyance flickered over his face—he still hadn't perfected the trick of hiding his emotions. "I didn't make a portal that night. And my portals are green, not purple."

Ivy fingered a stone in her ear and nodded to let me know he was telling the truth.

"Normally, yes. But are you sure it wasn't yours?" What else could it have been?

"Of course I'm sure. You were there—you didn't see one, did you?"

True, but the vampires I'd questioned weren't able to lie, not with Lola all up in their chakras. "But you were trying to create one, weren't you?"

Shade shrugged, looking annoyed.

"You've never failed before," I persisted. "Why was this time different?"

"Who knows?"

Austin leaned forward. "When we arrived, you were gesturing toward the altar room, where Alejandro disappeared. Do you think you did it by accident?"

"I doubt it."

Austin's question reminded me what else Shade had been doing. "You looked like you were saying the words to a spell. Were you?"

Shade cast a glance at Micah, as if wondering if he should say anything more.

"Please," Micah said. "Anything you can share may help us find Alejandro."

"Yes," Shade said curtly. "I was trying to use a spell. It didn't work."

"What spell?"

"It was something the books helped me with."

Sheesh, this was like pulling fangs. "*What* spell?" I asked more forcefully.

"How was it supposed to work?" Micah added.

"It was supposed to make a one-way portal."

"What the heck for?" I asked, surprised.

Shade pressed his lips together, looking as though he didn't want to answer.

Austin squeezed my hand. "Didn't you tell me that Shade can't go through one of his own portals?" At my nod, he added, "Then I imagine he was trying to find a spell that would allow him to send himself through a portal, so he could retrieve Sharra's body."

Of course he was. I closed my eyes momentarily in disbelief. I didn't need to see Shade's expression to know that was true.

"Is that what you were doing?" Micah asked, looking annoyed.

"Yes," Shade said, the word short and biting.

Ivy nodded—he was still telling the truth.

"Why?" Micah asked, looking baffled. "When it's so dangerous?"

"Because no one would go through for me—I had to find a way to get to the demon dimension myself."

"And how were you planning to get back?" the Underground leader demanded.

"The same way I got there—by using the spell. The book said it would work on the other side, too. But I must have done something wrong."

Yeah—thinking he should go unprotected to the demon dimension in the first place. "I don't think you did, Shade. I think it worked and that you sent Alejandro and Vincent instead."

He narrowed his eyes at me. "How?"

"I don't know—maybe this particular spell opens portals at a distance, instead of right next to you. Or opens closest to the nearest other person. Is that possible?"

"I have no idea," he said.

Annoyed, I stomped out of the room and went to retrieve the encyclopedia. Setting the books on the coffee table, I talked to them. "Show me the spell that you told Shade to use to open a one-way portal."

One of the books quivered, as if wondering whether to answer me or not. Crap—was this the price I'd have to pay for the books' waffling about letting me stay as keeper?

MAYBE YOU SHOULD ASK NICELY, Fang suggested.

"Please?" I asked, feeling silly about needing to be polite to a set of books, for heaven's sake.

The book shook a little more, light coming from its pages. I opened it where the light was coming from. "Is this the spell you used?" I asked Shade as the light faded so we could read it.

He skimmed it quickly. "Yes. But see, it doesn't say anything about it working at a distance."

"That doesn't mean it didn't work that way. We all know the books are sometimes incomplete." As if whoever wrote them thought we'd know things we didn't.

"Does it matter?" Austin asked. "It looks as though this might be where Alejandro disappeared to."

"Yes, it does matter," I said. "We need to test it, make sure that's what happened. You can't just go haring off into the demon dimension without knowing how it works."

"I can't open portals anymore," Shade reminded us. "You made sure of that with the amulet, Val."

"No, I said you couldn't open portals anymore without Micah's permission," I reminded him.

"That's right," Austin said and glanced at Micah in triumph. "So, if you'll give him permission to test it, please?"

Micah frowned, thinking. "It sounds dangerous. If you're right, Shade sent Alejandro and Vincent through by accident. We can't test it here—you don't want to send your neighbors off into a demon dimension."

I DON'T KNOW, Fang drawled. I WOULDN'T MIND GETTING RID OF THE GUY NEXT DOOR. At Ivy's questioning glance, he added, HE HATES DOGS. THINKS I'LL CRAP ON HIS LAWN OR SOMETHING.

Do you? I asked curiously.

Fang wouldn't meet my eyes.

I shrugged and told Micah, "That's why we need to test it." I thought for a moment, then said, "Let's go to the high school. They have a big football field, so we can see what's happening." I checked the time—a little after four. "No one will be there this time of the morning."

Micah still looked hesitant, so Austin said, "Please, Micah. We must know if this is what happened. You wouldn't want to leave the New Blood Movement leaderless, would you?"

"Plus the portal is only one-way," I added. "So no demons can come through. The book is clear about that."

Micah nodded reluctantly. "Okay, we'll test it, but if I say stop, you'll close the portal immediately, Shade."

Shade nodded, looking strangely eager.

OF COURSE HE IS. HE PROBABLY SEES THIS AS A WAY OF RETRIEVING SHARRA'S BODY.

Yeah, I knew that.

We headed toward the local high school in two cars, scarfing down pizza on the way, and piled out at the football field. It was strange being at this bastion of normality, especially since I'd been homeschooled and never attended a football game. Not that I wanted to. After the danger and excitement of fighting vamps and mage demons, the thought of watching two teams of humans fight over a piece of pigskin was quite a yawner. I didn't understand the attraction, especially on television when you couldn't even see the pigskin in question half the time.

MAYBE IT'S HOW NORMAL PEOPLE SAFELY CHANNEL THEIR AGGRESSIONS AND FIND SOMEONE TO CHEER FOR, TO GIVE THEM A SENSE OF BELONGING TO SOMETHING BIGGER THAN THEMSELVES, Fang suggested. YOU DON'T NEED THAT—IT'S BUILT INTO WHAT YOU DO.

Maybe, but I still didn't get it.

We set up at the center of the field, to give us plenty of room to see what might be happening in all directions. Shade faced one set of goal posts, and Micah told him, "Go ahead, try it—create a one-way portal."

I couldn't see Shade's expression, but he raised his arms, and I could hear him muttering under his breath. The rest of us stood close and watched the area in front of him and everywhere around us, just in case.

"There, I see it," Ivy said excitedly.

Sure enough, a purple cloud was forming about fifteen yards in front of Shade. It took less time than I remembered. Apparently, Shade's ability had been enhanced by the shattering of the crystal as well.

"Keep it small," Micah said, "so no one can come through."

"They shouldn't be able to, anyway, if what the books say is true," Shade reminded him.

"Just in case," Micah said warningly.

Squinting, I said, "It doesn't look the same as his other portals." It wasn't as close, obviously, and it was a different color. But there was something else different . . . the shape, maybe?

I'LL CHECK IT OUT, Fang said. He trotted down the sidelines and peered at it from the side. HUH, YOU'RE RIGHT. THEY'RE NORMALLY SHAPED LIKE A BALL, BUT THIS ONE LOOKS LIKE A FUNNEL FROM THE SIDE. LIKE A WEIRD SIDEWAYS PURPLE TORNADO.

I repeated his observations to Austin. "Is the smaller side toward us or on the other side?" he asked.

I repeated Fang's answer. "The smaller end of the funnel is toward us, right in the center."

Austin nodded and picked up a green toy football some kid had lost under the bleachers. Then, with nary a wasted motion, he arrowed it straight into the center of the cloud.

AND HE SCORES!

"Did it go through the portal to the demon dimension?" I asked.

IT MUST HAVE, BECAUSE IT SURE DIDN'T COME OUT THE OTHER SIDE HERE.

"Yep, it went through," I told Austin, though I wondered idly what the demons on the other side would think of a football coming out of nowhere. Would they choose up sides and play a game? The mind boggled.

THEY'LL PROBABLY JUST EAT IT, Fang said.

"Please, shut it down," Micah told Shade.

Slowly, the purple funnel cloud shrank and disappeared.

"Well, I guess that explains it," Austin said. "The distance from here looks about the same as it was between the staircase and the altar room. Shade must have sent Alejandro and Vincent through to the demon dimension." He sounded relieved, yet grim.

YEAH, HE'S PROBABLY GLAD TO KNOW WHAT HAPPENED TO HIS BOSS, BUT JEEZ, THE DEMON DIMENSION? WHO WANTS TO WIND UP THERE? DOESN'T SOUND LIKE MY IDEA OF A PICNIC.

Mine either.

"I didn't do it on purpose," Shade said stiffly.

"We know that," I assured him.

"So, do we go through and get him?" Ivy asked.

"Not here," Austin replied. "We'll need to go back through in the same place to have a hope of finding him. He'll probably stay close to the portal, in hopes we'll rescue him."

"Even then, it's iffy," Shade said. "Time can run differently in other dimensions. You could arrive a few minutes later or months later."

I hadn't realized that. "I see what you mean. If it's been months for them, they might not be close to the portal anymore."

Austin's jaw tightened. "Nevertheless, we have to try."

"And retrieve Sharra as well?" Shade asked stubbornly.

"Of course," Austin said. "The sun will rise soon, so I can't do it now. Can you meet me at the blood house after sundown tonight and open a two-way portal?"

"Yes," Shade exulted.

Micah frowned. "No."

"That's okay," Shade said. "I know you have to perform at the club. Just give me permission now to open a portal tonight. That should meet the requirement to get your permission first. Right, Val?"

"Yeah, it should." But I didn't think that was why Micah was hesitating.

Micah shook his head, his lips firmed. "I mean, no, I won't let you do that."

"Why not?" Austin asked, his gaze narrowing.

"Because it's still dangerous," Micah said. "Remember, the reason we didn't let Shade reopen the portal in the first place was because there were too many full demons waiting on the other side to come in and lay waste to this world. You saw how much havoc one full demon wreaked during his time here. How can I risk the lives of my people, your people, and the whole city again?"

He was right, but I kept my mouth shut, not wanting to come between my boyfriend and my boss.

YEAH, THAT'S A NO-WIN SITUATION, Fang said in agreement.

"Demons on the other side?" Ivy said faintly. "And they want into this world?"

"Yes," Micah said. "Full demons—can you imagine the destruction they'd do?"

"But it's been days," Austin protested. "They're probably not massing at the portal anymore."

Micah shook his head. "As Shade just told us, time works differently over there. You could be going back only minutes later. We barely kept the demons at bay last time. I'm not confident we could do it again—especially for the length of time it might take to keep the portal open."

"It does sound dangerous," Ivy said.

"It's more than dangerous," Micah said. "It's suicidal."

"Well, it'll be our lives at risk," Austin said.

"I'm willing to risk it," Shade added.

"But it's not just your lives in danger—it's the entire world."

"What if we use the one-way portal to get there so they can't come through to this side, then open another one-way to come back?" Shade suggested.

"You can't be sure it'll work that way," Micah protested.

"And what if you get killed on the other side, and Austin is stuck over there with no way to get back?" I retorted. "Or demons follow you back through the portal?"

"Whose side are you on?" Shade asked.

Austin looked annoyed, as if he'd wanted to ask the same question.

"I'm on the side of keeping danger to a minimum," I said firmly.

"What if we can minimize the danger?" Austin asked. "Ensure no demons cross over to this side?"

Micah shook his head. "I don't see how you can guarantee that."

"But if we can, you'll allow it?" Austin persisted.

"Maybe."

Austin nodded as if Micah had said yes. I knew better.

"I'll figure something out," he said decisively.

We headed toward the cars, and I slowed. Austin slowed his pace to match mine. "I'm not sure Micah will agree," I warned him quietly. "He can be really stubborn." Not to mention protective of the Demon Underground. He was serious about his position as their leader and keeping the secret of their existence.

Austin's jaw clenched. "So can I."

"You're not thinking of forcing him, are you?" Because I couldn't allow that.

"No, but if I bring Luis in on this, he might."

"Then don't bring Luis in."

"I might have to, in order to put a plan together that Micah will go for."

"How about I help you, and we only call in Luis for reinforcements when we actually put the plan into action?"

"And if we can't come up with something Micah will agree with?" Austin challenged. "What then?"

I soooo didn't want to answer that question, especially not given the heat with which he'd asked it. "Are you really asking me to go against the wishes of the Demon Underground leader, my boss?"

"I'm asking who you'll back—me or him?"

I shook my head. "It's not a matter of—"

"No more evasions, Val. Who will you support?"

I'd never seen him look so angry. I sighed.

YOU'RE GONNA HAVE TO ANSWER HIM SOONER OR LATER, Fang said, looking sympathetic.

Yeah, might as well bite the bullet now. "I'm sorry, but I have to agree with Micah on this one. Letting demons into this world is too dangerous to risk unless we have a foolproof plan to keep them out."

I couldn't see Austin's face because he'd sped up, his back to me.

"Austin?" I asked.

"I need to get back," he said over his shoulder, his voice clipped. "The sun will rise soon. Get a ride back with Micah." And, just like that, he took off without me.

UH-OH. LOOKS LIKE THERE'S TROUBLE IN PARADISE.

Chapter Twenty-Two

Val

MICAH DROPPED Shade, Ivy, Fang, and me back at the townhouse. Instead of heading home or back to work, Shade asked if he could come inside for a bit.

"Why?" I asked. I was tired and wanted to go to bed. Plus I wanted to think about what had just happened, about Austin being pissed that I'd agreed with Micah and not him. I couldn't really blame him for being upset, but was this going to be a repeat of what happened with Shade? I didn't want to deal with any more pouty men. And I sure didn't want another relationship to fizzle just when it seemed to be going so well.

But I didn't want Austin going in to his duel with Luis upset, either. We probably wouldn't be able to retrieve Alejandro by midnight tonight, so they'd meet on the dueling grounds in about nineteen hours.

"I just want to talk about getting Alejandro back," Shade said.

Not to mention his twin sister's body.

"It's not me you have to convince—it's Micah." And I wasn't up for arguing right now.

"I know," Shade said eagerly. "But I have some ideas I want to run by you. Go over some options I've been thinking about."

HE'S NOT GONNA GIVE UP AND GO HOME UNTIL HE HAS A CHANCE TO TALK AT YOU, Fang warned me.

Unfortunately, I knew Fang was right. "Okay, come in for a little while."

We all settled in the living room once more, Shade petting Fang so we could all see him.

"Okay," I said, "let's hear it."

"Well, Micah's big fear is that we're going to have demons pouring in from the other side, right?"

"Yes, and since that's what happened the last time you opened a two-way portal, can you blame him?"

Ignoring that and the fact that Ivy looked disturbed by the notion,

Shade said, "So what if we check to see if there are demons on the other side first?"

"How? Got a handy-dandy demon detector on ya?" Okay, I was tired, so feeling a bit testy.

"Yes, I do," Shade said. "And so do you."

"Huh?"

"The hellhounds—they can detect demons *and* hear their thoughts. They do it all the time."

I glanced down at Fang. "Yes, but across dimensions? I don't know if that's possible."

Fang seemed to shrug, but Shade was excited. "Yes, they can. Remember Diesel's hellhound, Max? He heard demons on the other side during the battle at the blood house."

I thought back to that night. I did remember Max saying something along those lines. I glanced at Fang. "Is that true?"

THAT'S WHAT HE SAID.

His phrasing was odd. Suspiciously, I asked, "What do you mean, that's what he *said*?"

I MEAN, MAX SAID HE COULD HEAR ON THE OTHER SIDE. I DON'T KNOW IF IT'S TRUE.

Since Shade had blocked his ability to talk to Fang directly, I translated. "Fang doesn't know if Max was telling the truth."

"Of course he does," Shade protested. "Max said there were demons massing on the other side." He paused, his fingers clenching in Fang's fur. "You said Max was telling the truth, Fang."

Fang wouldn't meet my eyes. I ASSUMED HE WAS TELLING THE TRUTH, SO I BACKED HIM.

"You *assumed* he was telling the truth?" I asked, flabbergasted. We'd left Sharra on the other side on Max's word alone?

Shade looked as though he was about to blow a gasket. Not that I knew what a gasket was, but blowing one couldn't be good. Smart Fang—he eased away from the shadow demon's grip on his fur.

"Who's Max?" Ivy asked.

Absently, I replied, "Another hellhound. Belongs to the Albuquerque Paladin, Diesel."

I DID WHAT I HAD TO, Fang said defensively. THERE WERE DEMONS COMING THROUGH THE PORTAL, AND WE HAD TO STOP THEM.

"What's Fang saying now?" Shade demanded.

I didn't want to admit to Fang's potential part in leaving Shade's sister stranded on the other side. *Did you hear the demons on the other side?* I asked Fang privately.

NO, BUT I DIDN'T TRY. I WAS TOO BUSY KICKING BUTT ON *THIS* SIDE.

"He took Max's word for it," I told Shade.

Ivy's eyes widened.

Wild-eyed, Shade leapt to his feet, swirling faster in agitation. "Max is the one who said Sharra was dead. That means she could still be alive," he exclaimed. "Even more reason for us to mount a rescue operation."

"You don't know that. Max might have been telling the truth."

"And he might have lied to convince us to close the portal," Shade pointed out.

Ivy chewed her lip. "Sharra's a shadow demon like you, right?"

"Yes, she's my twin."

"Then . . . if she's still alive, wouldn't she be able to open a portal on the other side to come back?"

"She can't come through a portal she created," I told her.

"But couldn't she create one to let us know where she is?" Ivy persisted.

"If she can," Shade said, sounding desperate. "She might be unconscious or too weak."

He was grasping at straws. "Even if Sharra was alive when she went through, that doesn't mean she still is," I reminded him.

"It doesn't mean she's dead, either," Shade said. "What's Diesel's number? I want to call him right now and find out."

"I don't have it, but Tessa does." When he pulled out his phone, I added, "You might want to wait to call her, since it's still kind of early." Trying to distract Shade and calm him down, I added, "And who's to say Diesel would tell you the truth even then?" It wasn't as if Lola could compel him through the phone lines.

Shade glanced at Ivy. "Can your stones tell?"

"Not on the phone—it has to be in person. Sorry."

Shade muttered some curses under his breath and paced.

PROBABLY WONDERING HOW HE CAN GET TO ALBUQUERQUE AND WRING THE TRUTH OUT OF DIESEL AND MAX.

No doubt. "You'd probably get the truth if Micah asked him," I said.

"And why would he do that?" Shade asked bitterly. "Micah doesn't want to do anything that might open the portal."

"Actually," Ivy said gently, "I believe Micah is concerned about how safe it is, first and foremost. Your idea is a good one. If hellhounds can sense the presence of demons on the other side, it might help him agree to a plan that includes those abilities."

Everyone's gaze turned to Fang.

I DON'T KNOW IF I CAN OR NOT, Fang said, sounding sulky.

I shrugged for Shade's benefit.

"Then we have to test it," Shade said.

"How are we going to do that safely? And get Micah's permission to open a portal to test it in the first place?" Shade was so single-minded, he wasn't thinking straight.

"What about the books?" Ivy asked. "Would they be able to help?"

Shade shook his head. "I've already asked. They can't. But you—can you help?"

"Me?" Ivy asked. "How?"

"Maybe one of your stones can sense demons in another dimension," Shade said.

"How would she know that?" I asked him as Ivy shrugged helplessly. I'm sure it wasn't something she'd ever thought to try.

"We can test that, too," Shade insisted.

Sighing, I said, "But how will it help to know how many demons are on the other side? Especially since we wouldn't know the range?"

"I'm sure the Movement will supply people to mount a rescue operation, probably even bring in Lisette's vamps from Austin. We can make sure we're not outnumbered and keep the demons at bay. Come on, Val, we have to try."

Feeling a little guilty that we might have abandoned Sharra alone in the demon dimension, I said, "Okay, if you can do it safely and Micah allows it."

"We might not need Micah's permission," Shade said slyly.

"You think you can get around the last order I gave with it? How?"

"What if you use Lola to force me to open a portal?"

Huh. I didn't know. Which would be stronger? The command I'd given him using the amulet days ago, or a chakra-binding command with Lola? "I don't know if that'll work."

"But you'll try, right?"

He sounded so eager, and this was one thing I could finally do for him, after all the crap I'd had to do *to* him. "If you can find a way to do it safely, without endangering Ivy." No way was I risking a demon horde coming through here and now.

"Do it now," Shade urged. "Just to see if it'll work."

"Is that safe?" Ivy asked.

"It is if I keep it small so no one can come through," Shade assured her. "And I'll make sure it's a one-way portal to a pocket dimension where there are no demons. Come on, Val. Try."

Micah hadn't expressly forbidden us to try this. . . .

THAT'S BECAUSE HE DIDN'T THINK OF IT. TRY IT, VAL. IT'S THE ONLY WAY YOU'LL BE ABLE TO GET RID OF SHADE SO WE CAN BOTH GET SOME SHUT-EYE.

I did kind of wonder if it was possible. I glanced at Ivy. She shrugged. "Since part of the demon in the crystal went into you, it might work." Quickly, we explained what we thought had happened to Shade.

"So that's why the last portal on the football field formed so quickly," he mused. "This should work then. Let's do it."

I sighed. "Okay, but keep it as small as possible. And make a regular two-way one so we don't have to worry about the neighbors."

Shade stood at one end of the room while the rest of us stood behind him. "I'll make a tiny one right over the coffee table."

"Try it first," Ivy suggested. "See if you can do it without Val or Micah."

I wasn't sure I'd encourage that, but Shade raised his arms out in front of him, obviously already trying.

He lowered his arms. "I can't. Val's last command is still in place, and I can't even begin. Try Lola."

He must be desperate if he was actually asking me to use Lola on him. Slowly, I eased Lola's energy tendrils into him, trying not to make him feel too much lust. Neither of us wanted to go there. I clamped onto his chakras and said, "Create a two-way portal, Shade. No bigger than a baseball." I reinforced the instruction with Lola, to force him to do it.

Slowly, a minute green cloud formed. Not as fast as it had on the football field, but apparently, it would work. "Okay, close it down."

It disappeared immediately. "It worked," Shade said excitedly. "It was harder than normal, but with Lola's help, I could do it." He turned to Fang. "Did you sense any demons on the other side?"

Fang shook his head, so I didn't even have to translate.

"Does that mean he can't communicate through a portal?" Ivy asked.

"Not necessarily," Shade said, sounding overly optimistic. "I chose a dimension without demons, remember? Let's experiment—"

I held up my hand to stop him. "Not right now. I'm tired. Let me get some sleep first."

"Then call me as soon as you wake up," Shade said. "I'll figure out a way to make sure you and Ivy are safe."

I glanced at Ivy who shook her head. "I promised your mother I'd come by her store tomorrow," Ivy reminded me. "Plus I need to do some research to see if there might be any gemstones that have the kind of capability you're looking for."

"Then when?" Shade asked impatiently.

I deferred to Ivy, since she was the one with the commitments. "How about seven tomorrow night?" she asked.

"Can't you make it sooner?" Shade asked.

Defending her, I said, "It's a good time. Austin should be awake by then, and we can plan everything together." If Austin was talking to me. Heck, I'd make him listen—I didn't want to give him any reason to get Luis involved too early, or the Spaniard would probably hurt Shade or Micah in his zeal to get answers. I was pretty sure I could count on Austin not to harm them but wasn't sure about Luis.

"Okay," Shade said reluctantly. "That'll give me time to set up a good test. Where shall we meet?"

I thought for a moment. Depending on what kind of portal he tried to open, we might need more open space, not to mention privacy. At that time of day, I didn't think it was possible. "I don't know. Let me ask Austin, see if he knows of someplace. I'll call you."

"Okay," Shade said and left, almost bouncing in enthusiasm.

Sighing, I said goodnight to Ivy and headed for bed.

YOU KNOW WHAT YOU JUST DID, DON'T YOU?

Agreed to something I really don't want to do?

YEAH, AND YOU JUST PROVED YOU CAN GET SHADE TO OPEN A PORTAL WITHOUT MICAH'S PERMISSION. YOU CAN'T BLAME YOUR DECISION TO LEAVE IT CLOSED ON YOUR BOSS ANYMORE—TO AUSTIN OR ANYONE ELSE.

Oh, crap.

Chapter Twenty-Three

Austin

AUSTIN ROSE AFTER the sun went down. A day of slumber had left him feeling more optimistic. Now that they knew what had happened to Alejandro and Vincent, it was far more likely they could rescue the two of them unharmed. If he could just convince Micah and Val . . .

His phone rang. Speak of the devil. . . . "Yes?" His voice came out a little more curt than he'd intended.

"You're still mad at me, huh?" she asked.

He sighed. In his surprise at Micah and Val's refusal to let Shade open a portal, Austin had been less than polite. In fact, he'd been downright rude. "You have a right to your opinion," he said stiffly. Even if it didn't agree with his. That didn't mean he had to like it.

"I didn't say I wouldn't help you—just that Micah is right in saying you need a plan to deal with the demons that might come through along with Alejandro. In fact, wouldn't Alejandro insist on that himself?"

Probably. "Maybe."

"Well, Shade and I talked about it last night, and we did a little testing to see if Fang can detect demons in other dimensions," she said.

Relaxing a little at this evidence she was trying to be reasonable, Austin asked, "Did it work?"

"We're not sure and want to do some more testing. We're planning to meet at seven. Do you know of someplace we can practice undisturbed . . . where there's enough space to see the portal?"

Austin thought for a moment. "Do you remember the old theater where we first met? Where we held the rally on All Hallow's Eve?"

"Yes, but can you get it on such short notice?"

"The Movement owns it now, and it's being repaired, so it's not open to the public yet. We should be able to use it, no problem."

"Okay, good." She hesitated, then said, "Isn't this the night you have to meet Luis?" She sounded tentative, as if she was trying not to piss him off any more than he already was. He appreciated the thought but wasn't ready to let go of his mad just yet.

"Yes, unless we can rescue Alejandro before then. But we have plenty of time before that. The traditional time for duels is midnight, and Rosa has set it up for then."

"Okay, good. We'll meet you at the theater in an hour. Don't bring Luis."

Val hung up, and Austin realized she was right about Luis. If he told the other lieutenant the truth about where Alejandro had most likely gone, he wouldn't rest until he'd forced the shadow demon to do his bidding. In this case, that meant forcing the leader of the Demon Underground as well . . . not exactly the best course of action for maintaining diplomatic relations with the demons. If the Movement was to survive and flourish, they definitely needed the support of as many people as they could get.

So, he enlisted the help of a few of his followers to watch the outside of the theater without explaining exactly what he'd be doing inside and headed there to meet Val.

He arrived a little early to unlock the theater and turn on the lights. The repairs were proceeding nicely, and the construction workers were gone for the night. There was plenty of space to do their tests, and the stage itself was pretty much free of construction materials. It would work.

Val and Ivy arrived shortly after that along with Fang, and Shade came a little later with Andrew—the redheaded fire demon who had almost burned down the mansion with all the vampires in it. True, he'd been under the influence of a mage demon at the time, but Austin still wasn't sure he could trust the boy who had no love for vampires.

"Why is Andrew here?" Val asked.

Shade's voice came from beneath his hoodie and the swirls that made up his face. "We need someone to go through to the other side. I plan to use an unoccupied dimension, but there may be other dangers there. I figure a fire demon will be able to handle himself."

"Are you okay with this?" Val asked Andrew.

The fire demon shrugged, looking way too cocky. "I can handle it."

He glanced aside at Ivy to gauge Ivy's reaction, and Austin realized he was posturing for her. Unfortunately for Andrew, Ivy looked amused.

Austin didn't have as much confidence in Andrew as the others did but kept his thoughts to himself. "Where's Micah?" Austin asked.

"He's working," Shade explained. "But we experimented a little yesterday and realized that Val can use Lola to force me to make a portal without Micah's consent."

Austin raised an eyebrow at Val. Had she changed her mind about supporting Micah? "You mean he doesn't know what you're doing?"

"Yes, he does," Val said defensively. "I talked to him earlier and got his consent after I promised to do this safely."

It annoyed him that she had to seek Micah's approval, but it was also the very thing he admired in her—she stuck to her principles, even when it might not be comfortable for her. Too bad it wasn't comfortable for Austin either.

"Let's get started," Shade said, sounding impatient. Glancing around, he said, "Where should I do this?"

"Why don't you create the portal on stage?" Austin suggested. "It has less construction debris, and that way, we can all see what's going on."

Shade went to the stage without answering.

"What's the plan?" Austin asked Val.

"We want to see if Fang can detect demons on the other side of a portal. That way we'll know if it's safe to open one when we look for Alejandro."

"That's why I'm here," the redhead said self-importantly.

Val and Fang rolled their eyes in unison, but Austin wasn't amused. He just hoped Andrew didn't do anything stupid while showing off. "Good," he said aloud. "Having advance notice of your enemy is always a good thing. But what about the issue of time passing differently in the different dimensions? Will that cause a problem with hearing each other?"

"No," Shade said. "Time syncs while the portal is open."

Good—that would make it less confusing.

Ivy came forward with a small silk bag in her hand. "Before we start, I have something for you, Val."

Val pulled a necklace from the bag—an oddly shaped spear of clear crystal and a turquoise nugget set together in a gold wire freeform setting. "It's beautiful. What's it supposed to do?"

"The crystal is a shard from the amulet. It's cleansed now, and I thought it might continue to resonate with you, since you wore it so long. Turquoise helps to enhance communication, so I thought it might help during your tests."

Val nodded and slipped the necklace over her head. "Can't hurt. And even if it doesn't, it's pretty."

She seemed very pleased by the gift, and Austin realized he'd never seen her wear any kind of jewelry before. Odd.

"Here's one for you, too," Ivy told Andrew. She pulled off one of her rings and handed it to him. "This way, I'll be able to see if I can communicate with it when it's in another dimension."

Andrew nodded and tucked the ring in his pocket.

"I also checked the bloodstone in the athame," Ivy said, turning to Austin. "It's more coherent now but seems focused on what the blood demon used it for and Guillaume's death. I don't think it'll be any help in confirming what happened with Alejandro."

"That's okay," Austin said. "I'm confident we know what happened now."

Fang poked Val's leg, and she grinned down at him. "He's telling us to get started instead of standing around BSing."

"Stay off the stage, please," Shade said. "I don't want to get any of you caught in the portal by accident."

As everyone did so, Val hitched her backpack more securely on her shoulder, then clasped the pendant in her fist and stared at Shade, using Lola, he assumed. "Create a two-way portal to another dimension, Shade. Not the demon dimension—a safe one."

Austin glanced toward the stage and saw a small green cloud forming in front of Shade. Since it was his normal two-way portal, they didn't need as much room for this.

"Make it big enough so Andrew can go through," Val said, obviously concentrating.

Everyone went up the stairs to join Shade on stage, keeping behind him, out of the way of the green cloud that was slowly growing to the proper size.

"Please explain to Andrew what we're doing," Val told Ivy.

Ivy smiled at Andrew. "We're going to test to see if Fang can hear you on the other side. If he can hear you, he can hear other demons as well. Fang will also talk to you, so just keep communicating with him."

"That's all?" Andrew asked.

"Yes," Val said. "If you can't hear him, come back immediately. If you can hear him, we'll do some additional testing." Quickly, she added, "Come back when he tells you to."

The fact that he needed to be told that said way too much about Andrew's level of maturity.

Once the portal was large enough for Andrew, the fire demon stepped boldly through it, his hands sparking as if he were readying his fire to ward off any danger.

"Fang asked me to translate for him since Val needs concentration to keep Lola pushing Shade," Ivy said with a grin. "Fang can hear Andrew—he says it's daylight over there, but misty. He's having problems making out landmarks."

"Can he see the portal on that side to come back?" Austin asked. He didn't know if they acted the same in other dimensions, and since they'd never tried this before, neither did anyone else.

"Good question." She paused for a moment. "Yes, he can, but it's blue on that side instead of green."

Okay, good. "Tell him to move slowly away from the portal so we can get a range, see how far Fang's ability to hear extends. If he can no longer hear Fang, have him move back closer to the portal." Realizing that Andrew might need more instruction, he added, "Have him go slowly and count his paces so we know how far Fang's ability extends."

"Good idea," Ivy said. She grinned. "He's arguing, but Fang is putting him in his place." Then she counted slowly. "One . . . two . . . three . . ." She got up to twelve, then abruptly cut off.

Fang leapt to his feet and growled at the portal. Or was it Andrew he was growling at? "What happened?" Austin asked.

"Andrew stopped counting, but Fang can still hear him. He stopped for some reason." She gave Austin a rueful grin. "He seems to be distracted by something. No, wait." She gave Austin a stricken look. "Fang said he felt a burst of pain, then Andrew's mental voice cut off. My gemstone felt the pain, too."

"Does Fang or the stone know what happened?"

"No, Andrew isn't answering." Ivy glanced at him. "I think he's in trouble."

Austin nodded decisively. "I'll go through, see what the problem is."

"No, you can't," Val said. "Andrew said it's sunny over there, remember? You'll fry."

"Then who can?" he asked impatiently. He wouldn't ask it of Ivy, and Fang needed to be here, to relay information back to the others. "Can you call Micah, ask him to send someone else?"

"No," Val said. "Lola has a good hold on Shade, so I'll do it."

Alarm bells rang in his head. "No, wait," Austin told her, but it was too late. Val had already stepped through the portal . . . and it snuffed out behind her.

Fang barked furiously, and Austin whirled on Shade. "Open it," he commanded.

"I can't," Shade said in surprise. "When she went through, it cut Lola off, so I had to close it. I can't open it again without Micah's permission."

"Then get it," Austin bit out.

The doors to the theater burst open, and two of his followers ran to him. "You have to get out of here—a group of rogues tracked you down. We'll try to hold them off, but they called in reinforcements."

"I can't," Austin said. He couldn't abandon Val in another dimension.

"You have to," Jeremy insisted. "It's not safe." He glanced at Ivy and Shade. "Especially for them."

He was right. Shade was his only hope to get Val, Alejandro, and Vincent back, and he didn't want anything to happen to the gemstone whisperer.

What the hell was he supposed to do now?

Chapter Twenty-Four

Val

I REALIZED MY stupidity the moment I stepped through the portal. Hearing Fang's and Austin's voices cut off in mid-word was one clue, but the biggest was the sudden severance of Lola's hold on Shade. I whirled, but the portal was gone. No blue cloud or cloud of any color anywhere. Just featureless gray mist—chill and damp.

Crap. What had I been thinking?

Obviously, I hadn't been thinking, as Fang would tell me if he were here. Or, rather, I had been thinking about entirely the wrong things. I was so worried about Andrew being injured, and how I was responsible for him as the Demon Underground's Paladin, and how Micah would never forgive me if something happened to him, that I hadn't thought about anything else.

It had simply never occurred to me that Lola might not work across dimensions. In retrospect, that, too, was stupid, but knowing that the sunlight—weak though it was—was dangerous to Austin, and that I didn't want to endanger anyone else, I somehow felt I had to be the one to save Andrew.

Hero complex, much?

Dumb. But, speaking of Andrew, where was he? I thought about calling out but froze, just listening. Shade had deliberately chosen a dimension free of demons, but that didn't necessarily mean it was free of danger. This wasn't the same pocket dimension where we'd exiled the two mage demons, was it?

For a moment, I stood still, not even breathing, trying to hear, to learn everything I could about this world. Nothing. No animal or insect sounds, no sounds of water or wind. The audio of this world was as devoid of meaning as the visual one. Hopefully, that also meant devoid of danger, but not of Andrew.

What had happened to him? He had gone approximately twelve paces before his counting had stopped, but in what direction? Though

Lola obviously couldn't reach across dimensions, would she work here?

I felt inside of myself, trying to assess Lola's strength. Weird—deep in my gut where the spells I'd invoked had resided, it was empty, as if the spells had been stripped away the instant I'd gone through the portal. So Lola was back at full strength now, not having to share any of her capacity with the spells. I sent her out in all directions, searching, and sure enough, she found one male in front of me, slightly off to my left, not far at all. The faint footprints in the sand supported that.

"Andrew?" I called cautiously. He was close enough, and this misty, foggy dimension was quiet enough that he should be able to hear me.

No answer.

But I didn't want to go haring off after him without knowing how to get back to this spot. The people I'd left on the other side were no dummies. They'd figure out right away that all they had to do was call Micah so Shade could get permission to reopen the portal. They were also smart enough to open it at the same location, so I needed to be able to find it again. But after whirling around in this fog, I was a bit disoriented. Where, exactly, had the portal opened?

I couldn't be sure, but one thing I knew—it was within a couple of feet of where I stood now. Unfortunately, all I could see was a couple of feet in front of me. I looked at my surroundings to see if there were any landmarks. The ground was sandy, with scattered gray rocks and a few boulders. I kicked at a couple of the smaller rocks, wondering if I could build a cairn, and realized they were embedded deep in the ground, sticking up like mini icebergs with only a small percentage of the rock actually above the surface. I didn't see any loose ones. So, a cairn was out.

However, I did have my backpack. I didn't really want to leave the whole thing behind but rummaged around inside until I found my flashlight. I turned it on and placed it on the ground as a beacon, pointing in the direction I wanted to go. Its beam wouldn't reach all that far in the dense mist, but with any luck, I'd be able to follow Fang's voice back to the portal once it opened again. This was just to mark the approximate place it would open. Besides, Andrew had to be close.

I headed in Andrew's direction, following in what I hoped were his faint footprints, scuffing my feet in the sand as I went. It was slower going, but at least this way I'd leave a trail we could easily follow back to the flashlight. I'd gone about ten dragging steps when I saw him lying on the ground, blood on his head.

I approached cautiously, stake in hand, but when I saw the small rock at his foot and the big boulder at his head with a small splash of blood on it, it was obvious he'd tripped and fallen over one of those iceberg rocks and hit his head—nothing more sinister than that.

Lola already knew he was alive, and I knelt to feel his pulse. It was strong and steady, and his head had already stopped bleeding. With any luck, the head wound wouldn't be life-threatening.

I debated what to do. I didn't want to drag Andrew's dead weight back to the portal location, so I'd wait until he regained consciousness or the portal opened again—and hopefully have help getting him out of here. Besides, I didn't know what would happen if I misjudged the portal location, and it opened right on top of me. I put my stake away and sat down next to him, my back against the boulder that had knocked him out.

It was eerie, sitting in the mist, isolated from our own world, unable to see or explore this one, hearing only my own thoughts. It was kind of weird, just sitting still with no Fang to talk to, no one to fight, and nothing I had to do right this minute to save someone else.

I ought to be worried, chomping at the bit to return to my own place, but I had to admit, I kind of enjoyed the enforced peace and quiet for a change.

With nothing left to do but wait and think, my mind wouldn't stop moving, reviewing the events of the past few days, fretting about Austin's standoffishness, worrying whether we'd ever find Alejandro and Vincent . . . and wondering if this job was really worth all the pain.

Without bidding, the images I'd tried to bury flashed into my memory. Those girls . . . the blood . . . the carnage . . .

I rubbed the heels of my palms over my eyes, trying to will the mental pictures away, but they wouldn't go. I couldn't unsee those horrific scenes now, much as I wanted to. And my own imagination supplied still shots of what it probably looked like after the vampires took care of their torturers. After I'd held them still so they could be slaughtered. That horror was on me—a black mark on my soul.

I'd have to carry that the rest of my life. Could I continue doing this job, knowing that I'd see many more such scenes, enter more black marks on my soul? Could I—?

Andrew stirred and moaned, thankfully pulling me out of my reverie.

"Quiet," I admonished him. "You knocked yourself out." I knew head injuries could be problematic, but it had been less than twenty minutes between the time he'd fallen and I'd found him. Regaining consciousness so soon had to be a good thing, right?

"Val?" he said, blinking up at me in confusion, then looked around. "What are you doing here?"

"Helping you." Apparently, he hadn't lost his memory either.

"I can't hear Fang anymore. Did I go beyond his range?"

I squirmed but had to admit my mistake. "No, the portal closed when I came through after you."

"What?" He sat up abruptly then moaned. Holding his head, he squinted at me, obviously in pain. "You *closed* the portal?"

"Not on purpose. But Lola lost her hold on Shade . . ."

He used words I'm sure his mother wouldn't have approved of.

"Don't worry—they'll come after us."

"How long have I been out?"

"No more than twenty minutes," I assured him.

He scowled. "Shade should have reopened the portal by now."

Yeah, I kind of thought so, too. "Well, he can't unless Lola is forcing him, or he gets Micah's permission."

"That's dumb. Why would he wait for permission?"

"He kind of has to," I admitted. "I forced him to agree to it with the crystal amulet, before it was destroyed."

"Well, that was just plain stupid."

I thought about defending my actions, but I couldn't argue with the consequences. "It seemed like a good idea at the time," I said lamely. "And if Micah's on stage, they'll wait until he gets off to bring him to the phone."

"So we wait?" Andrew asked.

It might not be a good idea to move Andrew just yet, and Fang had been able to hear him from here, so why not stay here where it was at least a little comfortable? "You have a better idea?"

"You have any aspirin?" he challenged back.

"I might in my backpack, but I don't have any water." And even if there was water here—there had to be, with all this mist—I sure as heck wouldn't feel safe drinking it.

"I don't need it," he assured me.

I messed around in my backpack and came up with a bottle of aspirin. He took three, swallowing them down dry. "Thanks." He scooted around to sit next to me and lean against the boulder.

"Sorry I'm such a screw-up," he muttered.

I glanced at him in surprise. "This wasn't your fault."

"Yes, it was. If I hadn't tripped and knocked myself out, you wouldn't have needed to come rescue me."

"Much as I'd like to give you credit, I'll take this one on myself."

"I just wanted to do something good for the Underground for a change, you know? After all, I tried to blow up Micah's club."

I sighed. "Everyone knows you were under the blood demon's influence then."

"And before that, I tried to burn down the vampires' mansion."

"You were mourning your sister's death," I reminded him. "And mistakenly blamed the vampires. The mage demon took advantage of your grief and anger to control you and try to destroy the vamps. Not your fault."

"That's nice of you to say," he muttered. "But if I hadn't been so angry in the first place, none of that would've happened."

My, my, was Andrew growing up? "Can't argue with you there," I admitted.

"I just wanted to be helpful for a change, more like you."

"Like me?" I repeated in surprise.

"Yeah. We're about the same age, but no one treats you like a stupid kid. Everyone respects you."

"It's only because I'm Paladin."

"Yeah, well, they wouldn't have chosen you as Paladin if you didn't deserve it."

Deserve it? I didn't even want it. I'd only taken the job because if I hadn't, they would have made Shade into a Memory Eater—a Lethe. The Demon Underground required either a Paladin or a Lethe to enforce justice. Paladins did their job with a sword, while Lethes stripped memories and abilities from the offender's mind. To do so, the Lethe had to become the demon equivalent of the boogieman—a crazed half-vampire, half-demon hybrid. After seeing what being Lethe had done to Elspeth before I'd exorcised the demon within her, I wouldn't wish that horror on anyone.

Not knowing how to respond to Andrew's comment, I made a noncommittal noise.

"You're also the Keeper of the *Encyclopedia Magicka*, *and* you're in good with the Movement and the SCU. You save the world on a daily basis, and everyone trusts you, respects you."

Was that jealousy I heard? "Is that really how you see me?" I asked in disbelief.

"It's how everyone sees you," Andrew said, sounding sulky. "Val Shapiro, slayer of bad guys, champion of the underdog, and friend to freaks everywhere—a true legend. Me, I'm just a legend in my own mind."

"My life isn't all glory and sunshine, you know."

"Well, it's better than mine." He leaned his head back against the rock. "How long do you think it's gonna take to reopen that portal?"

"I don't know." I'd assumed it would be open by now. "This could be one of those dimensions where time passes differently—a minute in our world might equate to an hour here." Or much more, but I didn't even want to voice that possibility.

"Great," Andrew muttered. "The aspirin is starting to kick in. I think I'm gonna be quiet for a while and let it do its thing. Let me know when the portal opens again."

"Okay."

As Andrew lapsed into silence, I took stock of my life over the past six months. Yes, I had the power and "prestige" he'd mentioned, but with it came a great deal of responsibility—more than I'd ever wanted or asked for. It hadn't happened all at once but had come on gradually, like a bad cold. Somehow, it seemed as if one day I was living at home, working for my parents, and slaying the occasional vampire, and the next, I was out on my own, independent, and everyone's go-to person for hunting and killing bad guys.

I had to admit I liked being valued and respected, but the constant violence and stress was beginning to wear on me. The charnel house scene at the farmhouse had left me heartsick—one of the reasons I was now questioning my life choices. Was this what the rest of my life would be like? And, if it was, would I crack under the pressure?

Fifty or sixty years of fighting, bloodshed, and danger—was it worth it?

Maybe not, but if I didn't do it, who would? I tried to imagine what Fang would say about now. Probably something about how I wasn't a special little snowflake, and someone else could do the job as well.

No, that Fang was imaginary. The real Fang had more confidence in me than I had in myself and would probably tell me to suck it up and do my job. The thing was, I was becoming weary of the whole life. Maybe I should just quit.

The thought was blissful for one wonderful moment but didn't last. Since I had the ability to help rid the world of evil, I knew I had to use it. What I really needed was a vacation. I entertained myself with planning the perfect trip. I'd buy a car, take Fang, and head off through the Southwest, visiting all those cities I'd always longed to see.

Planning kept me busy for a couple of hours, but then my butt grew numb, and I had to stand and give it some relief.

Andrew cracked open an eye. "Did the portal open?"

"Not yet." I tried to sound upbeat but was beginning to worry. I knew the time dilation aspects made it possible that not much time had elapsed on the other side, but I couldn't help but feel uneasy, abandoned.

"What if it doesn't open?" Andrew asked in a small voice.

"It will," I said, sounding more confident than I felt.

"But it could be a long time. I'm getting thirsty. If time is passing here way too slowly compared to our world, and it takes days or weeks to rescue us, what are we going to drink . . . or eat in the meantime?"

Good question, and one I didn't have an answer for. "It won't come to that," I assured him. But the last thing I needed was for the fire demon to panic. "Don't worry." I enforced that as a command with Lola, so subtly that I hoped he wouldn't notice. He relaxed, closing his eyes again.

Too bad I couldn't reassure myself as easily. Up until now, I'd had utter confidence in Fang and Austin insisting on my rescue. But as more time went on, I wondered. What if something had happened to Shade so he couldn't open a portal anymore? What if something had happened to Micah, and he couldn't tell Shade it was okay to open the portal?

We'd be stuck here forever, with no way home. We could probably find water, but would it be safe to drink? And I hadn't seen anything edible in the small area I'd explored. How long would it take us to die without food or water? And with only Andrew to talk to, how long before I strangled him just to shut him up? I sighed. Killing ourselves might be better than starving to death.

My gut clenched, and I tried to calm myself, but the longer the time went on in this silent, eerie place, the more panic threatened to overwhelm me. I was able to keep Andrew calm with Lola but had no way of doing that for myself. Worse, I was starting to get thirsty and hungry myself.

Finally, when I was beginning to worry about my sanity, I heard a voice.

VAL?

"Fang?" I said aloud, my heart vaulting into my throat. Was I imagining things?

I'M NO FIGMENT, BABE. DID YOU DOUBT WE'D COME FOR YOU?

I almost wept in relief. "Not at all." It had just taken way longer than I'd expected.

Andrew scrambled to his feet. "Where's the portal?" he demanded.

"Wait," I said. "I left a path back."

With nothing to mar my tracks, I was able to follow them back to the flashlight easily, Andrew leaning on me for support. And there, thank heavens, was the blue cloud. Forget testing to see how far Fang's voice would reach—I was so out of here.

I surged through the portal, keeping Andrew upright, and came to an abrupt halt.

It looked as though a tornado had gone off inside, with shattered construction materials, new holes in the walls, and stuff strewn everywhere.

"What happened here?" Then, registering the fact that only Shade and Fang were there to greet us on the other side, I asked, "And where are Austin and Ivy?"

Chapter Twenty-Five

Val

CHILL, FANG TOLD me. THE ROGUES ATTACKED RIGHT AFTER YOU WENT THROUGH THE PORTAL. AUSTIN AND HIS FRIENDS FOUGHT THEM OFF, AND NOW HE'S OFF DEALING WITH THE AFTERMATH. WE SENT IVY HOME, AND IT TOOK A LITTLE WHILE TO FIND MICAH.

Andrew staggered toward Shade, and I dropped to my knees to hug Fang. I'd missed the furry little beast. "Austin and Ivy are okay, then?"

THEY'RE FINE, he assured me. AND I MISSED YOU, TOO. BUT DON'T EVER DO THAT AGAIN.

"I'll try not to." Shade handed us both bottles of water, and I downed mine gratefully. Wiping my mouth, I asked, "How long were we gone?"

MAYBE TWO HOURS.

I nodded. "Felt more like a hundred over on the other side."

THAT LONG?

"Okay, maybe six in reality. Shade's right—time does pass differently in some dimensions."

Shade interrupted. "We need to get out of here, complete the tests."

"We can't—Andrew's hurt."

The fire demon scowled at me. "I want to finish what I started. And Shade can heal me, if you'll help."

"His wound is minor," Shade assured me. "But I want to make sure there's no concussion. You know we can't take him to the ER. You'll need to be the template."

Yeah—if they ran any blood tests, they'd learn real quick how unusual his blood was. If his wound really was minor, we wouldn't share memories during Shade's healing . . . much. Sighing, I said, "Okay, you can use me."

"Good." Shade dragged over a couple of unbroken chairs and had Andrew and me sit in them.

Quickly, Shade touched the back of Andrew's head, then mine. I was ready for the sensation of Shade's healing energies cycling through me, but this time it went much faster, and Andrew was healed so rapidly, we didn't even share more than each other's surface thoughts, which were pretty much what we'd already talked about. Had it gone so quickly because the injury was minor, or because the crystal had sped up Shade's ability?

PROBABLY BOTH.

"I feel much better," Andrew said, rubbing his head in wonder.

"Good," Shade said. "Let's go."

"Where are we going?" I asked.

"Austin said to tell you to come to the clearing near the mansion where you and he trained. It's being watched at all times now, so it will be safer to finish our test that way. Especially tonight. He'll meet us there."

Austin had kindly left one of the vampmobiles for us to use, so Shade drove us to the mansion. I nodded at one of the guards outside the front door, saying, "Austin told us to meet him in the clearing."

He nodded, and I showed Shade and Andrew the way through the trees on the side of the house to the clearing. Austin was there ahead of us, pacing off the distance.

When he saw me, the tension in his face and shoulders seemed to disappear. He was beside me in an instant and grabbed me into a hug. "I knew you'd be okay," he whispered.

Well, I was glad he was, because I hadn't been all that sure of it myself. But I really needed that hug and the reassurance that he still cared for me. "The rogues attacked again?" I asked when he finally released me.

"Yeah, it's getting so we're tripping over them everywhere."

"You think you have a traitor inside the Movement, giving away your location?"

Shade entered the conversation. "They may just have a lot of watchers out, like Micah uses me and others."

Austin nodded. "That's the conclusion I came to. They seem determined to take out our leaders."

"Best way to kill an organization is to chop off its head." I glanced at Austin. "You guys might take a lesson from them. Find this Zachary who's telling them to attack you."

"That's my plan," Austin assured me. "Right after we find Alejandro."

"Good. Speaking of plans . . . what have you come up with to convince Micah to let Shade open a portal?"

Austin scowled. "Beyond finding out how many demons are on the other side, and massing enough people on this side to catch any that come through, I don't really have one. There are too many unknowns."

Had to agree with him there.

"I'll help," Andrew said. "But we need to finish the testing first."

He was obviously eager to continue being of service, and we did need to know how far Fang's range would extend. As before, we all stood on one side of the clearing while Shade did his thing, and Andrew went through the portal into that same dimension. This time, there were no glitches, and we soon learned that Fang could sense Andrew on the other side within about fifty feet in any direction.

Andrew returned, and Austin clapped a hand on his shoulder. "Thank you. This will help a great deal."

Andrew puffed up like a proud rooster, and I hid a smile. I was glad the fire demon had gotten the approval he craved. It was as if Austin had sensed he'd needed it.

NAW, JUST THE MARK OF A GOOD LEADER, Fang said. HE WOULD'VE SAID IT WHETHER ANDREW NEEDED IT OR NOT.

Wasn't going to argue there. Then a thought suddenly occurred to me. "But this is a different dimension than the demon one. Will the distances be the same?"

Consternation showed on Austin's and Andrew's faces, but Shade said, "Yes, they would. My father taught us that time may change, but distances and locations are fixed. Otherwise, portals wouldn't open in the same spot each time."

Well, that was a relief.

Austin glanced at the two guys. "Can you find your way out? Val and I will see if we can come up with a better plan."

"I can help with that," Shade said stubbornly.

"I know you can," Austin said, more patient than I would've been. "But we should have a lot of vampires arriving starting about eleven thirty, and you don't want *him* around when they do." He nodded at Andrew.

Yeah—some of the vampires might still hold a grudge against the fire demon who'd tried to burn down their home, even though he'd helped save it later.

Andrew looked a little sick. "Yeah, better go."

"Why don't you come with us?" Shade asked Austin.

"Because I have to meet Luis at midnight."

Oh, crap, I'd forgotten this was the night of their duel.

"Can't it wait?" Shade asked.

"No, I have to do this," Austin said sternly.

"He really does," I told Shade. "We'll contact you later."

He nodded, then grabbed Andrew's arm, and the two of them left, Fang following to make sure they made it okay.

Austin pulled me into the darkness of the trees, and I glanced up at him and asked, "So what's the plan?"

"We still have twenty minutes before Rosa arrives, so . . . this," he said and leaned down to kiss me.

I definitely approved. Austin pulled back and regarded me in the dim light. "I'm sorry I acted like such a turd. But when you went through that portal, and I thought I'd lost you . . ." He shook his head. "Well, let's just say I don't ever want to go through that again."

Well, didn't that make me feel all tingly and warm inside? "It's okay," I told him softly and tilted my head for another kiss.

We made out for a few minutes in silence, until a buzzing against my hip brought me back to the here and now. Austin pulled out his phone, read it, then showed me the message: *Someone's coming.*

He tapped the time—forty-five minutes until showtime—then put a finger to his lips. I nodded silently. It was a little too early for the others. Who was this? Someone overeager to arrive early for the duel? What would be the point?

I heard the murmur of voices as they approached the clearing—a man and a woman.

IT'S LUIS AND LISETTE, Fang told me. WITH A COUPLE OF HER TWEEDLES FOLLOWING A FEW PACES BEHIND. DON'T WORRY—I'VE GONE TO GROUND. THEY DON'T KNOW I'M HERE.

When they got closer, I could make out their words.

"—got to win," Lisette said.

"Don't worry, I will," Luis said with utter confidence as he stepped into the clearing. "I have to, for our plan to succeed."

Luis and Lisette were in on something together? What? And why the hell was she wearing a filmy, floaty pink dress to a duel, for heaven's sake? Someone might choke her with that wispy scarf around her neck.

YOU VOLUNTEERING?

Maybe.

I figured we'd stay quiet and hope they'd spill their whole nefarious scheme, but Austin stepped out of hiding and asked, "What plan?"

Okay, that worked, too.

Luis scowled. "What are you doing here so early?"

Austin lifted an eyebrow. "I could ask the same of you. But I, for one, am working with Val to find a way to save Alejandro. What's *your* plan?"

Lisette tossed her head as her two "bodyguards" came up behind her. "We do not need to tell you anything," she said in her snooty French accent.

Fine. If she wanted to play hardball, I'd score before she did. Thrusting Lola into the tweedle on her right, I commanded him, "Tell us her plan."

Obediently, he blurted out, "Her plan is to help Luis win so he can take over the Movement."

Luis lunged for the tweedle, but Lisette shoved him aside before he could damage her pretty boy toy. "Stop. The succubus is forcing him."

Luis glared at me, and I shrugged. "I could force you instead, if you prefer."

Lisette gestured airily. "There is no need. You will find out soon enough once Luis wins."

OVERCONFIDENT MUCH? Fang sneered and came trotting in to stand next to me.

"Are you behind the attacks?" Austin asked Lisette.

"Mais non," she exclaimed, looking genuinely surprised. "You are allies. I would not do such a thing."

Twenty questions could take forever to get to the truth. Impatient, I told the tweedle, "Tell us why she wants Luis in charge."

He obediently responded, "Because she no longer supports Alejandro's desire to bring us to the public's attention."

Austin glared at Luis. "Is that why you've been so incompetent in getting anywhere on the political front? You agree with her?"

Pointedly ignoring Austin's insult, Luis said, "I have begun to believe as Lisette does, that coming out to the public is a bad idea. Public hysteria over the so-called *chupacabra* attacks in her city proved that. No one wants another Inquisition."

So that was a yes.

I WONDER WHAT SHE PROMISED HIM, Fang drawled.

Yeah, I wouldn't put it past Lisette to use her body to get her way. "So, if you no longer support Alejandro's objectives, why are you looking so hard for him?" I asked.

"He isn't," Austin drawled. "He talks a good game, but if you notice, he hasn't done a damned thing to help find him."

"You don't believe in the Movement's aims anymore?" I asked incredulously.

"Some of them," Luis snapped. "Alejandro is correct in providing blood banks to sate the hungry, in refusing to drink from unwilling victims, because it helps to keep us hidden from public view. But revealing our existence will do nothing but frighten the sheep. And when sheep become frightened, they turn into wolves. There would be a bloodbath unprecedented since the burning times."

No wonder he was so harsh in training the new recruits—he was anticipating widespread carnage.

"Are you saying you don't *want* Alejandro back?" Austin asked.

Luis didn't answer, which was an answer in itself.

"Did you try talking to Alejandro about this?" I asked Luis.

"Of course I did," he all but spat. "He is adamant. He will be the death of us all."

Micah had made similar arguments in keeping their existence a secret. I had to admit that Luis had a good point. But though I kind of agreed with him, I hated his methods. "That's no reason to leave him stranded in another dimension," I protested.

"What do you mean, in another dimension?" Luis asked.

Oops. I'd forgotten he didn't know. He was unlikely at this point to wring secrets from Shade, but I didn't need to point to the shadow demon as the crux of solving the problem, either. I shrugged, keeping it vague. "We have figured out that he was accidentally transported to the demon dimension. We know where he is and how to retrieve him."

"Perhaps we should leave him there," Lisette said.

"Out of the question," Austin snapped.

Luis's eyes narrowed. "You are not the leader of this organization."

"Neither are you," Austin countered.

Rosa stepped from out of the trees. "That is enough," she said, eyes sparking with anger. "If you know how to rescue Alejandro, you must do so immediately."

Luis whirled on her. "*You* are not the leader, either. That is what this duel tonight is going to establish. And when I win, you will all do as I say."

And that meant not rescuing Alejandro. Crap.

Rosa took two more steps toward him, her fists clenched. "The duel is no longer necessary. Once Alejandro comes back, he is in charge."

Luis scowled at me. "Is there a guarantee he is alive and well in a dimension full of demons?" he asked in an imperious tone.

"No, but—"

Austin interrupted me. "It's okay, Val, Rosa. I've had enough. Let's do this." Turning to Luis, he said, "If I win this duel, you swear to help rescue Alejandro?"

Luis fought with himself for a moment, then said, "Yes. But if I win, we will not."

Rosa almost growled. "If Luis wins, I will fight him myself."

"That is your right," Luis sneered, but everyone could tell he didn't consider her a threat. In fact, he didn't seem to consider Austin a threat, either. What was up with that?

HE PROBABLY DISCOVERED HE'S STRONGER THAN HE WAS BEFORE, Fang suggested. BUT DOESN'T REALIZE AUSTIN IS, TOO. AND AUSTIN WAS MUCH CLOSER TO THE AMULET.

Ah, yes, he didn't have the benefit of Ivy's insight on what had happened after the shattering of the crystal. Maybe Austin could use that to his advantage.

"Don't worry," Austin told Rosa. "I'll win."

"How?" Luis asked. "By using your pet demon to force me to submit to you?"

"No, I'll win fair and square," Austin said. "Val, will you agree to not interfere?"

I hesitated for a moment. "Is this fight to the death?"

Obviously understanding the duel was going to happen whether she wanted it to or not, Rosa said, "No, the Movement's rules do not allow that, and as arbitrator, I will enforce them. The fight is over when one is unconscious or submits to the other."

"What about her?" I asked, glancing pointedly at Lisette.

"She will not interfere, either," Luis said.

Lisette looked annoyed but jerked her head in a nod.

"You do not know our ways," Rosa said to me, "so I will explain. During the duel, no one may interfere. Anyone who does will be punished. Severely."

Oooookay.

AGREE, VAL. AUSTIN DOESN'T NEED YOUR HELP.

"Okay, I'll abide by your rules if everyone else does." Otherwise, I was afraid they'd kick me out, and I wouldn't be able to watch the outcome for myself.

"Thank you," Austin said softly.

Rosa checked her watch. “We still have fifteen minutes before the duel is scheduled to begin. I suggest you ready yourselves.”

Oh, crap. This was really going to happen.

Chapter Twenty-Six

Austin

FINALLY, THIS WAS going to happen. Austin had resisted the duel out of respect for Alejandro and to keep order within the organization, but he couldn't deny that it had been a long time in coming. Perhaps too long.

The stakes were never higher. Alejandro's life and the future of the organization were at risk, and Austin owed it to Rosa and Alejandro to win—decisively. For this to work, there could be no question in anyone's mind that Austin was the better leader.

Though, in Austin's opinion, Luis demonstrated his unfitness for command on a daily basis, many in the organization still held to the old ways, where might meant right. The ancient way of handling leadership challenges and disagreements still held strong in the organization, no matter how outdated it was. Luckily, Alejandro had modified the rules to outlaw killing opponents in duels and challenges. Otherwise, they might have greatly reduced numbers, given the amount of testosterone saturating the membership.

At this moment, though, Austin could see why duels to the death had been allowed in the past. Even if he won, he'd have to worry about Luis subverting his every move in the future.

Well, he'd deal with that when it happened. For now, he had to defeat Luis so he could rescue Alejandro.

"What kind of duel is this?" Val asked quietly, looking worried. "Crossbows at twenty paces? Or do you have your choice of weapons?"

"No, it's hand-to-hand combat—no weapons allowed. Just brute strength and the ability to outthink your opponent."

Val seemed to relax. "Then you've got it in the bag." She glanced up at him. "Unless he cheats."

"He can't," Austin assured her. "Any fighter who does so automatically forfeits, and if they kill their opponent, they, in turn, will lose their life."

"Not exactly reassuring for the person who's killed in the first place."

"It won't come to that." Luis was too proud to risk humiliation. And that had given Austin the basis of his strategy for the coming duel.

"What if Lisette or one of his followers tries something hinky?"

"They won't. The penalties are almost as severe for interfering with a duel."

"Okay," Val said. Austin hoped she'd be satisfied with that explanation—he didn't want to go into the ancient forms of torture considered acceptable as punishment.

He nuzzled her neck, whispering under the cover of the crowd's noise. "And I'm counting on you to stop him or Lisette's men if it goes that far."

Startled, Val stared at him open-mouthed. "But I promised—"

"*Only* if someone tries to kill me," Austin stressed. He knew he could count on Val to ensure nothing "hinky" occurred. "And Fang didn't promise anything."

Val glanced down at her hellhound. "He wondered why everyone else was ignoring the other sentient being in the clearing. But you weren't, were you?"

"Nope."

"Okay," she whispered. "But I hope it isn't necessary."

Rosa was beginning to shoo people into position. Time to face the music. "It's starting soon. Are you going to stay and watch?"

"Of course! I have to cheer you on, right?"

Pleased, Austin smiled down at her. "I hope you don't mean that literally. Noise and shouts can sometimes be misconstrued as interfering."

"In that case, I'll keep all the 'rah, rah Austin' comments between Fang and me."

"Good plan. But there's nothing wrong with a combatant accepting a favor from a lovely lady . . ." He nodded to where Lisette was pulling the filmy pink scarf from her neck and tucking it into Luis's shirtfront.

Val's eyes narrowed. "I'd give you a wooden stake, but that's probably not allowed, huh?"

He suppressed a chuckle. "Definitely not."

"Well, I'm not taking any clothes off in front of this crowd," she said, trying to make a joke, but Austin could tell it bothered her that she didn't have something to give him.

"It's not really necessary," Austin reassured her. He'd just wanted to give her a way to feel a part of what was going on.

She glanced down at Fang. "Oh, Fang reminded me I do have something." She pulled off the necklace Ivy had given her. "Here—this has the piece of the amulet that broke." She reached up to undo the clasp.

Accepting it, Austin placed the necklace in his front jeans pocket where it probably wouldn't be damaged. "What I was really hoping for was a kiss," he told her with a grin.

Val's eyes darted back and forth. "In front of them?"

"Why not? Everyone knows how I feel about you, anyway."

"Okay, if you insist," Val said, and her cheeks turned a rosy shade of pink discernible to his enhanced vision even in the dark of the night.

He kissed her firmly, not lingering in a show for the prurient, but not a slow peck, either. Leaning back away from her, he flicked his finger against her soft cheek. "There. That should help me win all manner of tournaments, m'lady."

"This will even more," Val said softly. She kissed him again, but this time, sent Lola surging into his chakras. Instead of draining energy from him, Val did something unexpected—she sent energy into him, making him feel strong and vibrant.

When she finished, Val pulled away and murmured, "Just giving you back what you gave to me. Now you're at full capacity."

He couldn't argue with that and didn't want to. She'd made him feel powerful, supremely male, able to do anything.

"Gentlemen," Rosa said impatiently. "If you're ready?"

Austin pulled away from Val and was happy to see there was no fear in her eyes—only acceptance, encouragement, and utter faith in him. It made him want to live up to that belief. He removed his Stetson and plopped it on Val's head. "Hold that for me, darlin'."

"Everyone but Luis and Austin will now leave the clearing," Rosa instructed.

Austin had been so busy with Val that he hadn't noticed the multitude of people who had come to watch the duel. It seemed everyone in the Movement wanted to see the outcome for themselves. The circle was ringed with spectators packed shoulder to shoulder, with others peering over their heads and some climbing onto the convenient low branches of the live oak trees.

It annoyed him a little that they were so eager to watch the duel, then realized this was as important to them as it was to him. It made him even more determined to win. Leaving Luis in charge of the organization would be a huge mistake.

Rosa made room for Val, Fang, and Lisette next to her at one point of the circle, no doubt so she could keep an eye on them. Once everyone was in place, she called out, "The first combatant to lose consciousness or yield to their opponent loses the bout. If you receive assistance or use a weapon other than your body, you will forfeit the match with dire consequences. Spectators will remain silent so as to not distract the combatants. Anyone who interferes in the match in any way will be severely punished. Is this understood?"

Austin and Luis said, "Yes," in unison. There were murmurs in the audience among those who hadn't witnessed or heard of duels before, but they soon subsided.

"Then take your positions," she ordered.

Austin faced Luis, both standing about ten feet in front of the spectators, on opposite sides of the circle. That left about ten feet between them. They were pretty evenly matched. Luis was a little heavier and more vicious, but Austin had a longer reach and a cooler head. He'd need both to win this bout.

As Austin shook his arms and legs to loosen up, he tried to gauge Luis's most probable move. Austin hadn't paid all that much attention to Luis's fighting style, but, knowing the man's personality, Austin figured he'd try to take him down as soon as possible, counting on the element of surprise and the added advantage he'd received from the shattered crystal to defeat Austin in the shortest time possible.

Austin didn't have a plan so much as a strategy. Keep calm and humiliate Luis to make him so angry, the Spaniard would make stupid mistakes. Luis would never yield, so the only option was to render him unconscious. Contrary to popular belief, blood still flowed in a vampire's veins, so cutting off blood flow to the brain would render him unconscious, and so would giving him a concussion or cutting off his air.

"Begin," Rosa exclaimed.

Luis bellowed and charged Austin like a bull, trying to blitz him with sheer strength.

Just as he'd expected.

Austin sidestepped with a lightning-fast fluid movement, and, as Luis stumbled past, Austin struck him across the face with his open palm—a gesture of contempt. Shocked exclamations came from the crowd, along with a couple of chuckles. *One point to me.*

"Silence," Rosa reminded them all as Luis staggered to a halt.

He turned to face Austin, his face red and his expression outraged. "You dare?"

Austin merely grinned at him, using beckoning motions to egg him on.

That's when Luis lost it. He whirled with a snarl, and, without telegraphing his move, he leapt up for a roundhouse kick to Austin's head.

Austin deflected it—barely—and grabbed Luis's leg, throwing him onto his back on the ground. With a roar, Luis leapt to his feet and onto Austin like a madman. Damn, the man caught him off guard. They both slammed to the ground, Austin underneath, as Luis grappled with him, attempting to immobilize him.

No way would he let that happen. Luis's hold wasn't as good as it should have been since he'd lost his cool. Austin retained his and struck the inside of Luis's elbow so his grip loosened, and Austin was able to jump free.

From the ground, Luis kicked out and tripped him. Austin fell backward but used his sharp elbow to cushion his landing in Luis's stomach. The contact left Austin off balance for a moment, and though Luis let out an *oof*, he got in a punch to Austin's head. Though he'd thankfully missed Austin's temple, Luis had scored a hard hit to his left eye, and it was bleeding.

Realizing he'd probably lose half of his field of vision soon, Austin careened to his feet and took an instant to brush the blood out of his eye as Luis surged up from the ground, his head barreling toward Austin's stomach.

Austin turned to avoid the head-butt, but though Luis missed his stomach, he caught Austin on his side, in the ribs. In fact, it felt like at least one of them cracked. It hurt like hell but didn't knock the wind out of him.

He'd had enough, and Luis was enraged enough now, so Austin took the offense. He chopped down hard on the back of Luis's head, then kneed him in the face. Luis started to fall, then regained his footing and reeled away backward, shaking his head.

Following up on his advantage, Austin advanced on Luis and hit him with an uppercut, hoping the blow to his chin would cause a knockout. No such luck.

Luis surged back and attempted another punch of his own. Just where Austin wanted him. He deflected Luis's arm by shoving it aside and trapping it between their bodies, then caught him in a choke hold, cutting the flow on his carotid arteries.

Luis tucked his chin and pulled on Austin's arm in an effort to get more air and blood flow, to no avail. There was no way Austin was giving in. When that didn't work, Luis tried to distract Austin and make him lose his grip by using his heavy boots to stomp on his foot, then slugged his free arm into Austin's head and ribs. Austin grunted but held on. Getting desperate, Luis got in a couple of punches to the kidneys and even a shot to the groin.

Austin held on grimly, taking the pain and punishment without letting go or giving in. Luis's struggles slowed, then ceased altogether. Austin held on a second longer, just to make sure Luis wasn't bluffing, then let go. Luis slumped to the ground, clearly unconscious.

He wouldn't be out long, but he didn't need to be—the fight was over, and Austin had won. He rested his hands on his thighs, trying to control the pain and get his bearings back.

The roar of approval was immediate and deafening. Surprised, Austin glanced at Rosa out of his right eye, since the left was rapidly swelling shut. She strode to the center of the clearing and grinned at him. Raising his arm in triumph, she yelled, "Austin is the winner!" He could barely hear her above the roar of the crowd.

The crowd rushed the clearing, but Val got to him first. She grabbed him in a hug as if she'd never let go. He winced.

"You're hurt," she said, pulling back and reaching up to touch the wound above his eye.

Though his many aches and pains were screaming at him, Austin said, "It's nothing," and removed his hat from her head to plunk it back on his own. He wasn't entirely lying—he might be in pain, but he'd heal soon enough, and it was worth it to get this settled once and for all. If Luis honored his word, of course.

Some of Luis's followers dragged him off to the side so he wouldn't be trampled, and Rosa held her arms up. "Silence, everyone, please." When they all finally quieted, she said, "Austin, as winner of the duel and the de facto leader of the San Antonio New Blood Movement, do you have anything to say?"

Though he'd known it was necessary to keep Luis in line, Austin had humiliated the man enough for one day. Instead of crowing about his victory, he said simply so everyone could hear, "The true leader of the organization is Alejandro. We have discovered where he is and how to rescue him. With everyone's help here, we can do so first thing tomorrow night. Will you help me?"

Another roar of approval filled the air as Luis rose shakily to his feet, assisted by his minions.

"What about Luis?" someone asked from the back.

Austin wasn't sure exactly what the man was asking but chose to believe he was inquiring about the rescue. "Luis has agreed to assist with saving Alejandro."

He heard a couple of snorts of disbelief, and Luis drew himself up to his full height, his nose in the air, his expression hard as stone. "I have given my word. I will assist in freeing Alejandro from his imprisonment."

He didn't promise more, and Austin didn't expect it. That was all he wanted from Luis—for now.

"We will all meet at the blood demon's house immediately after sunset tomorrow," Austin said dismissively. "Go, prepare yourselves."

Val stood off to the side as many lingered to slap him on his back or congratulate him on his victory—many more than he'd expected, in fact.

When Gwen and Elspeth approached at the end, he asked in surprise, "You came?"

"We wanted to support you," Gwen said. "Did you doubt it?"

"No, but I didn't think you'd want to witness the fight, especially given the way Luis . . . trained you." Scared the hell out of them was more like it.

"And that is precisely why we came," Elspeth informed him. "We needed to know immediately if we could continue belonging to this organization."

There was a wrinkle Austin hadn't considered—how many would have left if Luis had won? Or been allowed to leave? And how many would leave now that Austin had won?

Gwen, ever the nurse, didn't give him a chance to think about it as she peered up at his eye. "You need to get that looked at."

He waved away her concern and tugged his hat lower. "I'll be fine. I wouldn't want to battle full demons right this moment, but I should be fully healed after a restoring sleep."

Elspeth patted Gwen's arm. "He's right. He'll heal without us. Come, let us return to our duties."

"Okay," Gwen said, then reached up to kiss him on the cheek. "You have no idea how relieved everyone is that you've won."

Bemused, Austin watched them leave. Now, no one was left but Val and Fang. He pulled her necklace from his pocket and inspected it. "See? No damage."

Val refastened the necklace with an odd expression on her face.

"What's wrong?" he asked.

"Oh, nothing. I'm glad you won and that you've rallied everyone to rescue Alejandro. But there's just one problem—you haven't convinced Micah to let Shade open the portal yet."

Austin tried to raise an eyebrow, but it hurt too much. "Is that really necessary now that we know you can force Shade to open the portal . . . if you choose?"

"Yes, it's necessary," Val said firmly. "Micah is my boss. Would you go against *Alejandro's* wishes?"

"If it was the right thing to do," Austin said stubbornly.

Fang snorted, as if the hellhound knew he was lying. And if Fang thought it, Val knew it, too.

"Alejandro and I helped rescue Micah when he was kidnapped," he reminded her.

"From *one* demon, not a freakin' horde of them. And the rest of the world wasn't in danger." She shook her head. "You'd better come up with a doable plan fast, or Micah will never agree."

"He'll agree," Austin said with confidence. He had to.

Chapter Twenty-Seven

Val

I HEADED HOME after the duel, glad it was done and that Austin had won—not that I had any doubt he would, but I hadn't been sure Luis would play it honestly. In any case, I was exhausted and wanted to rest.

Unfortunately, Ivy had let Shade into the townhouse, and they were both waiting for me when I got home, reading the encyclopedia.

"What's the matter?" Ivy asked, seeing my face. "Austin didn't lose, did he?"

"No, I'm just tired." I gave her a weary smile. "Those two hours you guys spent in this world while I was trapped in the other were more like six to me." I hadn't done anything physically demanding, but it still felt as if I'd been up for days.

WORRY WILL TAKE A TOLL ON YA, Fang said sympathetically.

Yeah—and I'd done plenty of that in the other dimension and while watching Austin fight—not that I'd let him see anything but confidence in his ability.

"Where's Austin?" Shade asked. "Aren't we going to do the rescue now?"

His eager puppy bounciness made me want to slug him. "Austin and Luis were both injured in the fight and need a little time to heal."

"I can—"

"No," I said, stopping him with a raised hand. "They want to heal on their own. Besides, Austin has already rallied everyone to meet tomorrow night at the blood mansion." I dropped into the soft cushions of the couch, which felt really good right now.

"Val needs rest, too," Ivy reminded him.

Amen to that. "Besides, you still need a plan Micah will agree to."

"But—"

I shook my head. "Enough, Shade, please. I've thought about it, and I'm not going to go against Micah's wishes. If he feels it's too dangerous, and that he doesn't want to risk many people to rescue a few,

I'm not going to argue with him." Before Shade could put forth another argument, I said, "It's him you need to convince, not me. I'll do whatever Micah says."

WAY TO DUMP THE RESPONSIBILITY ON SOMEONE ELSE, Fang snarked.

Yeah, well, that's why Micah gets paid the big bucks.

"I already called and asked him to meet us here," Shade said stubbornly. "If you'll call Austin and have him come over, we can settle this now. There are still a couple of hours until dawn."

"He's healing and just settling in to his new job—"

"That's BS, and you know it. This is the most important thing to Austin right now—and to me. Let's get it settled."

HE'S NOT GOING TO GIVE UP, Fang warned me.

"Okay, okay." I texted Austin quickly, and he texted right back. "He's coming over," I said wearily. "Can I rest now?"

The doorbell rang, and Ivy answered it, letting Micah in. Guess not.

"We're waiting for Austin," Shade told him. "I'm sure he has a plan by now."

DOES HE? Fang asked me.

Not so far as I know. At least, not one Micah will buy.

AH, I SEE. SHADE IS IN THE LAND OF WISHFUL THINKING. WE ALL LIVE THERE SOMETIMES.

Truth.

Micah nodded, and Ivy took over hostess duties, offering our guests drinks. When she brought us each a soft drink, Micah glanced down at the books on the coffee table alongside Shade's laptop. "Are you about done compiling the digital list of known demons, Shade?"

"Yes, I'm done with that, but a list of the spells would come in handy, so I've been trying to record them, too."

It would be handy, but. . . . "The spells?" I said in disbelief. "That's not—"

"Just a listing for an index," Shade assured me. "None of the details. And none of this is connected to the Internet, so you don't have to worry about it getting into someone else's hands." He shook his head. "But it's getting harder and harder to read them. Sometimes it's as if the book doesn't want me to know what the spells are."

I nodded. "The books are supposed to open up fully only to the Keeper." And Shade was only an alternate.

"But Ivy doesn't seem to have a problem reading them," Shade said.

I glanced at my roomie. "One of your stones helping you?"

She shrugged. "I don't know. Maybe. But the text doesn't seem to blur and twist for me the way Shade said it's doing for him."

"But I thought you used some spells, Shade." He'd used the one-way portal, blocked Fang, talked to the books, and who knew what else.

"I did," Shade said. "But it's harder now. I only seem to be able to read one complete spell at a sitting, though I can skim the titles, a bit."

Odd.

MAYBE THE BOOKS DON'T LIKE HIM SO MUCH ANYMORE, Fang suggested.

Could be. Fang must have broadcast that to Micah and Ivy as well, because they glanced down at him.

Micah looked thoughtful. "Didn't you say before that only potential keepers can use spells in the books?"

Shade answered him. "Yes—and mage demons, of course, but we've taken care of those. It seems the Keeper can use any spell, but potential keepers can only use some of them."

"Which ones?" Micah asked.

"I don't know—it seems to change at the books' whim."

Micah nodded. "You think Ivy might be a potential keeper, and that's why she can read it?"

"Why don't you ask the books?" I suggested. "Shade can talk to them with a spell they gave him."

Micah raised an eyebrow, and Shade opened one of the books to a place he'd bookmarked. "Is Ivy a potential keeper?" he asked.

Yes.

"Why do you need so many?" Shade asked.

We don't. We only need one keeper. And we choose Ivy Weiss.

Everyone looked stunned, especially Ivy. "What? What does that mean?" she asked.

"Explain," Shade told the books tersely.

The keeper has a great responsibility—to use our power wisely, keep us safe, and keep herself safe. With mage demons no longer a threat, our need is less for protection than it is for continuity and reliability. The demons known as Val and Shade have risked themselves too much and plan to do so even more in the future. Ivy Weiss will be a wiser Keeper.

Well, I couldn't deny I was a bit offended that they didn't want me anymore, but since the demon from the broken crystal had restored my powers, I didn't really need the strength spell the books had provided. I also had to admit to some relief. I wasn't a scholar like Shade—I hated doing research in them. And I hated the balancing act I had to perform between Lola's powers and the spells I'd used. Now that crossing dimensions had stripped the spells from me, I didn't have to worry about them anymore either.

"I don't even know if I want this," Ivy protested.

"Why Ivy?" Shade asked the books, sounding annoyed. He had more to lose than I did.

Because she has the gemstones to assist her, along with the wisdom and maturity to handle the responsibility without harm to herself or others.

Huh. Did the books just call me immature?

Fang snorted. SURE SOUNDED LIKE IT.

Fine. I didn't need them anyway.

AAAAND YOU JUST PROVED THEIR POINT.

Micah looked thoughtful. "Ivy, I believe you were planning to stay here in San Antonio?"

"Yes," she said cautiously. "But I'm not sure about this. What does being Keeper entail?"

I shrugged. "Well, they're not worried about mage demons anymore and don't need protection, so mainly, it means looking up spells in the encyclopedia and using them to help the Underground when necessary." I paused, then added, "So far, I've used a locator spell, a strength spell, and an exorcism one. None of those are dangerous in and of themselves, unless you put yourself in harm's way." Which is what the books were probably getting at. "The books are selfish in getting what they need to survive," I added. "They were made that way deliberately, to protect themselves at all costs. And it looks like they think you are the best person for the job. Keep them safe, use them wisely, and I think you'll be a great keeper."

"I agree," Micah said. "And you would be doing us a great favor in taking on this job."

Ivy blew out a breath. "I . . . okay. I was wondering how I'd fit into your organization here, anyway. Looks like the books made the decision for me."

And with her agreement, it felt as if a great weight had been lifted from my shoulders. Interesting—I hadn't even realized it had felt like a burden before.

A knock came at the door then, and Ivy let Austin in. It hadn't been all that long since the fight, but he looked better already—the bruising around his eye looked days old, and the cut was nearly healed.

"Come tell Micah your plan," Shade urged.

Austin took off his hat and sat next to me, his arm along the back of the couch behind me. Lola burbled happily, making me feel all smooshy and girly inside.

HE'S GOOD FOR YOU, Fang said. A VAMPIRE BOYFRIEND . . . WHO WOULDA THUNK IT?

Certainly not me. Six months ago, I hadn't even realized there was such a thing as a "good" vampire, and I'd pretty much slain every bloodsucker I met.

"The plan is simple," he told Micah. "Tomorrow night, Shade will open a portal, small enough that no one can come through from the other side. Fang will be able to tell us how many demons are there, so we'll be prepared and know how many people we need to take through to combat the demons on the other side, if any. After my strike force goes through, Shade can reduce the size of the portal again so no one can get through, but Fang can still monitor what's going on over there."

"How can Fang monitor anything?" Micah asked. "He can't read your mind."

"No, but he can Val's."

Micah raised an eyebrow. "You will not risk my Paladin without my permission."

Austin glanced at me, but I kept my mouth shut and held my hands up in surrender. I wasn't going to get in on this argument. "It doesn't have to be me," I said, trying not to sound as if I were taking sides. "Any demon will do. I'm sure Andrew would volunteer."

"I know he would," Shade said eagerly.

"*If* I agree to let you open the portal," Micah reminded him.

"Why wouldn't you?" Shade asked.

"Because the plan is flawed. You may know where Alejandro went through, but there is no guarantee he'll still be in the same spot days later. And you have no idea what's waiting for you on the other side."

"I might be able to help with that," Ivy said. When we all turned to look at her, she added, "When Andrew went through the portal, I gave him a stone to enhance communication. While he was there, I was able to still hear the stone. It was able to give me some intel on the situation on the other side. If we toss a stone through the portal, we could get at least some information that way."

"And I will have personnel massing on this side," Austin said, "ready to strike down any demons who make it through. With the help of some of your people, we should be able to keep the danger contained."

"See?" Shade said, as if the question was settled.

Micah shook his head. "The problem still remains that you don't know how long it will take to find him or how fast time is passing over there. How long can you keep a portal open, Shade? Can you do it for hours? Days? If you can't, what happens to the people on the other side when they need to come back?"

Shade kept silent for a moment, as we all thought about how complicated this could get. But he wasn't about to give up so easily. "If I create a one-way portal to take us through, with plenty of provisions, I can bring us back with another one-way portal when it's safe."

"If you're still alive," Micah countered. "There's no guarantee you'd survive, and if you're dead or unconscious, the rest of the team will be trapped there, forever."

Dang, Micah had some good points.

"There are always problems with any plan," Austin gritted out. "We won't know what we need until we get there and assess the situation."

"And that's why I can't agree," Micah said, looking regretful. "My first duty is to the Demon Underground, then to the people of San Antonio. You know how much damage Emmanuel did—and he was only one demon. Imagine what a whole horde could do. I can't risk the lives of everyone in the city to rescue one man."

"Two men and a woman," Shade reminded him. "Did you hear back from Diesel yet?"

"Yes," Micah confirmed. "Diesel called me back. His hellhound Max admits he may have lied when saying Sharra was dead."

"May have?" I repeated. "Was she alive or not?"

"He doesn't know. He said what he had to say to keep the portal closed."

"I knew it," Shade exclaimed. "Sharra is alive."

Micah shook his head. "You don't know that for sure. Nor do we know if Alejandro and Vincent are still alive."

Austin took a deep breath. "Alejandro didn't hesitate when it came to assisting in your rescue," he said softly. "Won't you do the same for him?"

OH, MY. HE WENT THERE, Fang said admiringly.

Well, he was a hard man who tried hard to be civilized, but that didn't mean he backed down.

Micah stared down at his hands. "Before I left the club, Tessa gave me a prophecy about this situation. She said, 'Trust in the Paladin's judgment.' " He glanced up at me, apology in his eyes. "So, Val, you have all the data, both pro and con. What should we do?"

Fang hooted. SO MUCH FOR ABDICATING RESPONSIBILITY.

Well, crap. I didn't want to make this decision, didn't want to screw anything up, or tick off anyone I cared about.

Everyone assumed I was going to take their side. "Can you let me sleep on it?" I asked, stalling for more time.

"No," Micah said. "You have all the information you need. Decide now, please."

What should I do? I asked Fang plaintively. No matter what choice I made, it would piss someone off.

TESSA SAID TO TRUST THE PALADIN'S JUDGMENT, NOT FANG THE WONDER DOG'S. BUT WHATEVER YOU DECIDE, I'LL BACK YOU. AND SO WILL MICAH AND AUSTIN.

I sighed and gave in. "Okay, give me a minute to think."

I closed my eyes and let the details flow through my mind. Both sides had excellent arguments. I would definitely like to see Alejandro and Vincent back in this dimension. Not only because I liked them, but because Alejandro could help stabilize the uncertainty that was threatening to tear his Movement apart. And bringing Sharra back—dead or alive—would do a lot toward making me feel less guilty about screwing up Shade's life.

But Micah had a good question. Was it worth risking the lives of many people to save just a few? Especially when the outcome was so in doubt?

The arguments went around and around in my head, and I didn't know what to do. *Help me*, I begged Fang.

TESSA HAS CONFIDENCE YOU KNOW THE RIGHT THING TO DO. WHAT IS IT?

I had no idea. What *was* right? Going with my feelings and bringing them back despite the consequences? Or using cold, hard logic and abandoning them there?

Abandoning . . . that word struck a nerve. When I'd been lost for only a few hours in the other dimension, the thought of not being able to return home had frightened me more than any vampire or demon I'd ever faced, and I hadn't even been in danger. I couldn't get an image of Sharra out of my head, huddled in a corner, wondering how long to wait. Wondering if anyone would come.

I couldn't abandon anyone to that sort of fate. No matter what the consequences, I knew I would've desperately wanted someone to rescue me. I looked at Austin. I looked at Shade. I looked at Fang, and I knew. As surely as they came for me despite the consequences, we were coming for Sharra. For Alejandro. For Vincent.

They were family. You came for family. It was the reason I was Paladin—to protect my family. I had to remember that. I had to stop putting up walls and protecting myself by pushing them away and assuming they couldn't love me, forgive me . . . trust me to be more than just a Paladin. I was Paladin because they trusted me to come for them. No matter what.

I took a deep breath and announced, "I've decided. We're going in."

Austin expelled a relieved breath as Shade shouted, "Yes!"

Micah sighed and nodded. "I trust you as well as Tessa's prophecies. We will give the members of the Underground the opportunity to assist if they wish, but I will not require them to do so. Shade, I give you permission to open whatever kind of portal you need tomorrow night. Val will make the decision as to when, where, and how long, and you will abide by her decision."

"You got it," Shade said exultantly.

"And Austin," Micah continued grimly. "I must insist that whether Alejandro returns or not, you must agree to talks with demons and humans about revealing yourselves to the world."

"Done," Austin said instantly, giving me a one-armed hug I wasn't sure I deserved.

YOU MADE THE RIGHT DECISION, Fang assured me.

Yeah, I thought so too. I just hoped it wasn't too late.

Chapter Twenty-Eight

Val

IVY, FANG, AND I drove up to the blood house an hour after sunset the next day. There were a lot of black vampmobiles parked on the surrounding streets, along with other less discreet vehicles owned by demons. I'd called Lt. Ramirez last night, and he'd agreed to provide some members of the SCU to run interference with the neighbors and provide a last line of defense. Lord, I hoped they weren't needed.

That's when the fear hit me. Not of the fighting, not of the raving demons on the other side, but of having made the wrong decision. Who was I to choose a path that might result in some people losing their lives or being trapped forever in a demon dimension?

YOU ARE THE PALADIN OF THE DEMON UNDERGROUND, Fang reminded me. THAT GIVES YOU GREAT POWER. AND, AS THEY SAY, WITH GREAT POWER COMES GREAT RESPONSIBILITY.

Yeah, well, I didn't want it.

NO GOOD LEADER TRULY DESIRES IT.

Not helping.

Lt. Ramirez himself was directing traffic, and when he saw me inside Ivy's MINI, he directed us to a spot in the driveway they'd saved for us. As I got out with my backpack and sword, I realized what Austin meant about having an appropriate car. Hard to command respect when you arrived in a vehicle resembling a chubby baby bumblebee. Luckily, only the cops were outside. The rest must be waiting inside.

I controlled my apprehension and stepped into the foyer, crowded with vamps and demons.

"There she is," Andrew shouted from the stairs, where he'd apparently been set to watch for me.

Everyone turned to stare at me, no doubt assessing me, weighing me and my ability. I gave them a curt nod, trying to look confident and competent. They were all here because of me.

BECAUSE THEY WANT TO HELP, Fang corrected me.

Andrew charged down the stairs toward me. "They're waiting in the altar room for you. This way," he said.

He was so excited about being a part of this, I didn't let him know I already knew the way.

Sure enough, Austin, Luis, Rosa, Diego, Jeremy, and a couple of Luis's minions I didn't know represented the vampires, and the Underground was represented by the massive water demon Ludwig, Josh, the phase demon, Micah, Shade, Ivy, and me.

I'd left the planning of the actual strike force to Austin, and he looked totally prepared and in charge. "You have the supplies we might need?" I asked.

Austin nodded. "Rosa has outfitted the six of us with sustenance in case we need to spend a lot of time over there, and I understand Micah has brought food and water for the four of you."

The vampires all carried packs and swords, but the rest of the demons needed only packs, since swords would interfere with their powers. "Four?" I hadn't expected Micah would go through since his power only worked on female demons.

"Yes—you, Ludwig, Josh, and Andrew."

"I didn't know you were going through," I said to Andrew.

"I can fight," he said stubbornly.

"I know you can," I assured him. "But I hoped you'd stay on this side to watch over Ivy." She had to be here to read her stone, but I didn't want to put her in any danger beyond that.

"The fire demon will be a good asset on the other side," Rosa said. "I am staying on this side to prepare for anything they might need. I will watch over her."

ME, TOO, Fang said.

That's right—I'd forgotten Fang would have to remain behind to let Ivy and Micah know what was going on in the other dimension. It would be odd fighting without my faithful hellhound by my side, but it had to be this way. "Okay."

Austin nodded briefly. "That makes ten of us, and I have more in reserve in case we need them."

"What's the plan?" I asked him.

"I figured we'd have Shade open a portal here in the altar room since this is where Alejandro went through, but the rest hinges on what's on the other side. We'll only send through as many as we need. Are you ready to get started?"

They couldn't go anywhere until I gave Shade permission to open the portal. I glanced around at them. "Everyone who is going through is aware they may not come back?"

They all nodded—the younger ones with an eagerness they might soon regret and the older ones with grim certainty. Except for Luis and his minions. Their expressions held more of a sneer laced with contempt.

Fine. I didn't care for them, either. "Anyone not going through should stand back." Rosa, Ivy, Micah, and Fang withdrew to the other side of the room. "We'll only use the personnel we need. Austin will let us know who he wants." I glanced at Ludwig, Josh, and Andrew. "The three of you, listen to Austin—he's in charge. Fang will keep us posted as to what the demons are doing."

They all nodded. I trusted Ludwig to do as we asked, but Josh and Andrew were unproven. "The primary objective here is to rescue our people—that is of paramount importance. No grandstanding. Got it?"

"Got it," the two said in unison, and I had to be content with that.

"Okay, Ivy, you have a stone?"

"Yes." She pulled a large turquoise from her pocket and handed it to me. "Bring it back if you can?"

I nodded and gave the stone to Austin. "Here, you were so good with a football, let's see how you do with this. Shade, open a small portal, please, only big enough for Austin to throw the stone through." I didn't know how far the portal's field extended and didn't want anyone sucked through prematurely.

Shade nodded and, with no evidence of strain, immediately formed a small, baseball-sized green cloud. Good—it looked like the amulet was providing him some extra oomph.

Austin weighed the stone in his hand, then chucked it through perfectly the first time.

"What do you get from the stone?" I asked Ivy.

"Dry, hot, wind. Nothing too out of human tolerance, or the stone would be screaming."

"Day or night?"

"Twilight, I think."

Austin nodded in relief. He'd been afraid of full day, when it would have been impossible for them to go through.

"How many demons?" I asked Fang.

I COUNT TWELVE WITHIN MY RANGE.

That was a relief—we could handle twelve. "Pick up anything else?" I asked Ivy.

"Stones aren't good at material details, but they do recognize emotions. They're picking up some fear and anticipation. Oh, and a sudden spike of excitement just now."

Fang leapt to his feet. THEY JUST SPOTTED THE PORTAL. THEY'RE SENDING FOR REINFORCEMENTS. SHARRA'S THERE, AND SHE'S THINKING ABOUT ALEJANDRO AND VINCENT, SO THEY'RE THERE TOO.

We had to go now, before more showed up, and we were inundated. Making an instant decision, I shouted at Shade, "Open wide."

"Everyone goes," Austin ordered.

Shade opened the portal wide, and the ten of us jumped through one at a time, pausing only an instant on the other side to get oriented. Once everyone was through, I yelled, "Shrink it," at Fang.

He passed the order to Shade via Micah, and the writhing blue energy of the portal became the size of a baseball once more. It was reassuring to know it was still there.

Briefly, I noted the world was just as the stone described—hot and dry, with red sand everywhere and rock monoliths looming like hoodoo stones as far as I could see. Which wasn't all that far. The howling wind drove sand into our eyes, and I scrubbed them clean with the back of my hand. I squinted to keep the dust out of my eyes and tried to make out details of the demons charging toward us.

"Spread out," Austin yelled. "Find them."

THE DEMONS DON'T WANT YOU, THEY WANT THE PORTAL, Fang yelled.

"They're after the portal," I screamed into the wind. "And two of them are getting away to bring their friends."

I pointed in the direction of the two demons, and Luis bellowed, "After them!" They had to be stopped before there were too many to handle.

His two men raced after the retreating demons with vampire-enhanced speed. After that, the other demons converged on us like starving locusts on a wheat field.

"Sharra's here," Josh yelled, "behind the—"

A snatch of wind carried the rest of his words away, and I had no time to feel relief as a demon appeared out of a red dust devil, a fireball in his fist. Ludwig was suddenly there beside me, dousing the flame with a huge splash of water. The soaked demon paused in astonishment, and I was able to chop off his head with a single stroke. "Thanks," I hollered at Ludwig.

He nodded and went on to slam water at another demon coming toward us.

JOSH SAYS SHARRA IS BEHIND THE ROCKS ON YOUR LEFT, Fang said.

Seeing that the others had the fight well in hand, I darted around the rocks. Here, three monoliths leaned against each other, forming a sort of shelter from the wind. Josh was on one knee next to Ms. Swirly Face herself, holding a bottle of water to her lips. Relief filled me, and I passed the news on to Fang, knowing that would help Shade hang on.

"She's alive," Josh said in delight.

"What about Alejandro and Vincent?"

"They're fine," Sharra said. "When they heard you, they went to join the fighting."

"Good. Can you get her to the portal?" I asked Josh.

"But I want to fight," Josh said. "With my phase ability, I can reach in and pull out their hearts."

That meant getting way too close to them. "I don't think—"

But he was gone, and I was left with Sharra.

"Don't worry," Sharra said, pushing herself to her feet. "I can walk, no problem." She took a big slug of water. "Just point me in the right direction."

I touched her, so I could see whether she was telling the truth. She was in much better shape than I expected. Caked with red dust but able to walk. "Follow me. The portal is small now but will open wide again when we signal Shade."

She nodded and followed me back into the wind. I saw people struggling with demons, plus a few figures lying motionless on the ground, but couldn't make out who was who in the whirling dust. "I have Sharra," I shouted.

Austin shouted back, "Alejandro and Vincent are here. Gather our wounded and retreat!"

Wounded? Crap. I sent notice back to Fang to have Shade be ready to open the portal. I couldn't see it in all this whirling dust, so I told Fang to have Shade open it to basketball size.

"Found it," Ludwig bellowed. "To me!"

We all headed in the direction of the man-mountain's large form, Luis and Austin holding off two more demons, their swords flashing with their speed.

"All here and accounted for," Ludwig said as I reached him.

Ah, there it was—the portal. "Open it wide," I yelled at Fang. The blue cloud widened, and I told Ludwig, "Let me know when everyone is through," before I turned to help Luis and Austin. Austin was battling a huge demon with long claws, teeth, and horns. He was holding his own, but those sharp things could impale him at any moment.

I let out a battle cry of pure fear and frustration and swung my sword at the monster's arm—the only part I could reach. I almost completely severed its arm at the shoulder, and it roared, turning on me, blood spurting out of its arm. Austin leapt up, and with a two-handed blow, cleaved its head off its shoulders.

Austin didn't pause but went to assist Luis. Before I could even move to help them, they'd skewered the demon front and back. It fell to the ground, and I motioned them toward the portal. "Let's go!"

Seeing we were coming, Ludwig said, "You're the last," and leapt through the portal.

The three of us followed close behind. "Close it," I told Shade in the relative silence and peace on the other side.

When it reduced down to a pinpoint then disappeared, I breathed a sigh of relief. It was done. The wind was gone, too, and all that was left of the other dimension was the red grit covering every surface of our bodies and even finding its way into way too many crevices for my comfort.

I glanced around. The twins, Shade and Sharra, were locked in a swirly knot together, and Alejandro was wrapped in Rosa's arms. Vincent was being given back-slapping man hugs by a couple of vamps . . . but not everyone was exultant. One of Luis's followers was cradled in Diego's arms, run through the heart by his own sword, it looked like. Diego shook his head sadly as he gazed up at Luis. "He's gone."

Oh, crap. I didn't even know his name. Was he the only casualty?

ONE MORE, Fang said sadly.

I whirled around to see Andrew collapsed on the ground next to Josh, tears making streaks in the red dust on his face. Josh's head and shoulders were covered in blood. "Josh . . . ?"

"He's dead," Andrew wailed. "He tried to phase through a demon to grab its heart, but he got too close, and that clawed demon ripped his throat open."

I closed my eyes in pain. I'd done this. They were dead because of me.

NO, BABE. YOU DIDN'T KILL THEM. THE DEMON DID.

But it was my decision to mount the rescue.

AND IT WAS THEIRS TO PARTICIPATE. YOU CAN'T BE RESPONSIBLE FOR JOSH'S STUPID DECISION.

Couldn't I?

"How long were you there?" Shade asked Sharra. "It was about three weeks our time."

"Only about a day for me," Sharra said.

I did a quick calculation. So, about an hour had passed there for every day here. Thank goodness.

Alejandro nodded. "It was only a few hours for us."

"Why didn't you open a portal so we could find you?" Shade asked Sharra. "And why did they leave you alive?"

"Because I was knocked out at first. And they knew I was a shadow demon, so they were trying to force me to open a portal." She shook her head. "I refused. Knowing their plans for coming through and inundating this world, I couldn't let that happen."

And now I felt even more guilty for not rescuing her earlier.

STOP TAKING THE BLAME OF THE ENTIRE WORLD ON YOUR SHOULDERS, Fang said in annoyance. YOU THOUGHT SHE WAS DEAD, FERGAWDSAKE.

"The demons stayed close to the portal, hoping you'd open it again to rescue me. I figured you wouldn't unless you had enough firepower to take them on. I didn't know you thought I was dead until Alejandro told me." Sharra glanced at Alejandro and Vincent. "They helped keep the demons from hounding me and kept my hopes up."

Well, we'd done one thing right at least, in bringing the three of them back. I gave Ivy a regretful look. "I'm sorry, I was too busy to retrieve your stone."

"That's okay," she said with a smile. "I didn't really expect you'd be able to, but Ludwig found it while he was waiting at the portal. He brought it to me."

Ah, good.

Austin left Alejandro's side to come hug me tight. "Thank you," he whispered fiercely.

I hugged him back, happy that we'd been able to rescue Alejandro for him. I watched from a distance as Luis stood stiffly and spoke to Alejandro and Rosa in the dining room.

"What's that all about?" I asked Austin.

"He may be discussing our duel."

"What will happen to him?"

"Nothing. He acquitted himself honorably and kept his word. He has nothing to be ashamed of."

EXCEPT HIS HUMILIATING LOSS TO AUSTIN, Fang snarked.

Yes, there was that.

When they finished speaking, Luis and his remaining minion left abruptly, taking their friend's body, and Alejandro and Rosa came to join us. Alejandro clasped Austin's hand with a rueful expression. "I understand you two fought a duel for leadership of the Movement, and you won."

"Only as a temporary stopgap until you returned," Austin assured him.

Alejandro smiled. "Yes, I understand." He placed an arm around Rosa—the first time I'd actually seen him show affection toward her in public. And she was eating it up like he was peanut butter, and she was intent on licking the spoon.

VAMPIRES DON'T EAT PEANUT BUTTER, Fang reminded me.

Maybe, but the proper image grossed me out. *It still works as a metaphor, or simile, or whatever you call it.* English wasn't my best subject.

"It has been coming for a long time," Alejandro continued, "and I'm glad you two settled it without my interference."

Austin nodded, but though he obviously didn't feel it necessary to ask any more questions, I did. "So what will happen now? Is Austin your deputy or something?"

"Yes. I see the wisdom in having a permanent deputy, especially in light of my recent absence, and Austin will fill that position admirably."

"What about the lieutenants?" I asked, since Alejandro didn't seem to object to me asking questions.

"I still need three. Rosa will continue in her current position, Vincent will take over the duties formerly done by Lily—I've waited too long to make that decision—and . . . who would you recommend to take your place, Austin?"

He thought for a moment, then said, "Diego, I think."

"Good choice," Alejandro approved.

"But what about Luis?" I asked. Was he reduced in rank now, or what?

"I will absorb his political duties." Alejandro hesitated a moment, then added, "Luis has informed me he intends to leave San Antonio and join Lisette in the capital. Immediately."

Well, that was a relief.

FOR EVERYONE, Fang agreed.

I gave Austin a one-armed hug in congratulations, and he smiled down at me.

But our satisfaction was short-lived as one woman pushed her way through the crowd, saying, "Josh? Where's my boy?"

"Over here," Andrew said in a choked voice.

The woman was slight with wavy blond hair—and looked just like Josh. Obviously his mother. Oh, crap.

She dropped to her knees beside Josh's body and wailed. "No, no. He's dead. My boy is dead."

Pain filled my chest, almost more than I could bear.

She wiped tears from her eyes and looked wildly around the room. When she spotted me, her eyes narrowed, and she rose from beside her son's body. "You," she spat. "This is your fault."

She phased out and leapt for me. How the hell could I defend against an insubstantial female demon? I couldn't do more than dodge, and I tried to do just that, as Austin and Fang futilely leapt in front of me.

"Stop," Micah yelled, his hand outstretched toward Josh's mother.

She halted obediently, unable to resist the command of his incubus.

"This is not how we settle disputes," he said sternly.

She phased back to her substantial form, her fists clenched and face twisted in rage. "Then I demand a Judgment Ritual to prove her guilt and pass sentence. Someone needs to pay for Josh's death."

"You're not thinking clearly, Cora," Micah said soothingly. "The entire Underground appointed Val as Paladin. You can't call a ritual to condemn her for doing her job."

Cora forcibly calmed herself. "No. It was her decision to open a portal to the demon dimension. She didn't know the shadow demon's sister was still alive, so her sole purpose was to help her boyfriend—a *vampire*—rescue two other vampires. Then she took three of *us* with her, endangering their lives and leading my son Joshua to his death. Not only that, but she opened the portal not knowing what dangers lay beyond or how many vicious, violent full demons might come into this world to wreak havoc upon us and the humans around us." Cora raised her chin and pointed accusingly at me. "She used her power as Paladin for private gain, recklessly endangered the demons in her care, and is responsible for the murder of my son." She ended on a triumphant note, looking around for support at the crowd that had gathered.

Acid churned in my stomach. Good heavens, did the woman really believe that?

YES, Fang said soothingly. SHE IS GRIEVING AND NEEDS TO BLAME SOMEONE. IT MAKES HER THINKING A BIT WONKY.

"That's not entirely true," Shade said, to my surprise. Andrew kept his hand on Shade's arm, so everyone could see his expression. "I was the one who badgered Val into letting me rescue my sister." He glanced at Sharra and kept her hand in his as if he didn't want to let her go. "Though we initially believed she had died, we all—including Val—had learned it was possible that she was still alive. So, it isn't true that she thought Sharra was dead when she agreed to do this. She knew Sharra could have survived and, in fact, knew my sister was alive before she went through." He hesitated, then added, "Val didn't ask Josh to fight—he volunteered. Ask Andrew."

Shade elbowed Andrew, encouraging him to talk.

Andrew stared down at his hands. "Josh and I wanted to help," he said in a voice hardly louder than a mumble. "To save Sharra and the rest of the Demon Underground."

They wanted to be heroes. I could understand that, but it had led to such a tragic outcome. I hoped everyone learned something from this.

Andrew cast Cora an apologetic glance. "Val told us about the danger and warned us not to grandstand, but we didn't listen. Once we were over there, I heard her tell Josh to take Sharra to the portal and safety. But he ignored her . . . and attacked a demon instead. That's who killed him, not Val."

He dropped his eyes again and wouldn't look at anyone. I respected his willingness to put himself out there for me and the truth.

"The boys speak the truth," Ludwig said in his deep voice. "Joshua was reckless and did not listen to the Paladin. She is not responsible for his death."

That made me feel a lot better. I wondered if Austin would say anything.

I DOUBT IT, Fang said. CORA LABELED HIM YOUR BOYFRIEND, SO ANYTHING HE SAYS WILL SEEM SUSPECT. I WOULDN'T EXPECT HIM TO.

I winced. In that case, I wouldn't, either.

Ivy gave Cora a pitying glance. "The assertion that Val did it for her 'boyfriend' is untrue. I was present on at least two occasions when she denied Austin's and Shade's requests because she refused to go against Micah's wishes. It was only when Micah forced her to make a decision that she decided to mount a rescue. And she used all assets at her disposal to learn as much as possible about what was waiting for her on the other side."

Alejandro stepped forward. "I, too, lost a dear friend, but I do not blame Ms. Shapiro. Though I did not witness the events leading up to her decision to rescue Vincent, the shadow demon, and myself, I can confidently say that she does not let favoritism or personal bias guide her decisions. Emotion may sway her, but it's always in the direction of what is right for everyone involved. She does not agree with all of the aims of the New Blood Movement, but she has worked with us when necessary to protect the members of the Movement, the Underground, and all the people of San Antonio. You could have no better Paladin."

How nice of him to stand up for me. I felt tears pricking at my eyelids.

Lt. Ramirez nodded. "What he says is true. Val Shapiro has been a force for good in this city. She has not only helped the vampires and the demons present here today, but full humans as well. She acts as unofficial liaison between the three factions, though I have long thought we should make her position official."

What? I wasn't sure I wanted that at all, though I appreciated his support, too. I hoped no one else was going to say anything more. If anyone else was nice to me, I was afraid I'd burst into tears.

"No, no, it can't be true," Cora said, choking back a sob. "You didn't have to do it. You didn't have to go. *Why?*"

With all eyes upon me, I cleared my throat of the emotion clogging it, then said, "Yesterday, Andrew and I were trapped in another dimension for many hours, hoping someone would come to our rescue, but not knowing if it was possible. It was a horrible feeling, wondering if we were abandoned, doomed to spend our lives, or what little might be left of them, in another dimension." I stopped for a moment, willing my voice to stop wavering.

When Andrew nodded with feeling, I added softly, "I realized that I couldn't let something like that happen to anyone else if it was within my power to stop it." I raised my chin. "I wanted everyone to know that I, as your Paladin, will always come for you, no matter what the risks are to me, personally."

GOOD SPEECH, Fang said admiringly. YOU'VE GOT THEM IN THE PALM OF YOUR HAND NOW.

I was just telling the truth.

AND THAT'S WHY IT WORKS.

I turned to Cora. "I think Josh felt the same, and that's why he insisted on coming with us. You can be proud of your son—he's a hero."

Cora burst into tears, and I pulled her into my arms. "I'm so sorry,"

I whispered. She clutched at me, and the tension eased in both of us, though I knew we'd both feel the pain of his loss for a long time to come.

Gently, Ludwig pulled the sobbing woman away. I glanced up at Micah, needing . . . something. Absolution, maybe?

"You did your job well, Paladin," he said gently.

Sweet, giddy relief filled me. They didn't blame me.

NOW YOU JUST HAVE TO STOP BLAMING YOURSELF.

That might take a bit longer.

"But I do want to address something Lt. Ramirez said," Micah continued. "I agree that you are an excellent choice to act as liaison between the three factions to maintain harmony and communication. What do you think? Are you up for the job?"

Wait—I'd just survived one challenge after I assumed too much responsibility, and they wanted me to do it more often? I glanced up and saw Alejandro, Lt. Ramirez, Austin, and Micah grin at me as if they thought the idea was just peachy.

IT IS, VAL, my faithful hellhound said. YOU'RE DOING THE JOB ALREADY. MIGHT AS WELL GET THE AUTHORITY ALONG WITH THE RESPONSIBILITY.

It looked as though I had no choice. "I—I will," I said shakily.

Micah beamed at me, and I accepted Austin's hug along with Alejandro's and Ramirez's congratulations. "Gee, guys," I drawled. "Thanks for setting me up."

They all laughed, and I said, "Can I at least take a vacation first?"

"Absolutely," Micah said. "I'd say you deserve one."

"Don't worry, darlin'," Austin said with a grin. "Everything in your life has been leading up to this point. Don't fight it—it's your destiny. And you're going to be damned good at it."

HE'S ALMOST RIGHT, Fang said. TO HELL WITH GOOD. YOU'RE GONNA BE AWESOME!

The End

Dear Reader

Thank you so much for continuing to follow the adventures of Val and Fang as they take on the baddies of the world. You'll notice I added a new character this time—Ivy Weiss, the stone whisperer. Ivy was originally a character in a totally different universe, but I didn't have the time to both write it and get this book out in a timely manner. Then I realized—duh!—she could be a demon in *this* universe. That happy thought made this book much more fun to write, so you'll probably be seeing more of her in the future.

Thanks for spending time in my world, and let me know how you liked Ivy, Austin, Val, Fang and the rest of the gang by leaving a review or contacting me on Facebook . . . and come visit my website at parkerblue.net to sign up for my newsletter!

—*Parker Blue*

About the Author

Parker Blue lives in Colorado Springs with her three rescue dogs where she spends her time reading, writing, beading, and watching way too much TV.

CPSIA information can be obtained at www.ICGtesting.com
Printed in the USA
LVOW08s0022250715

447619LV00002B/358/P